5/10

GEM
X

Other books by Nicky Singer

The Innocent's Story

GEM X

NICKY SINGER

HOLIDAY HOUSE / New York

Printed in the United States of America

www.holidayhouse.com

First U.S. Edition

1   3   5   7   9   10   8   6   4   2

Library of Congress Cataloging-in-Publication Data

Singer, Nicky, 1956–
GemX / by Nicky Singer.
p.   cm.
Summary: Sixteen-year-old Maxo Strang, the most perfect human ever made,
suddenly discovers a "crack" in his face, which leads him to expose his
community's dark underworld of secret scientific research and
the city's corrupt supreme leader.
ISBN 978-0-8234-2108-4 (hardcover)
[1. Genetic engineering–Fiction.   2. Cloning–Fiction.   3. Political
corruption–Fiction.   4. Science fiction.]   I. Title.
PZ7.S61728TGem   2008
[Fic]–dc22   2007014975

For my darling Molly—
who is all spirit and soul.

1

Maxo Evangele Strang, sixteen-year-old GenOff of Dr. Igo Strang and Ms. Glora Orb, ascended in the exterior glass elevator of his apartment block with his right hand attached to his right temple as if he were injured or in pain. Normally he enjoyed the ride; his building was situated on one of the Heights higher reaches and had a commanding view over the west side of the Polis. On a clear day one could see all the way from the Enhanced Sector down to the Dreg Estate 4. But on this day Maxo felt not that he was looking out over the world but that the world was looking in at him, more particularly that the world was focused on whatever it was that lay beneath his right hand at his right temple.

This wasn't exactly true.

Far from having his gaze fixed on Maxo's shielding hand, Bovis Frank, a fellow GemX who happened to be ascending in the same glass elevator as Maxo, was staring so hard out of the window you might have thought his life depended on it. And if Bovis also had one hand clamped to his face (which he did, though in his case it was his left hand that seemed welded to the little gap of skin between his eyebrows) Maxo didn't notice. It wasn't that those of the GemX genotype weren't intelligent. They were, preposterously so, in fact. It was just that other people's lives didn't feature very much on their radars. So if Bovis was glad to get out at SkyFloor 6 or Maxo glad to travel on unhindered, then that's just the way it was.

At SkyFloor 15, the elevator door opened and Maxo stepped into the small gap between the elevator shaft and what looked like a large flat sheet of steel. Maxo presented the iris of his left eye to a small red scanner and the steel sheet slid noiselessly aside. At no point did Maxo's hand leave his temple, not even when he stepped into Living Space 1 and the two ordinary walls, picking up on his mood, immediately changed from enlivening pink to soothing green. The most soothing of the eight green options, Maxo noted grimly; things must be bad. Wall 3, which was a fifteen-foot plasma TropScreen, sensed his shadow and turned the volume up on the Announcer: *It has now been one hundred and twelve days since the last Atrocity. Leaderene Clore, may her name celeb forever, and you, the Pure Germline Members of the Polis, are winning. Together we are winning the fight; the Polis is strong, the Polis is healthy, we progress each and every day toward perfection. But we must never once let down our guard; vigilance is everything. . . .*

"Shut up," said Maxo without conviction, and the TropScreen continued, oblivious.

Maxo headed for WashSpace2, his en suite shower and personal refreshment room. He went inside, checked he'd shut the door behind him and then checked again, even though he knew his GenParents were never in the apartment at this time of day. He paused, took a slow breath, and then leaned toward the mirror. Sensors automatically

2

measured his distance from the glass and swiveled four spotlights onto the part of his body he was presenting: his face. Maxo Strang took away his hand. The shock made his head dip, made it bounce and reel. The spotlights readjusted themselves, wheeling with him, dipping and bouncing, trying to keep the light (or so Maxo thought) on the hideous obscenity, for there it was (there it was!), the tiny indentation that stretched from the corner of his eye for about half an inch toward his hairline.

It was true then.

It was worse than true.

Could things be worse than true?

As Maxo pushed down hard on the mica basin to steady himself, he heard the sudden purr of his body-hugging ambisuit, a sure sign that the suit's thermostat had been triggered. He must be sweating. He tried to regulate his breathing, to control himself, to concentrate on the rest of his beautiful GemX face. His GenSire had chosen well, he had what was still considered, even after sixteen years, to be the premier bone structure, the 740; it had never been superseded. His gray eyes were top of the range Gentype 5.5 and his skull (currently shaven, as was the fashion) unmistakably model 47. Put simply, his perfection was not something he'd ever had to think about, it just existed. It was.

But now there was the line. The half-inch line that had drawn itself on his perfect face. Maxo could not ever remember being so revolted. It was a physical thing; it made him feel that, but for the ambisuit, he might throw up. The suit was working overtime, the high collar was like a thin layer of ice around his neck, it was cooling him, freezing down his emotions. And yet—that Clodrone driver! That's when Maxo had first known there was something wrong. He'd seen it on the face of some lowly sector driver; the surprise, the disgust, on the face of a Clodrone, for celeb's sake! And that's when he'd put his hand up, he'd felt the little crack, and, of course, he wondered, because it was so unlikely, so horrible, he wondered if there was just a mistake, a pale thread just caught on his temple, nothing to do with him, nothing to do with his body at all. And that's how he'd managed to get home, by covering it up, by not even being tempted to look, by refusing the reflections in the glass of the elevator—which could just have been shadows. But now he was at home, and he was standing in front of a mirror with four spotlights telling him the awful truth: he had a crack in his face.

Maxo Evangele Strang opened his mouth and screamed.

2

In Dreg Estate 4, not many miles (but a very great distance) from the Heights, fifteen-year-old Gala Lorrell vowed never to go to Hospital 17 again. What was the point? It only exhausted her mother and they learned nothing that they didn't know already: Namely, that Perle Lorrell was dying and there wasn't anything anyone in the Polis was prepared to do about it.

Her mother was sleeping now, at last at home, at last in her own bed, but she did not look at ease; her frail body was angular and wrong beneath the thin blankets. Gala wanted to see—needed to see—the strong limbs and the generous, laughing face she remembered from childhood, but here was something gray and sucked-in. Gala watched her mother's gaunt fingers twitch restlessly about her neck as if to clutch the sheet tighter, ward off the cold. The fifteen-year-old went to her own room and took the final blanket from the bed. She could sleep in her clothes, what did it matter?

The blanket was as threadbare as her mother's other covers, but Gala tucked it in as tenderly and as warmly as she could. Then she tidied a few little wisps of hair from her mother's forehead. A moment later, she found herself running soft fingertips down her mother's sunken cheek, as if she could make things well by just by wanting. Perle Lorrell exhaled, a very small sound, but there was something of contentment in it, and Gala felt a sudden wash of gladness.

"Mama," she said. Perle did not respond, but her sleeping, so Gala thought, looked more gentle.

Time to fix the window, then. The cardboard that Gala'd taped over the broken pane had almost worked loose again. She went to the tiny kitchenette and looked in the relevant drawer.

No tape.

Of course, no tape. Who would have bought tape but her, and she'd forgotten, hadn't she? As if to console herself she reached out and turned on the kitchen tap.

No water.

And she could kill for a cup of something hot. She screwed the tap on full and put the plug in the basin. There would be water sometime between now and morning, that's how it worked in the Estates, you got water on a rotational basis. Only you never knew in advance which hours you would have water and which hours not. People hoarded water, of course, she did it herself, it was the only way to survive. But you couldn't leave the taps running when you were out (and she'd been five hours at the hospital) because, if the basin overflowed, if water ran down into the apartment below, well, you never knew, you never knew who was living beneath you, how violent they might be. She'd have to stay awake then, listen out, all night if necessary, because they had to have water, not just for drinking but for washing, she needed to keep her mother clean. What now?

Tape.

No tape.

Water.

Gala went to the bathroom; normally there was always at least a cupful of water left in the bucket. But not today. If Daz had used it to clean his paintbrushes, she'd kill him.

Daz.

Where was Daz? He should be home by now.

Gala turned the taps on in the bathroom, she put the plug in the basin, and the bucket under the showerhead.

Towel. Her brain was thinking slowly, in single items. She was very, very tired. She took the small hand towel from the bathroom to her mother's room. The broken window had never shut properly anyway, there was space between the window and the window frame. Maybe if she was clever, she could wedge the towel somehow, make another layer between her mother and the outside world. She eased the material into the window gap, securing the towel edge around the window catch. Not bad. It might hold, so long as there wasn't too much wind.

When she'd finished, she stood a moment looking out over the sprawling estate. Eastward was totally dark, the buildings blind except for the strange behind-the-curtains flickering of candles and the low, uncertain light of flashlights. She should be grateful about that anyway, grateful that it was her area that had electricity tonight. Electricity wasn't rotational, there were just random power outs, when the system overloaded somewhere. They said there were power outs in the Heights as well, but she'd never seen the lights off there. Never.

But she was grateful. It would have been quite impossible to support her mother up the four flights of stairs to their apartment with one hand taken up with a flashlight. Of course, it would have been better still if the elevator had been working, but the elevator had been out of action for fifteen months. She didn't see how it would ever be repaired, since no one seemed to know who was responsible for repairing it. In earlier days her mother might have known, might have been able to talk to someone, get a contact, make something happen by force of will. But her mother was ill and no one else seemed to care.

Still, at least they lived on Floor 4. If they'd been allocated Floor 17, well, then things would be desperate. She couldn't afford to think of the people who lived on Floor 17. Gala closed her mother's curtains, pressing them close against the towel, trying to make things as draft proof as possible. She had to hope there wouldn't be Sudden Onset Snow. Since the Global Warming Catastrophe, weather had become both unpredictable and dangerous. No, they couldn't have a Sudden Onset, they couldn't have that much bad luck.

She was parched, she needed to drink something. She returned to the kitchen; looked in the desolate fridge. The remaining half-pint of milk she'd bought as a treat for her mother was sour. There was no keeping milk fresh when the fridge power was so uncertain, she knew that well enough, but she'd wanted her mother to have that milk, the taste of it, its wholesomeness. Only her mother couldn't drink much and now it was sour. In the cupboard was canned milk, but she needed to keep that for her mother's morning tea. Gala put chocolate powder—a lot of chocolate powder—into a pan and heated it with the rancid milk. As she waited for it to boil, she thought again about the hospital.

The consultant assigned to her mother was Dr. Parks. He was young and tall, but with a stoop, as though some weight on his shoulders was gradually, relentlessly, crushing him down. The doctor had looked at Perle Lorrell's notes. He had looked at Perle Lorrell. He had shaken his head.

"I'm very sorry," he had said, "but cancer is not an officially recognized disease in the Polis anymore." His shoulders sagged further. "Cancer," he said, "is on the eradicated list, you understand what I mean?"

She did understand what he meant. He meant that, because the Enhanced Sector were protected against cancer, because they no longer got cancer, it wasn't worth the drug companies making the cancer medicines. There wasn't enough money in it. The money was in the little pink stabilizers the Enhanced used to control the side effects of their anticancer modules. If she had wanted stablizers . . .

"But cancer isn't an absolutely eradicated disease," Gala had burst out, "even in the Enhanced Sector." Everyone knew that. There were still pre-enhanced and proto-enhanced people with dodgy cancer cover, with immunity from breast cancer maybe but not from lung cancer. The eradicated list—it was all just TropScreen lies! "So there must be some drugs," Gala said.

"Yes," replied the doctor. "At a price." He sighed. "I'm so sorry."

Gala stirred the dark milk.

Pain. She wasn't being quite fair about that. Because Dr. Parks had given her mother something for pain. In fact, Dr. Parks had given her a bottle twice the size of the one he was allowed to prescribe her—diamorphine. Gala knew what it was, her friend Parsha's mother had died of it. It was a kind of heroin: It stopped the pain but it stopped your life, too. Gala had the bottle concealed beneath her pillow. It would stay there until the very last, until after the Agaricus Blazei bloomed. If they bloomed, Gala's mushrooms, the "cure" for which she'd paid such a price and tended daily with such hope.

The milk bubbled and frothed and smelled bad. Gala was pouring it into a mug when she heard the front door. Stretch.

"And just where the hell do you think you've been?" she burst out as her brother came into the room. She hadn't realized she was still so angry.

Stretch was as good a name for her brother Phylo now at fourteen as it had been when they'd nicknamed him at twelve, when he'd suddenly started to grow, to shoot up. He was as angular as his sister, but much longer and thinner. He moved like a young giraffe, uncertain of why it had such a strangely shaped body. But his eyes were piercing blue and very focused.

"Do you know what day it is," he flashed back at her.

"Yes," said Gala. "The day your mother had an appointment at the hospital. The day you said you'd stay at home and help."

"Oh." His face fell. She saw immediately that he counted himself to be in the wrong and her anger melted.

"How were the stairs?" he asked.

"We managed," she said.

"And the doctor?"

"As we thought."

"Nothing to be done, then," said Stretch.

"Yes," said Gala, and then, "No." The mushrooms had to grow. They had to work. She didn't mention the mushrooms. Stretch had laughed at them before.

"I hate them," said Stretch. "I hate them so much."

"The doctor was nice. Dr. Parks. I felt sorry for him."

"Not the doctor," said Stretch, his voice rising. "Them! Those little pieces of plastic that call themselves 'Enhanced.'"

"Yes," said Gala, cutting him off. "I know."

There was a brief silence, and then Stretch asked, "Can I have some of that?"

"It's sour."

"Yes," said Stretch. "So I smell." He looked longingly at the cupboard where the canned milk was, but didn't either ask for the good milk or criticize his sister for buying the fresh.

"Here," said Gala gratefully, and, taking a second cup, she divided what was left of the chocolate drink.

"So where did you go?" Gala asked.

"To the Lab," he replied.

"Not again."

"It's the anniversary. Today's the anniversary."

Now it was Gala's turn to be in the wrong. Was it possible that she had thought so much about her mother's appointment that she had forgotten to think of her father's disappearance? Four years to the day. He'd gone to the

Enhanced Sector in response to a call for Clean Genes, gone with thousands of other Naturals to the lab of Dr. Igo Strang to give skin cells in return for a few feligs. Only, while the others had returned, Finn Lorrell had not. Stretch believed that Dr. Igo Strang must know something, must be hiding something. Yet what could the man know? He was the chief scientist on the program, not the worker who would have logged her father in or taken the skin scrape or watched their father leave. They'd been through all that. Going to the Lab achieved nothing, just kept Stretch's anger lit.

But she still said, placating him, "And?"

"They've heightened security," he burst out. "Again! There's no talking to anyone. Especially not to Dr. Igo Strang."

Of course. He'd never get to speak to Dr. Igo Strang. But Stretch didn't understand that, wouldn't give up. Gala wanted to touch her brother, gentle him as she'd gentled her mother, but her hands remained around her mug.

3

Dr. Igo Strang was sitting in his laboratory staring down the lenses of his Micon 10 Scope at a petri dish of human eggs. It was, he thought, the most beautiful sight in the Polis, in the world, in fact. These eggs! When he looked at them, he did not just see the tiny, pale, gelatinous roundels the microscope presented, Dr. Igo Strang saw life itself. He saw each one of these pulsing little dots as the beginning of something new, something huge. Oh, these eggs, he could look at them all day! His whole life, he thought, was in these eggs, what he and the eggs could do together—once their nuclei were removed, of course.

Dr. Strang did not believe himself to be a vain man, but few individuals, he thought, could have journeyed so far with these eggs. After all, he did not have the advantage of an Enhanced brain, so everything he had achieved was entirely and only by his own ingenuity, his own merit. So no one, he thought as he looked at the squirming eggs, deserved more than he did the title of chief scientist at GemCorp, second only in importance to GemCorp's founding chairman, Llublo Quells.

Dr. Strang pulled his eyes from the eggs and took a moment to survey his larger empire. He had forty-four staff in (still in—though it was dusk) all of them pursuing tasks set with meticulous attention by the chief scientist. As they hovered over their test tubes or liquid hydrogen caskets, there was an air of extreme seriousness, of intense hush, each one of them set upon a path as exciting as his own when he had begun the Clodrone Program.

Ah, Dr. Igo Strang breathed out: the Clodrone Program. Of course he couldn't take credit for the initial research (that belonged to Llublo himself) or even for the idea (Llublo again)—and what a spectacular idea! To find strong, kind but docile, beastlike and not very intelligent human beings and clone them—again and again—for the benefit of the Polis, to be the Polis workers, to drive the cars and sweep the streets and check the securipasses. What a man Llublo was. He'd seen the advantages immediately, the moneymaking potential. It wasn't just the science he was interested in (science was more Igo's department) but the whole experiment, the range and possibility of it. It was Llublo who'd not just birthed the first Clodrones, but who'd overseen their upbringing, who'd developed the idea of the pods where all the Clodrones lived together with their Clomasters. They were well fed, well taught (they didn't need education as such, just obedience skills and driving diplomas and so on), and they were endlessly happy, because they didn't know anything else or want anything else. That itself was remarkable, thought Igo Strang, to be able to take away the need for striving. Marvelous. He himself strove all the time, he needed (not being Enhanced) to prove himself, to be better than the best.

But at twenty-four years old, after a productive life of a mere eight years, what had happened to Llublo's army of

Clodrones? They'd begun to deteriorate, that's what, they'd begun to degrade. Worse than this, some of them had actually died. It was such a terrible waste. When non-cloned humans were extending their lifespan year on year, here were the Clodrones irritatingly refusing to live. They were giving out, giving up. Llublo Quells was about to lose his investment, he was about to go broke.

Enter Dr. Igo Strang of the Heights University, only twenty-eight years old himself, but considered a brilliant student by his Enhanced tutors, a genius by those who had employed him since to think about genetics. What Llublo Quells wanted Llublo Quells got, and he wanted Igo Strang. It wasn't the money that attracted Igo, no, never the money, it was the science. What was going wrong with the clones? What could be done to halt their decline? It was a mission, Igo had thought, both of science and humanity.

Llublo had given him the run of the Lab; Igo was to have the most modern equipment and as many technicians as he required. Whatever Igo requested, authorization was to be immediate. Igo requested eggs. They were cultivated from the Naturals, who would always donate if the price was right. And then Igo sucked out the egg nuclei and began his work. The longevity gene code was well understood, although the patent for processing the gene belonged to a rival company—GeModify. Dr. Igo Strang was not disheartened. He had studied the nematode worm and he knew what he was looking for. People liked to think of themselves as very different from worms but, Dr. Strang knew, at a genetic level there was barely any difference at all. To identify the longevity marker in the human gene and find a new way of extracting it was simply a matter of time and (in Igo Strang's case) the luck of hitting on the exact segment, quite by chance, one Sunday afternoon, when he'd been watching Glora Orb open some exhibition on the TropScreen and his restriction endonucleased molecular scissors had slipped. It had happened to Newton with an apple and it had happened to him with Glora Orb and some scissors, that's how science worked.

Of course, that had been only the beginning. The faulty Clodrone gene that had been identified had to be cut out and replaced with the new longevity gene, and the resultant DNA spliced, electroshocked together. People said it couldn't be done, people said that even if the fusing worked, the Clodrone bodies would reject the foreign DNA. Certainly, this part of the process had been slow, and some Clodrones had died (but only in the service of science, only to make things better for their peers). His first mistake had been the use of one of his own skin cells. He hadn't paid attention to the difference even proto-enhanced cells made: They made things more unstable. It was often the obvious things, Dr. Strang mused, that passed one by.

It was an assistant (Igo couldn't quite remember his name) who had first suggested they might try Natural cells. Even now, Igo Strang felt a rise of excitement as he remembered cultivating those cells and then transferring them to the Minimal Human Tissue Media where (without dying) they stopped dividing and entered a state of quiescence. He recalled repeating the process with a single strand of Clodrone DNA, faulty gene removed. And then the beautiful eggs! He remembered sucking out the nucleus of one particularly handsome specimen and implanting a quiescent cell in the zona pellucid. Of course the skill (his skill) was lining up the two different strands of DNA and directing the surge of electricity, such a small surge really, but so perfectly directed! There was immediate fusion, there was! Of course, there were agonizing days ahead, waiting to see if the embryo grew, if the stems cells he was creating would be healthy enough to transfer into a Clodrone body. Day and night (he didn't go home at all during this time) Igo watched and waited. The cells grew, they divided. But he didn't tell Llublo, not at that time, he kept the excitement all bundled up inside him—and called for a Clodrone. It was 1312 who'd arrived—what a lucky individual Clodrone 1312 was!

Igo Strang selected blood as the carrier and primed a couple of Hox genes to aid the chemical signaling. Clodrone 1312 was injected and then kept in the Lab for observation. Even within a week the effects were evident. Clodrone 1312's memory improved (he was subject to rigorous testing), his energy levels rose by 27 percent, his physical strength returned (though the full effects of this were not seen for a number of months), and even his skin improved. It began to retain its oils and its elasticity, most noticeably about his face where his forehead wrinkles simply plumped away.

Dr. Igo Strang took his masterpiece to show Llublo Quells. Llublo Quells smiled widely. All they needed now, said Igo, was a fresh supply of Natural cells. Llublo said Igo could consider it done and 'catored his good friend Leaderene Euphony Clore (may her name celeb forever). The following day, Euphony arranged a Mass Call. The Naturals, offered a little money and the chance to defend the germline-line of the Polis (Igo didn't think the word *Clodrone* was mentioned, there wasn't any need), came flooding in to donate. Dr. Igo Strang was promoted from lab director to chief scientist of GemCorp International. With the title came new responsibilities. He was assigned the GemAlpha Program, to develop new gene possibilities for the next generation of Enhanced. In fact, Igo had personally overseen each evolution from GemT to GemZ. Although his proudest moment was the manipulation that had gone into Maxo's generation, the GemXs. Many of those enhancements had still not been superseded. They remained, Maxo remained, the best science and money could buy. In fact, if he said it himself, Maxo Evangele Strang was perfect.

Maxo Evangele Strang had stopped screaming. Remembering that he was enormously intelligent, he decided to do some research.

Crack.

Was that the right word? Is that what the Naturals called it? He didn't know, had never had to be interested. He retreated from the washroom back into the living space. Two of the walls were still green, the TropScreen wall was zooming in on Dreg Estate 2. *"Danger,"* intoned the Announcer, *"could come from any place at any time, only vigilance..."* The fourth, and least obtrusive, wall had the slight translucent shimmer of a dormant plasma screen. Maxo grabbed a small black audio control and barked into it: *global search engine: naturals; crack.*

The plasma screen began to glow. "In 0.3 seconds,"

hummed a soft female voice, "you have activated 1,444,582,212 possible links. Proceed?"

"Obviously," said Maxo sarcastically. How come his Gen-Parents were the only ones in the Enhanced Sector who didn't see the point of updating this worn-out, Dreggie system?

"I'm sorry?" said the voice. "Please repeat."

"Item one, Sappho," said Maxo. He'd given her that name. It had been a major selling point on the original system: You could personalize your search engine. Personalize, but not give her a personality, unfortunately. He'd chosen the name after one particularly frustrating day with her because, so HistoryData said, it was an ancient name, from about a million years back, not unlike, he reckoned, the system itself.

"Global encyclopedia brings you 830,416 'Natural, Crack' entries," said Sappho. "Do you wish to refine your search?"

"Just get on with it!"

"Each hit costs 0.04 TropCredits. Payment will be deducted immediately by LineScan."

"Yeah, yeah," said Maxo.

"Natural crack, Equivalent Defect Size and Residual Stress, natural cracks in seabed, natural cracks in software, retro wood has natural cracks say 'yes' buy immediately . . ."

"Not natural as in 'from nature,'" shouted Maxo. "Natural as in 'Dreggie,' as in lowest of the low, as in miserable, non-enhanced, subhuman being. Cracks on Dreggies. Get it?"

"Refined search," intoned the female voice, not at all aggrieved. "I did ask. *Natural Dreggie crack.*"

A picture assembled itself on the screen: It was a man's

face, large as the wall. He was covered in cracks. There were three deep cracks width ways across his forehead, three angry, vertical lines above the bridge of his nose, cracks from the splay of his nostrils in a horrible curve right down to the edge of his lips. And there were also cracks that radiated out from his eyes.

"Detail," said Maxo.

"Natural hominid, Dave Pearson, circa 2006, aged sixty-six."

Maxo whistled, only sixty-six!

"Historical picture," Sappho continued. "No enhancement."

"And the cracks?"

"Wrinkles."

So—wrinkles. Wrinkles!

"Natural occurring process for all Naturals."

"Funny ha-ha," said Maxo.

"Repeat?" questioned Sappho.

"Wrinkles, natural for Naturals, but not natural for the Enhanced. Not at all natural, in fact. Not at all Enhanced. Even GemAs last a hundred years. I'm a GemX, for celeb's sake! I've got a three-gene anticancer module, a stroke regulator, twenty-four antivirus modules, a cluster of high-blood-pressure and diabetes signalers not to mention unparalleled slow-release juvenile hormones, which extend my life expectancy to approximately one hundred thirty years and no wrinkles. Do you get that, Sappho, no wrinkles!"

Sappho might have said, "Oh, dear," or "keep taking the pills," or "perhaps it's not really a wrinkle at all," but, as she hadn't been given a command or asked a direct question, and she was only a machine after all (albeit an intelligent one), she said nothing.

"What do you suggest I do?" The shouting had made Maxo more focused.

"Suggest body sculpture plaster," said Sappho helpfully. The non-screen walls relaxed down to green pigment four, a mild soother.

"I could be dying," said Maxo. "Naturals get the wrinkles and then they die. I'm sixteen, Sappho!"

The walls immediately reverted to green pigment eight.

"For celeb's sake!" Maxo jumped up and hit a control panel mounted at hand height in wall two. All walls except the TropScreen went white; Sappho discreetly turned herself off.

He thought about reactivating her; he thought about calling MediAlert immediately. It was, after all, a crisis, wasn't it? But perhaps it would be better to call his Gen-Sire. After all, Dr. Igo Strang was chief scientist for Gem-Corp, there wasn't much he didn't know about the gene program. It could be just a little blip, there could be some small pink stabilizer pill that would do the trick. There were occasional blips, it was an inevitable part of progress, Igo said. Not everything could be thought out in advance, things had to be adjusted, one had to deal with situations as they arose. Maxo was already taking stabilizers for the high-blood-pressure cluster; in fact, there was talk (the Announcer always advised against talk, talk could be dangerous) that his particular cluster (the 23) was unacceptably volatile. But what option did anyone have? It was obviously better to have the cluster than not have the cluster. And no one said that being enhanced was risk free, it was just the only sensible option for those with intelligence and also cash. It was the right choice, the only choice. Otherwise, one would slip, one could find oneself sliding down from the top of the economic and social pile, well, to the unthinkable. It had apparently happened, people whose GenParents hadn't been prepared to pay the price, and where were their GenOffs now? Running riot in the Dreggie Estates, that's where. Or so Glora said.

Maxo flipped open his 'cator and said "GenPap." The pixels on the small screen assembled into the face of Igo Strang. It occurred to Maxo that he'd never really looked at his GenSire's face before, and although the image was only a couple of thumbnails wide, Maxo looked; in fact, he stared. It was a strong face, handsome, although slightly lopsided because Igo was only proto-enhanced, so facially he still retained some natural characteristics. Apparently, before the first genetically modified children, no one had ever really noticed this lopsidedness that all human beings used to have. Extraordinary really, considering how strange it looked now. Still, Igo's face was handsome. He was dark-haired, clean-shaven, and had the sort of architectural jawline any GenParent would be happy to pay for.

How old was he? Forty-five? Fifty? Birthdays were not much celebrated among the proto-enhanced, it made them aware of how time was passing, forced on them unpleasant comparisons with the Naturals, with whom they shared a short lifespan. But wrinkles, did Dr. Igo Strang have wrinkles? Of course not, even protos had the anticancer and the rejuvenation clusters. Besides, if he had had wrinkles, Maxo's GenDam, Glora Orb, would have screamed so loudly his own scream would have seemed quite insignificant. Glora Orb was ninety-seven years old (though, with her bright blue eyes, flawless skin, and mellifluous voice she looked a scant twenty-five) and on her fourth interface. Meshing with a man who was only proto-enhanced, that was one thing. But wrinkles? Oh no, Glora Orb could not have tolerated wrinkles.

The 'cator glowed. "Sorry," said Igo Strang's shimmering mouth, "Dr. Strang is currently not available. Thank you for your image which has been logged. Voiceprints may be left after the star." Dr. Strang's face dissolved, it whirled, it became a raining silver star. Maxo considered a message. He had three seconds. How could you leave a message about cracks? The seconds passed.

"Good-bye," said the 'cator, and turned itself off. Conserving energy, even of the solar sort, was imperative, everyone in the Polis (as the Announcer often said) knew that. Nothing lasted forever, after all. Maxo flipped the 'cator shut.

"It is now one hundred and twelve days since the last Atrocity," repeated the TropScreen Announcer. *"The credit for this goes, of course, to Leaderene Clore (may her name celeb forever) but also to you, people of the Tropolis, because it is your ears and your eyes that see into the dark places. How many faces on this screen now could you remember?"*

"None," said Maxo. "How can one remember Dreggies?"

He made his way to Washspacel, where he knew his GenDam kept the MediBox. Maybe this was the solution after all. There were a number of different-size body plasters inside, each one color matched either to his or his Gen-Parents' skin types: very pale for Glora, rather swarthier for

Igo, and somewhere in between for himself. He'd never really understood the body-sculpting technology that allowed the plasters, at the moment of application, to mold themselves flush and smooth the body surface.

"Is it important," his GenDam, Glora Orb, had asked once, "to know why the lights go on when the sensors detect your presence in a room? No, it is not. It is only important to know that they will."

Sometimes Maxo disagreed, sometimes Maxo (taking after his scientific GenSire, maybe) thought he should at least have some idea why things worked the way they did. But today he wasn't going to argue with his GenDam, he wasn't going to argue with Sappho. All one needed to know was that BodySculpt was there and it worked. Designed to heal minor cuts and abrasions, what it actually did was cover things up. Maxo took a small Maxo-flesh-colored strip of the plaster and, under the watchful gaze of his GenParents' mirror spotlights, applied it to his face. It felt warm and a little moist. He pressed and held the patch for ten seconds, during which time he felt it harden slightly (while still remaining perfectly supple), and then the crack was gone. The crack was gone! Maxo Evangele Strang was himself once again. One only had to look at his face to know that. He wasn't going to die after all. He was sixteen and he was perfect.

He bounced out of the washroom and hit the living space control panel. The walls went pink. The walls were happy.

Maxo Evangele Strang was saved.

4

On Dreg Estate 4, Stretch drank the evil chocolate. Gala might forget the anniversary—obviously had forgotten—but he could not forget. It was as raw to him as on the day four years ago when his father had set out for the Polis Heights and never returned. The only thing that was different was the speech. He knew exactly what he was going to say to Dr. Igo Strang now. He'd been eleven when his father had disappeared. Well, he wasn't eleven now, he was nearly fifteen and he was making plans. Gala thought he'd gone meekly to the Lab, to knock and see if they'd let him. In fact, he'd gone to look at security.

"They have Poldrones," he burst out suddenly. "Can you believe it! Not just some Clodrone wallahs minding the desks and asking for your securipass, but Poldrones, patrolling—marching up and down outside the building. Eight of them. And that's just the ones you can see."

"All security's up," said Gala evenly. "You can't go within twenty blocks of the Heights now."

Well, it wouldn't stop him. Poldrones might have a reputation for ruthlessness but, judging by the ones at the Polis CrossingPoints, they weren't much more than human robots.

He would be able to outwit them. It was only a matter of time. They'd see. Gala would see.

He'd imagined the scene so many times, when he'd stand in front of Dr. Igo Strang, taller than the doctor probably, look down on him and say:

"Do you know who I am?"

Strang would say "no," of course, but he wouldn't forget the meeting, oh no.

"I'm Finn Lorrell's son," Stretch would begin. "Not his GenOff, his blood-and-guts son. Finn Lorrell, who did his duty, who came to you because the Leaderene asked him to. Answered the call alongside a thousand other men and women from the Estates, agreed to donate Clean Genes because the germline was under threat, because the Polis—at last—recognized that Naturals had something to offer, something untainted, something you and the plastics needed. And none of those men needed to come, what did they owe the Enhanced? Nothing. Nothing at all. Less than nothing. What had the Enhanced ever done for them? Lied to them, deprived them, cheated them, lived off their needs, and tramped on their dreams. And yet, those men and women came, came out of the goodness of their hearts because it was the right thing to do. The honorable thing. For the Polis. And . . ."

"Where's Daz?" Gala said, interrupting his reverie.

"Daz?" repeated Stretch as though he barely recognized the name of their younger brother. And then: "Why didn't you ask him to help with the hospital visit?"

"Because he wasn't here," said Gala simply.

"He said he was going to the burned-out place. See if he couldn't paint there."

"Thanks for letting me know."

"He should have let you know himself!"

"He's only twelve, Stretch." Gala paused. "Which burned-out place anyway?"

"The Havkos'. The one that was firebombed. Apparently one of the rooms is big and pretty much untouched. Big enough to lay out all this new wonder work of his."

Gala sighed. "We should get him. It's late and the lights could go off anytime."

Stretch nodded. No one could say that Gala wasn't responsible, hadn't taken on her mother's mantle. As they tracked back along the corridor, he stopped to peer in at his sleeping mother.

"She looks awful, doesn't she?" Gala said, as if she wanted the truth to be different.

"I'm sorry I wasn't here," said Stretch.

Gala smiled then, her first smile of the evening, "I guess everyone does what they have to do."

"Like Daz," said Stretch.

"Yes, like Daz."

The Havkos' apartment was on Floor 2 of the adjacent building. Appropriating other people's property, even when burned out, was dangerous. There wasn't enough space on the Estates for any accommodation, in no matter what state, to remain empty for long. Technically, the author-ities would clean up the mess and allocate another family. In the meantime—and that meantime might be a year or more—it was first come, first served. Until the Top Boys came or the Mescats or any one of the other Estate gangs. Then you got out and got out fast.

As a matter of habit, both teenagers took flashlights. In

the Estates, one thing you made sure never to run out of was batteries. Gala had a stash in the kitchen cupboard and, unbeknownst to her brothers, another in her underwear drawer. She made small food sacrifices to have enough batteries. Stretch also took a knife, tucked into his right boot, close against his ankle. Gala said it didn't help, it made you more of a target. But Stretch knew what he knew.

Now it was dusk, the lights had come on, on the elevator stairs. It was a feeble, insufficient light, but neither Gala nor Stretch switched on their flashlights. They just walked more slowly, took more care, listening all the time for other footfalls on the stairs. If you met people on their way to Floor 17, they might be cursing, sweating, spoiling for an argument, so you made yourself thin and kept your eyes down. But Gala and Stretch were lucky, they met no one.

Out in the street they both paused and scanned the immediate vicinity. If there was a group of more than five young men together, it would be safer to take the longer route around to the back entrance of Block 214. The gangs were mainly concerned with their own turf wars, but it didn't do to get too close. As with the elevator, you didn't want to make eye contact, that was taken as a challenge, and the weapons would be straight out.

"Okay," said Stretch. "Go." The way was mercifully clear and they walked purposefully fast to the neighboring block. As a matter of routine, they kept in the TropScreen cameras' eye line though, as Stretch often said, unless there were Poldrones within twenty yards, he couldn't see much difference between being filmed while you were murdered and not being filmed while you were murdered, the end result would be the same.

"Did you know the Havkos?" Gala asked.

"No."

"So you don't know who did the firebombing?"

"Someone who didn't want them about," said Stretch simply.

He was right, of course. It was best not to inquire, not to know anything or to get involved. It was safer that way. The Block 214 elevator was working, but it was streaked with urine. Gala and Stretch took the stairs; it was only two floors, after all.

They emerged into the Floor 2 corridor to be hit with a smell both acrid and wet, the sharpness of burned metal doused with water.

"Your brother," said Stretch, putting his hand over his nose and mouth.

The door to the apartment hung off its hinges; Stretch and Gala walked in. Simultaneously, they switched on their flashlights. The hall area was totally blackened, a burned table collapsed next to a puddle of melted plastic, possibly an ex-chair.

"Daz," they called, Stretch's voice was muffled. "Daz!"

The only reply was a faint, low whistling and, up ahead, the glimmer of candles.

The passed a caustic-smelling kitchen and shone in their flashlights to see blackened metal bowls of water on the floor.

"Water," said Stretch ironically.

"Come on," said Gala.

They found Daz in what must have been the living room. Their brother's information (where had he got it? thought Stretch) was accurate. There was some smoke damage here and the windows were sooted up (although Daz had obviously rubbed himself some light when there had been light), but otherwise the room was strangely, miraculously, untouched. Daz was working in the flicker of about sixteen candles, some of them burning on bare wood.

"This place already got burned out once, Daz," said Stretch.

"Hi," replied his brother. "Come in!"

Daz had pushed what little furniture there was to the edges of the room and laid on the floor space five assorted "canvases," one of which was made of thin cotton.

"Daz!" exclaimed Gala. "That's a sheet!"

"It's my sheet," said Daz defensively.

"Daz, we are not made of money."

"No," said Daz, "that's why I had to use my sheet. Canvas being a bit thin on the ground in our house."

"Daz," said Gala despairingly.

Daz's sheet painting, which was clearly meant to join onto the equally large piece of cloth that abutted it, was a blaze of color. The design was abstract, it could have been a triumphantly rising sun; it could have been a whirl of red-and-gold fireworks; it could have been the sort of autumn your grandfather talked about.

"The paints . . . ," began Gala. It was a big canvas, there was a lot of paint.

"Gubbins gave them to me," said Daz quickly. Gubbins was an old man who lived on Floor 12 of their block. A painter and decorator by trade, he used to paint in his spare time. Daz had been running errands for him since the elevator broke.

"I thought it was just advice he was giving you."

"He wants me to have the paints," said Daz. "I didn't steal them, Gala, he gave them to me."

Stretch wasn't paying attention to this familiar altercation, he was looking at the painting.

"Why don't you paint what you see, Daz?" he asked.

"What?"

"This," said Stretch, pointing out through the smoke-blackened windows into the dark and the flickering danger of the Estate beyond. "All this stuff. Our lives. Why don't you paint that?"

"I do paint our lives," said Daz surprised. "Well, my life anyway. This is what I see. When I look about, I see this."

Gala looked properly then. Normally, she just saw the paint, the cost, the worry, and the fear, for surely it was only a matter of time before there was no more paint to beg or borrow, and then he would steal. She knew he would. The painting was an obsession. Now she looked at the picture.

"It's beautiful, Daz."

"Thanks," he said. "Thanks very much." He was so unlike his elder brother, Gala thought. There was more meat on him, less anger. He bloomed somehow.

"Come on," said Stretch. "We need to get home. Roll that thing up."

"I can't," said Daz. "It's wet."

"So what do you propose to do?" Stretch asked. "Stay here all night until it dries?"

"Yes," said Daz simply.

"No," said Stretch.

"Anyway I can't take it home wet, it's oils, this one, and you know Mom can't stand the smell now."

That was true, that was why he was sent out of the house to paint.

"Anyone could come in the night," Gala said. "It's not safe."

"I'm not leaving the picture."

"Fine," said Stretch suddenly. "Then I'll stay here with you, Daz. Thanks for mentioning about bringing a sleeping bag."

"There are sofas," said Daz happily.

"One seriously charred sofa," said Stretch.

And Gala, who wanted so much for there to be something more in her life than there was, nodded gratefully, perhaps at the painting, perhaps at one or both of her brothers, and then she left, returning down the stairs and across the concrete wasteland toward her mother.

Which is when the TropScreen cameras freeze-framed.

Gala knew it was a freeze-frame because the constant buzzing and whirling of the building cameras stopped for an instant and the noise went down a pitch. Normally she wouldn't have minded, it's not as if she wasn't used to it, the Enhanced Sector spying on them all, spying on itself, but suddenly it all exploded inside her: the money! The money they spent on those cameras, and on the verification process afterward. She couldn't imagine the amount of money that was being spent in that one minute, but it would be plenty enough money to buy her mother some cancer drugs, to extend her life, to ease her pain! Gala opened her mouth and she howled.

Not that there was anyone close enough to hear her.

5

At roughly the same time, in a Polis Heights apartment, the Announcer was announcing: *"There are people who are not concentrating. The Leaderene knows it. She requests a one-minute standstill. All members of the Polis to report to a Trop-Screen immediately."*

Maxo, in a happy mood, (after all, the crack was beneath the BodySculpt and he was saved) found himself in front of the screen. He saluted.

"Now," said the Announcer, *"this is a freeze-frame. Pay attention to every face on the screen. Your life and the life of the Polis could depend on your being able to recall the location or identity of one or more of these potentially dangerous people."*

The screen froze on a depressing little scene outside what appeared to be Block 213, Dreg Estate 4. It was dusk in the Estates and, as the Dreggies clearly didn't know how to enjoy a good night out, there weren't many people about: a small gang of youths with hoods up (deliberate obstruction of Verification was an offense against the Polis—they'd probably be dealt with later); an old man caught halfway through a stumble; a woman wearing what looked like some sort of sack; and . . . and . . . CelebHigh and live forever—an incredible girl! Maxo felt a huge and shocking surge of something pound through his veins. What a girl! He felt he was going to explode. Everyone else on the screen simply disappeared. In fact, there was no one else there at all, possibly no one else in the Polis, in the world, but this one girl. She had huge brown eyes, a lopsided face, an angular frame, and wild, disheveled black hair. Her mouth was half open as though she was screaming or crying out for something. For him, perhaps? Yes, she would be crying out for Maxo Evangele Strang. They were utterly meant for each other, she for him and he for her. In that moment, Maxo lost his perfect heart to her. He wanted an interface— more than this, he wanted a mesh!

The Announcer pressed a button, the world moved on. The girl moved on, was lost behind the edge of a building. But in Maxo's mind's eye, she was still there, the most synthentic of all the creatures he'd ever seen, he perfected her. He did!

His 'cator flashed. The image of the rather less perfect Bovis Frank appeared.

"Yes?" said Maxo, coming over curmudgeonly.

"Guess what?" said Bovis.

"What?" said Maxo.

"I've randomly been assigned your number and you need to describe to me one of the Dreg faces you saw for identification and verification purposes. You have six seconds to describe him or her and I'll need your security number for an input reference."

"Dreggies?" said Maxo. "Those people on the screen— they were Dreggies?"

"No fooling, Maxo," said Bovis. "This is for real. You really have been assigned to me for Verification and security. Polis safety, our safety, depends on all of us being vigilant all the time. You know that. Don't blow it for both of us, Maxo."

"Dreggies," repeated Maxo. He had fallen in mesh with a Dreggie. It was vile, it was revolting. It was also impossible. He must be ill after all. Beneath the BodySculpt, he was very, very ill.

"I don't believe it," said Maxo.

The walls, unable to keep up emotionally, flashed, sputtered, and finally settled on a kind of sick yellow.

Back in the Laboratory, Dr. Igo Strang was thinking of his long-term mesh, Glora Orb. Usually Dr. Strang didn't like anyone or anything to interrupt the flow of his rigorous scientific thought. But Glora Orb—Glora Orb! Even her name was delicious, almost as lovely as the word *eggs*. What a marvelous woman she was, he'd just have a little peek at her on his 'cator. He whispered her name aloud and the pixels on his screen immediately rearranged themselves into the face of his perfection. Her blue eyes were huge, they were pools, Igo thought, of beauty. The early genmasters had modeled the eyes (of girls, at least) on the eyes of babies. Why did people melt when babies were around? Because of their eyes, of course, those huge take-me-home-and-look-after-me eyes. Glora's eyes were so huge, you could see four different shades of blue in them. You could also see, around the pupil, an extraordinary starburst of golden yellow, which exactly matched the color of her hair.

The 'cator glowed as it contacted his MeshBaby. Glora Orb's perfectly pink mouth moved: "Glora Orb is currently involved in the final preparations for the Art of the Century

35

show, opening at the Glora Orb Gallery on October 31, Year of our Leaderene 34. No voiceprints may be left at this time. Please try later."

How many times had Igo accessed this message in the last few weeks? Four times a day, maybe five times, although he did it a little furtively, careful not to set the wrong example to Laboratory staff.

He was about to flip the 'cator shut when it began to glow the pale blue that indicated an incoming message. Llublo Quells! Igo moved quickly from the Lab bench into his admin office, shutting the door behind him. He pointed the 'cator's infrared at a wall screen's receptor and Llublo Quells's face became instantly huge. It was huge anyway, reflected Igo, and rather blubbery. The poor man had missed out on the antiobesity gene markers for which everyone beyond GemD was eligible. Perhaps his GenParents hadn't cared, perhaps they liked the idea of a fat son. Igo allowed himself a little laugh. Llublo was lucky that his massive status (and certainly Igo wasn't laughing at that) meant people were more forgiving about his massive body weight.

Llublo Quells's large lips wobbled.

"Are you alone, Strang?" he asked in his thick voice.

Igo winced, even now, at this patronizing use of his surname. But he was working on it, working hard in the Lab toward the point where he became not just chief scientist, but also "Igo."

"Yes," said Igo.

"Good," said Llublo Quells. "We have a problem."

This might be anything, but it probably involved money. Things usually became problems for Llublo Quells when they involved losing money. In his boss's pause, Igo wondered what part of the empire was beginning to shake.

"In the last eight hours, MediAlert has taken 3,017 hits from concerned GemXs. It appears that this generation is experiencing a mass degradation. Symptoms seems to vary from what the younger members are calling 'cracks' to unusual emotional disturbances. Have you a view, Strang?"

Strang had a view. Strang's view was that he ought to 'cator his GemX GenOff Maxo right away.

6

Maxo Evangele Strang, who had a plan, arrived at the Virtual Date Palace and entered the Males Only tunnel. The VDP Protector, assigned to check gender, ran a TestosScanner over the lower half of his body.

"Proceed," he intoned.

Maxo proceeded. This evening the lights in the tunnel were throbbing purple circles crisscrossed with white lasers, and the music was electric saxophone. Sometime Maxo wondered what they had in the female tunnel. Bovis had tried to check once and almost had his gender reassigned by a Palace heavy wielding an OestroWand.

Maxo emerged into the holding area and presented his eye to the Palace scanner.

"Strang, M," he announced. "GemX."

At the registration desk, a girl in a regulation brown Clodrone ambisuit checked his iris scan against the information held on the screen in front of her. Maxo clicked impatiently as he waited. He wanted to appear normal, but he was far from normal—the image of the Dreggie girl was flashing repeatedly across his brain.

Which is why he'd come. All decent, all proper interfaces began in a Virtual Date Palace. Keeping the purity of the germline was far too important a project, so the Leaderene said, to be left to chance. One needed control. HighElites, therefore, came to the VDP from the age of twelve. They came for fun—and also to learn the rules. In the VDP there were rules about everything from the use of 'cators to the exchange of genetic information. Rules, after all, kept you safe. As you got older, you were allowed to access the private rooms—though everyone knew the operator was always listening in. If you were near the age of gene-transfer (and Maxo was), your GenParents would be informed of any potential interfaces. That was right—people needed to be vetted, credentials checked. In the VDP therefore, there could be no sudden, unwarranted assault by some ludicrous Dreggie.

"All clear, Mr. Strang," trilled the Clodrone. "May I have you 'cator, please?"

Maxo was about to hand over the communicator when it started to vibrate. Igo.

"Do you want to take that?" Clodrone 2017 inquired helpfully.

"No," said Maxo, flicking his GenSire away. How could he have a conversation about cracks and repellent Dreggie girls in front of a VDP representative?

Maxo watched Clodrone 2017 log the 'cator against his name and place it in the Incommunicado Safe. It was forbidden to exchange 'cator numbers in the Virtual Date Palace—if you wanted another client's details, you had to log a request and, if it was accepted by the other party's GenParents, then you had to pay. The Incommunicado Safe was an extra layer of security, it prevented a client running a satellsearch on the building and logging the numbers of all users in the vicinity. It also prevented the VDP from losing money.

So—Igo wouldn't be able to track him either. That was good, Maxo thought, because, by the end of the evening, things might have changed. If Catspaw was in—if—there might be no need to talk about cracks or mental deterioration.

"Cubicle 26," said the Clodrone assistant, giving him a small white plastic card. "Payment is in five-minute blocks, or periods of five minutes. Private rooms cost double. Credit will be down-lined immediately. Have a virtually amazing time."

"Naturally," said Maxo ironically.

The cubicle was more like a small room, about eight feet long and four feet wide. At the far end was the desk and the options console. The rest of the room appeared empty. Maxo sat at the desk, slotted in the white card, and the wall screen in front of him sprang to life. Numerous options presented themselves, but Maxo was a seasoned campaigner and turned at once to the Palace Sign-In list and scanned the monikers of the girls. There were already forty-five of them and they were listed by arrival time, last in BetaBeauty, MeshGoddess, and X Marks The Spot.

"Rearrange alphabetically," barked Maxo. He scrolled down, his normally expert fingers fumbling. Please be in, please.

"Yes!"

There she was, right at the top of the Cs, Catspaw, the most synthetic of all the girls in the Polis. Of course, he'd only ever seen her padding around the Palace as a cat—but what a sight! She'd soon knock the image of that lopsided

Dreggie out of his brain! What an amazing piece of perfection she was, and how fitting she should be in the Palace right now, when it wasn't even her preferred (or purr-ferred, as she would say) night. It must be a sign. Tonight would be the night, he'd request her 'cator number, she'd accept, and then, at last, he could relegate his "feelings" for the TropScreen Dreg girl to the delete box, where they belonged.

Maxo hit the keyboard with enthusiasm (the VDP really took your mind off things), scrolled to the boys' sign-in list, and punched in "The Max." Next he selected the option "Full HoloMorph," put the screen in map-mode, and stood up. He positioned himself on the footprints marked in the apparently empty part of the room and lights and cameras began to whirr.

"Morphing shape?" inquired a disembodied voice.

"Human," replied Maxo, "model self." On the wall screen in front of him a life-size image appeared, a ghostly three-dimensional version of himself. You could choose almost anything you wanted: historical people, contemporary figures, vegetation. Bovis had once spent months as an extinct tree; the oak, Maxo seemed to remember. Typical Bovis; as a tree you couldn't move very fast and were often found blocking corridors, so girls had to start conversations with you, if only to ask you to move out of the way. But tonight, the stakes were high; Maxo needed to impress.

"Select," he announced to his image. He was handsome, Maxo thought, even as a series of three-dimensional lines.

"Color?" continued the voice.

"Rainbow," said Maxo.

The strands of himself on the screen twisted into red and

41

violet, blue and green, he looked vibrant, energetic, and, Maxo thought, a little as if he might be trying too hard.

"Rearrange blue," he said. Immediately his screen image toned down. Maxo turned slowly on the spot and his image turned with him. Blue was a sober, a serious color; Maxo thought Catspaw would like blue.

"Select."

"Any enhancement to features?" asked the voice.

"No," said Maxo. He wasn't being vain, he was simply being honest. Most people accepted that GemXs were about as perfectly formed as it was possible to be, so modification wasn't really necessary. It was the GemLs that needed that. And the GemKs—their jawlines, what a joke. Besides, Maxo wanted Catspaw to know what she was getting in advance, a top-of-the-range model. He was pretty sure (from her conversation) that she was also a GemX. She'd appreciate the brand.

"You are in the anteroom," said the voice. "You may move freely in all public rooms in the Palace. For private rooms you need to request access and log your name at the door. Any moving through walls is strictly forbidden and . . ."

"Yeah, yeah." Maxo pressed "skip" and then returned to his position on the footprints.

"Let's go." You could sit at the console and use the keys to move through the Palace rooms, or you could stand on the footprints and, by making seemingly insignificant gestures to the right or left, backward or forward, you could steer your own body. Novices tended to fall over, or bang into walls or other morphs, but that was part of the fun, part of the chat-up-line routine. Maxo wasn't a novice, but it didn't stop him, occasionally, banging into certain morphs.

Maxo, treading softly on the spot, moved out of the screen anteroom into the screen corridor. On the plasma wall his HoloMorph moved with a natural, easy stride. It made him feel good, it made him feel back in control again.

At the edge of the wall screen there was a ground plan of the Palace, but Maxo knew his way about well enough not to have to look at it. He made for the Grand Hall, where most Morphs would be dancing, and people like Bovis would be sitting on the sidelines pretending that's what trees did. Maxo had thought about trying a Direct-Access, which meant keying in his name and then Catspaw's and asking immediately for a private room meet, but he was pretty sure she'd refuse him. She liked playing games, especially the cat-and-mouse variety. "Why don't you actually come as a mouse, next time?" she'd asked him once. "Then we could have some real fun." But he hadn't fallen for that. In fact, if he remembered correctly, he'd spent the next purrfect night as an Alsatian. She hadn't entirely seen the joke. So—no DirectAccess, it would be better to just "happen" across her. He'd signed his normal name "The Max," so she'd know he was in.

He took the quickest route to the Grand Hall, which meant passing through the Games Room in which, as usual, people were flexing their morph skills, challenging one another for pinpoint accuracy in ball kicking or landing punches. It was really a room for the younger kids, he'd liked it himself when he was about thirteen.

As he approached the Grand Hall, he could hear both the music and the amplified buzz of conversation. The Palace DJ had the lights on fluorescent, and everyone's color was

43

heightened and throbbing. As he stepped into the room and saw his outline brighten, he was glad to have chosen a restrained blue as his base color. In the middle of the dance floor was the gyrating form of a rainbow anaconda, SnakeCharmer. Maxo tried to focus beyond her, scanning for Catspaw among the other couples. He could see a lioness or two, but definitely no cats. In the cubicle he swung his head this way and that, trying to identify the morphs gathered in groups at the edge of the floor. He was just hoping Catspaw hadn't gone to the virtual toilets for a girls-only chat, when he spotted her. She was curled on some cushion at the far end of the hall surrounded by men; well, by two human morphs and a shark. As he moved toward the group, Maxo checked their hovering names—all new to him. At Catspaw's feet sat a large purple human morph called Zen. Standing next to him was a regular-size historomorph, Alan Turing (some mathematician, Maxo thought, or perhaps the inventor of the computer?), and lolling to his right was an angry-looking, gray-green shark, simply called Teeth.

Maxo arrived. "Hi, Purrfect," he said.

"Are you talking to me?" asked the shark.

"Hardly," said Maxo.

Catspaw stopped licking her left foot. "Ooh," she said. "The Max."

"You know this guy?" asked Zen languidly.

"We have met," said Catspaw. "He used to be a dog."

"Still looks like a dog to me," said Teeth.

"You think?" said Catspaw, looking Maxo's perfectly formed GemX body up and down. "I rather think he might have just been hiding his light under a doggy bushel."

"Well, as I was saying," Alan Turing blustered suddenly, "how do you know I'm not a robot?"

"We have every reason to believe you are," said Teeth. "You move like a robot. You act like a robot. And your conversation is definitely robotic."

"Catspaw," said Alan Turing, "perhaps we should continue this conversation in a private room?"

"Meow," said Catspaw.

"The point is," continued Turing, "you can't prove I have a conscious mind and, by the same token, you can't disprove that the TropScreen, for instance, has a conscious mind."

"Chill out," said Zen.

"Are these gentlemen boring you?" asked Maxo.

Catspaw flicked her tail. "Maybe."

And that's how it would normally start, she'd give him some tiny scrap of encouragement and he'd spend hours (and a great deal of money) trying to eke it out into some meaningful 'cator connection. But tonight he just didn't have the time. He didn't. He suddenly needed to know right now. Was he sick or wasn't he? In the cubicle, his ambisuit was whirring.

"Catspaw," he said, "I need you . . ."

"Need her"—interrupted the shark, teeth bared. "Need her! Who the celeb do you think you are?"

"Need you, need to ask you something, Catspaw," stammered Maxo. "Something incredibly important, something . . ."

"Private room?" purred Catspaw. "Is that what you're saying?"

It was now or never. "Yes," said Maxo.

"Eleven months, six days, and about twenty-five minutes," said Catspaw. "I thought you'd never ask."

She rose from her cushion and arched her back. "Bye bye, boys."

"What?" spluttered Turing.

"We've been here hours," said Teeth.

"Plenty more fish in the sea, man," said Zen.

"This way," said Catspaw, and sashayed out of the Great Hall and along the corridor. Maxo followed, transfixed.

The first two private rooms they passed were engaged. What a malfunctionary I am, thought Maxo, I could have got her 'cator number months ago. Only had to ask. No, only had to appear in human morph form, me, Maxo Strang, GemX . . .

"Here we are," said Catspaw. Private Room 17 was free, there was a bleep in Maxo's cubicle as he entered the room, indicating the price rise, and a click in his ambisuit as the thermostat recognized his need for sweat control.

There were many private rooms in the Virtual Date Palace, each one different from the next. This one was decorated with virtual skins from extinct animals: the lion, the tiger, the puma, the black panther, and the leopard.

"Highly appropriate," murmured Catspaw appreciatively. She stretched herself out on the floor, her head against the mane of the largest lion in the room. "Now what?" she asked.

Maxo stood a little awkwardly. In the cubicle he found himself jigging uncomfortably from foot to foot. In the private room his holo-image looked a little unsteady. He was so close, he couldn't lose his nerve now.

"You wanted something," encouraged Catspaw. "*Needed* something . . ."

Maxo hopped.

"A little something beginning with *c*, maybe?" Catspaw continued. "As in *c* for 'cat . . .'"

"Cat," cried Maxo.

"'Cator," said Catspaw sternly. "'Cator number."

"May I remind you," interrupted a disembodied voice, "that any unauthorized exchange of 'cator numbers will result in immediate termination of cubicle contact. Gen-Parents will be informed and a fine will be payable before release of 'cators from the Incommunicado Safe . . ."

"Shut up," said Maxo. "We know. And yes, yes, yes to 'cator numbers but also *c* for cat. I mean, do you have to be a cat?"

A little fur rose on the back of Catspaw's neck. "You don't like me as a cat?"

"As a cat, you are utterly synthentic. You are the most perfect, purrfect cat I've ever seen. But I just wondered if I could, you know, see you, just once as . . ."

"As my human morph GemX self?"

"Yes," cried Maxo. She was a GemX. "Oh yes! And also maybe—know your name?"

"Meow," said the cat, "you ask a lot," and then she added, "Lydida."

Lydida. He hadn't known her name and now it was in his mouth, Lydida. Lydida! He didn't feel a bit ill.

"Lydida," he moaned.

"Desperate," said the cat. "Well then, shut your eyes."

Maxo did not shut his eyes.

"And you can tell me your name, morph. I don't think you introduced yourself."

"Maxo. I'm Maxo."

"Well, Maxo, I said shut your eyes, didn't I?"

Maxo shut them.

"Now what color would you like me?"

"Any color," said Maxo. "Your choice of color."

"Clodrone brown, perhaps?"

"No, no maybe not."

"Any color, you said," remarked the cat.

"Well, Clodrone brown then," said Maxo.

"No," said Lydida. "Gold. That's my choice. Gold."

There was an impossibly long moment while in her cubicle, Lydida selected her new morph form.

"Feature Enhanced?" she asked Maxo in response to the computer's question.

"Of course not," he said. "You're a GemX."

"Ah," she said. "So true. Open your eyes."

Maxo opened his eyes.

She was tall and glittering and gold. Her willowy figure had a perfectly cinched-in twenty-two-inch waist and her golden hair (blonde, presumably) was halfway down her back. She turned with catlike grace to show him her perfect GemX profile, her sculptured cheekbones, her limpidly large golden (blue in real life) eyes, her long neck, her perfectly proportioned teeth, and her utterly golden smile.

"There," she said.

"Oh no," he said.

"What?" she asked.

"No," he cried, "no, no, no."

Because she wasn't beautiful at all. She just looked like (and indeed was like) every other GemX girl in the Polis. The golden same. She didn't make him surge and pound—did that mean he wanted to surge and pound now, that he liked the feeling? No, it did not. But this girl in front of him, she didn't do anything for him at all, she wasn't important, she could have been just anybody, though she was, he realized suddenly, Lydida Malkin, someone he'd known since EduCate. By contrast, the girl on the TropScreen, the dark lopsided girl from the Dreggie estate, with her black eyes and her contorted mouth, she was . . . she was . . . in his blood! She was also in his brain. So, as he looked at Lydida Malkin, he saw only the Dreggie girl. The dark Dreggie girl filled his screen and surged through his veins.

"You don't like me?" cried Lydida, and she seemed to be trembling. "Mr. Maxo Strang. It is you, Maxo, isn't it? I'm not perfect enough for you?"

"No," said Maxo. "It's not you. It's me. I'm sick. Sick, sick, sick." And he was trembling too, in fact he was shaking from head to foot at the sheer, indescribable horror of it all.

"You're sick?" said Lydida. "You're sick?" She pulled at something near her golden temple and the virtual skin around her eye broke into a thousand tinier golden lines. "Look at me," shrieked Lydida Malkin. "I'm fifteen, I'm a GemX and I've got WRINKLES."

But Maxo wasn't looking, Maxo was running, out of the cubicle and along a real corridor and through the holding area and back down the tunnel out into the Polis where he thought, perhaps, he'd be able to breathe.

7

Clodrone 1640 sat outside the Virtual Date Palace in his master's car. Igo Strang had done a satellsearch on Maxo's 'cator and discovered its last active location had been very close to the entrance of the Virtual Date Palace. He'd ordered 1640 to go and pick up his GenOff if and when he emerged. So Clodrone 1640 was sitting and watching and waiting. He was also thinking. "It is not necessary for Clodrones to think," his PodTutor had often said, "it is only necessary for Clodrones to obey." And certainly 1640 had never been comfortable with thinking, because it often confused him. He started out with some important question (or a question he thought was important), but he never seemed to get to an answer, things just went around and around in his brain and then got tangled up. That was exactly what was happening with the issue of a second Degrade (if there was such a thing); somehow he wasn't getting anywhere with this subject.

He'd lain awake all the previous night wrestling with the conundrum. The seven other Clodrones in his pod had all been asleep. There were four LieDowns, stacked floor to ceiling, on either side of the very small space. He'd noticed (but only very recently) how the Masters had large spaces called rooms and the Clodrones had small spaces called pods. Why was that? The same reason, he supposed, that, in his Master's house, a piece of flat material jutting out from a wall was called a shelf whereas in the pod it was called a LieDown and you slept on it. Masters, on the other hand, slept on detached, square, comfy-looking things that stood in the middle of their pods (rooms) and were called beds. No wonder he couldn't think, when words shifted about depending on whose house (or Podcenter) you were in. Now where was he?

Oh yes, the existence (or not) of a second Degrade. He understood the Degrade itself, everyone understood that, it was part of Training. You started work at sixteen and then, after about eight years, your efficiency dropped. It wasn't your fault. No. But it was your responsibility to inform your PodMaster when you experienced any of the symptoms, (such as physical weakness or forgetfulness) because the eight years could be seven or it could be nine. There was no shame in reporting yourself and all that happened, when certain tests had been carried out to confirm the diagnosis, was that one day when you turned up to the Association Room to get your daily allowance of Food Pills, the Pod-Master would sign you off work for the day so that you could attend the Clodrone Medicenter for Rejuvenation. Here you would be subject to some injections and some medication (no one knew exactly what, but clearly it was in your best interests), after which you improved. Not immediately, it took a few weeks, but then your brain would clear and you'd become strong and able again, you'd be aching to demonstrate to your Master your new-found energy and efficiency. Yes, he'd got that right, he was sure.

So. So—should he be reporting himself now? All his Training suggested to 1640 that, with these new (and disturbing) symptoms he should be reporting himself, but he wasn't sure that he could explain to the Master what he couldn't explain to himself. Which was one of the reasons for all this thinking.

The problem was he wasn't feeling weak and he wasn't feeling forgetful, he was feeling . . . "not himself," that was the nearest he could get to it. When he'd heard the Masters talk about "not feeling themselves," it seemed to relate to some physical illness, whereas his not being himself, seemed more to do with feeling that he was in danger of becoming someone else, and not any old someone else either, but a very specific someone, a person who actually had a name: Finn. That was it really: Clodrone 1640 sometimes thought he was metamorphosing into a man called Finn. Which didn't make any sense, which was one of the reasons he didn't like to bother the PodMaster.

He even had a picture in his mind of how this Finn looked: middle-aged and tall and thin-boned, which was particularly disconcerting as he himself had always been a Regulation Medium. The Finn man also had piercing blue eyes, whereas 1640 had Preferred-Brown. Not that 1640's body had actually changed in any way (he kept a constant check on that, in the Master's mirrors, in the windshield of the Master's car, in the glass windows of the sky elevator), but he felt it might. Yes. He felt his body might, without warning, slip away and he'd find himself in Finn's. Which was frightening, but not nearly as frightening as being a vessel for Finn's emotions.

Finn's emotions were extraordinary, there were great

raging torrents of them. They ravaged him, they splurged and splattered through his normally sanguine blood. As a Clodrone, 1640 was not used to being hyped up about things. After all, there was nothing in life to get excited about. Finn, on the other hand, seemed in an almost permanent state of fury. Of course, 1640 had witnessed other people's fury many times. Glora Orb, for instance, was prone to towering tempers, which, although his Master called them "endearing," seemed to leave Glora in a state of extreme—Clodrone 1640 considered his expression with care—"foam" for some considerable time. Whereas he, Clodrone 1640, was a calm person. *"At all times and in all places"* (Code of Conduct 3, Rule 28) *"Clodrones are to remain totally calm."* He was calm because it was his duty to be calm and also because he knew and understood things: like the difference between good and evil (and how he needed to be good), and the importance of the UnquestionObey, and how to speak only when spoken to, and many other useful Training things, so the mad foaming stuff was not something he'd personally experienced before the advent of Finn. But now, almost daily, he got the foams. It made his head lurch, his stomach lurch; if he'd been a basin he would have felt inclined to pull the plug on himself, to let it all drain away. Because it was too much, this great uncontrollable wash of—stuff. And it wasn't his, it was Finn's, all Finn's stuff foaming through him. But that didn't make any sense, because there was no such person as Finn, there was only him, Clodrone 1640. So—so?

So put that aside, concentrate on the second Degrade, that's what he was trying to get to the bottom of. The Degrade (didn't the word *the* suggest there would only be the one?) was explained in Training, but a subsequent one where instead of feeling weak you got invaded by some random person intent on making you feel whatever it was that he felt—well, no one seemed to have talked about that. It wasn't in the manual.

This was a moment for asking questions, he supposed, but asking questions was not polite, it ran counter to Clodrone Lesson 2, Year 2, Rule 1. Besides, there was no one to ask. The obvious consultant would be an older Clodrone and he realized with a sudden Finn-like rush of horror, that there weren't any. Steady on, was that true? He considered the eight people in his pod and the six pods on his floor and the fourteen floors in his building. Yes. Of all those people, all six or seven hundred of them, he didn't think he knew a single one who was as old—or older—than he: twenty-eight years. Not that he knew everyone, in fact he didn't even know all the Clos on his floor, but you saw people about, and they were all young. Why had he never noticed that before?

The PodMasters were right. Asking questions, thinking, it didn't do any good, it just got things in more of a muddle. He blamed Finn. Surely there must be a rule against people like Finn? If the PodMaster knew, 1640 was sure he would ban Finn. People like Finn weren't fair, weren't appropriate.

So?

So Maxo Evangele Strang was coming out of the Virtual Date Palace; Clodrone 1640 might have missed him, so fast was Dr. Strang's GenOff walking, with his head down, apparently oblivious to everyone on the pavement around him. Clodrone 1640 clicked open the driver's side window and called: "Master Strang, Master Strang."

There was no reply. 1640 got out of the car. It made him feel wonderful to be doing what he did best, to be following orders.

"Master Strang!" repeated 1640, intercepting his quarry.

Maxo's head jerked up. "What the celeb are you doing here?"

"Your GenPap sent me to fetch you," said 1640 calmly. "Bring you to the Lab."

"What in celeb for?" The young master was very agitated, it was as though he couldn't stand still, keep still, his hand kept going to his right temple, scratching. "What does he want me for?"

That was a difficult question. 1640's job was to do what his Master, Dr. Igo Strang, asked. The doctor had asked him to fetch his GenOff from the Virtual Date Palace and bring him to the Lab. There was no reason given and no reason asked. Finn would have asked for a reason so Finn would have had an answer to the difficult question. But he was not Finn, he was Clodrone 1640. He was. He was!

Scratch, scratch, scratch went Maxo Strang at his temple.

"Please get in," said Clodrone 1640 doggedly, holding open the rear-seat door.

"No," said Maxo Strang vehemently, "not until you tell—" and then, quite suddenly, he stepped into the car.

"Thank you." As 1640 closed the door and climbed into the driver's seat, he felt a surge of Clodrone pride. *The pride of the Clodrone is a job well done.* Praise Rule 54.

"Only we're not going to the Lab," said Maxo Strang. "I want you to drive me to Block 213, Dreg Estate 4."

Clodrone 1640 felt the lurchy sensation. "I can't," he faltered.

"You can and you will," said Maxo Strang. "This is not a request, this is an order. I am ordering you to take me to Dreg Estate 4."

1640 understood the right thing to do. In situations like this, Training took over. A Clodrone obeyed his Master, Dr. Igo Strang was his Master. A lesser member of the family might give orders, but not in contradiction to the Master's. Clodrone Code of Conduct 3, Rule 1: *a Clodrone will obey his primary Master at all times.* Simple. He should drive immediately to the Lab. So why was he hesitating, why did it feel like someone else (Finn, presumably) was sputtering in his ear—go on, go to the Estates, you live there, don't you? It's your home!

"Now!" said Maxo. "At once."

Clodrone 1640 put the key card in the slot and the dashboard activated. He pushed the navigation system button: after all, he didn't know his way to the Estates.

"Let's go!" Clodrone 1640 heard himself say, rather uncharacteristically, and something foreign but extraordinarily pleasurable bubbled up through his body, something that finally arrived in his mouth as a kind of hiccup.

"Are you laughing?" asked Maxo Strang.

And Clodrone 1640, who'd never laughed before, was afraid (very afraid) that he was.

8

Stretch was up at dawn, but then he'd been up most of the night anyway. There had been no way to secure the front door of the Havkos' apartment so he and Daz had built a hefty barricade of burned furniture and booby-trapped it with delicately balanced light bulbs and pieces of thin china, anything, in fact, that they could find that might drop and smash if intruders were to try and find a way in. As soon as the work was done, Daz had announced that Stretch could have the sofa and then curled himself up on the floor next to his paintings and had promptly fallen asleep.

Stretch had not taken the sofa, he'd taken the two not too badly smoke-damaged cushions from the sofa and laid them close to the barricade. From his position in the hall-way, he could monitor the front door (or lack of it) and see out through the narrow kitchen to the Estate beyond. He lay down but he did not sleep. There was noise in the apartment above them; a man and a woman arguing in the apartment below; there were footfalls in the stairwell. He was still awake at 1:00 AM when the first of the Poldrone sirens went off. He got up to stretch his stiff legs and patrol the apartment. In the living room he shone his flashlight over the outline of his brother's sleeping body, marveling at how comfortable Daz looked on the unforgiving floorboards. Unwilling to wake his brother, but still curious, he moved the beam close to Daz's face. Even asleep Daz contrived to look happy. What was it about him that seemed to keep everything else at bay?

Stretch returned to his station and dozed briefly until, at 1:45 AM, a vicious fight broke out somewhere in street level darkness. He waited for more Poldrone sirens, but this time there were none. When the sirens went off again at 3:00 AM he wasn't sure whether he had or hadn't slept. There was a blaze on the third floor of the block opposite. He couldn't stop himself getting up and going to check out of the kitchen window whether his mother's block had also been hit, but it was thankfully dark. In the painting room Daz slept on, oblivious. Stretch returned to his makeshift bed.

Despite the cushions the floorboards felt sharp on Stretch's bones. Or maybe it was his bones that were sharp. "You're too like your father," his mother would say, "too thin. You'll eat yourself up, inside out." He liked it when she compared him to his father, liked the ease with which she still spoke of her husband after four years of absence. Sometimes he was afraid that his own memories of Finn would dissolve much as the man seemed to have. That's why he made a conscious effort to pin things down, remember as exactly as he could the big details and the little ones. Finn had been a Licensed ReGenerator—or Scavenger as they were known in the Estates—it was a dirty and dangerous job and Stretch knew (knew or thought? That's how slippery memory could be) that Finn should have had a different life, one that allowed him to dream. Scavenge Men couldn't afford to dream; from dawn to dusk they toiled at the Polis ReGeneration Plant.

"Polis ReGeneration Plant," Finn had said angrily. "It's a junkyard, a garbage dump." Once, only once, he'd taken Stretch to see for himself. The plant covered an area on the outskirts of the Polis nearly a mile square. It was a huge toppling edifice to the Enhanceds' waste. Scavengers clambered over the rusted skeletons of Clodrone cars and the smashed innards of technoputers, they picked their way over decaying soft furnishings and mounds of discarded (but slashed—as per Regulations) ambisuits. They wore gloves at all times, careful of the broken medicine vials, the sudden sharp wires, and the soft accumulation of detritus beneath (human? animal?), which everyone knew carried disease. The Scavengers retrieved what they could and sold it on: the bits of ambisuit to be resewn by the Estate seamstresses (Naturals weren't permitted to wear full ambisuits and, in any case, without the thermal controls, the material was actually far too thin to be of use in the Estates so it had to be reconstructed three or four layers deep); the digibits from old TropScreens or fridge memories that certain dedicated Estate programers could sometimes transform into drivers for worn-out washing machines or broken elevator switches. The prize though was the pixel unit from an abandoned 'cator. These made the most money because they could be used to upgrade the Estates' low-level mobile communicators. More than one man had been killed over disputed access to a pixel unit.

Lying on the sofa cushions, Stretch tried to crystallize that day at the plant. "They should deal with their own waste," Finn had said, his thin skin almost white over the bones of his face, "or pay us to do it. Not charge us for licenses to pick over their dirt." Then he'd paused and put an unaccustomed arm around his son.

"There are things that are right and things that are wrong, son," he'd added, and that detail had stuck in Stretch's mind because his father had said it quietly, without anger, as though it was a plain and simple thing.

Stretch coughed, a dry, rasping sound. Thirst had been nagging at him for some hours, but he'd been trying to ignore it. It was one of his control mechanisms. With water supply in the Estates so unreliable, you were often thirsty, so it made sense to try and train the body, curb its needs. But the desire was too strong now. With the exception of the rancid chocolate, he'd drunk nothing since noon the previous day. He got up and went to the kitchen sink. He delayed turning the tap for a full thirty seconds; this was control time but also dream-time, he could dream there would be water, couldn't he? He twisted the tap.

Nothing.

Of course nothing. Behind him was one of the bowls of blackened water, at least he believed it to be water. He knelt down and cupped his hands in the liquid, brought it to his nose, sniffed. It smelled of soot and metal, nothing else. He took a sip; it tasted of soot and metal and a powdery blackness stuck to his lips. But it was wet. He swallowed.

The bitter taste moved Stretch's mind to Dr. Igo Strang. In

the Enhanced Sector, in his apartment in the Heights, Dr. Strang would not be worrying about whether if he turned the tap there would be water. If Dr. Igo Strang turned the tap, there would be water. That's why Stretch would not give up—ever.

9

Block 213, Maxo had said, Dreg Estate 4. And, of course, that's where the Clodrone driver was obediently heading. But it was a good two and a half hours since Maxo had seen the picture of the Dreggie girl on the TropScreen Freeze-Frame. Did he imagine the camera had actually managed to freeze her and that after all this time there she'd be, standing exactly where he'd last seen her, waiting for him with open arms? No, he was not so foolish as to imagine this. So what was he doing purring toward the Estates in a Clodrone car? Scratching an itch, that's what. Being carried along by the image of that beautiful lopsided face at the same time as hoping, perhaps, that if he made the journey (which was not without risk) and came to the spot and the girl wasn't there (which she wouldn't be), then his rational GemX brain would reassert itself. In fact, he could already feel his superior brain beginning to assert itself. What were the chances of finding a girl whose name he didn't know in an Estate of a million such girls? No chance at all! So they should turn around and head for his GenPap's Lab? Yes! No! Not yet, anyway, because here they were at Crossing-Point R.

Maxo observed the stretching lines of pedestrians with

securipasses attempting to access the Polis from the Estates. There were no lines for cars wishing to go in the opposite direction. Maybe it was a warning. Who in their right mind would wish to cross into the Estates? But Maxo Strang was not quite in his right mind at the moment, he was aware of that. The Poldrone manning the barrier waved the car on through, executing a smart salute to Maxo as he passed. It was true what they said about Leaderene Clore, Maxo thought, she had increased respect right across the Trop.

The landscape changed immediately, became darker, denser somehow. Maxo realized, with a shiver of something that might have been excitement and might have been fear (everyone knew how dangerous the Estates could be) that, despite being sixteen years old, he'd never been out of the clean, grid-systemed Polis before. Of course he knew all about Estates, he'd seen the pictures, TropScreen after TropScreen of them. As for the people who lived there, the Dreggies (or Naturals as it was politically correct to call them), he'd learned about them in LifeSkills. You had to be careful with Naturals because they could be unpredictable. His LifeTutor had suggested the Enhanced look upon them much as they might on wolves. Naturals roamed in gangs and could be vicious, but it wasn't their fault any more than it was the fault of an animal that did the same. It was instinct that made them operate in packs and, in addition, they had substantially smaller brains than the Enhanced (again not at all their fault), so they were low on reasoning and their anger management was poor. This applied, apparently, as much to the girls as to the boys. Girls were dangerous, too.

How did Maxo Evangele Strang feel about that? He felt

his girl, the one on the TropScreen, was not dangerous. His head sang a little as he thought this, as though he'd been out for a glass or two of mescat. It's also helpful, the Life-Tutor's measured tones intruded, to think of Naturals as machines where the off-button sometimes malfunctioned and the lightest of touches could trigger Extreme Behavior. "That is why," the LifeTutor had explained, "the Naturals need to be kept under constant surveillance and why we need to be able to control them, because they cannot control themselves."

Maxo looked out of the window of his car, in fact, he stared out. He had never seen so many people on the streets at once. And such different looking people! In the Polis, notably among the young, there was a certain uniformity, a certain style of face, of soothing features, or elegant bodies and appropriate heights. Here were people as big as Poldrones or as skinny as the prehistory pictures of the starving. There were dark people, blond people, muddy-looking people, all of them with the tilted faces (beautiful in His Girl but not, alas, in these others). These others were, generally speaking, monsters; they were a series of strange grotesques like the gargoyles on churches from Defunct-Religions, each one horrifyingly, elaborately different. What's more, as they stared at the car, their features twisted about and a number of them, for some reason, were bunching their hands into fists and shaking them at him.

Maxo depressed the ActivateGlass button in the armrest beside him and the Reacterlite windows of the car automatically darkened. This meant he could continue to see out, but they could not see in. But even in his own private bubble of airspace, Maxo felt hemmed in, bustled about. The TropScreen images of the Estates, which he had been used to since childhood, these gave no real impression of the—Maxo struggled for the right words—the chaos of these streets. The roads here were not on a grid system, so you couldn't see ahead, know what was coming around the next corner, so all the buildings, all the cars (and there were many erratically driven, weirdly colored little cars, which looked as if they'd been welded together from pieces of scrap) seemed to roar out of the dark toward you.

The dark.

That was another thing—why was it so dark here? In the Polis it had been barely dusk, did they have some different day/night cycle in the Estates? No, he would have learned about that in CulturalDivision. It was the buildings! he realized suddenly. There were some huge blocks rearing up in total darkness. The occupants obviously hadn't arrived home yet and turned on the lights. Although there were candles; yes, in some of the blocks there were flickering lights behind closed curtains, which must be candles. Small brains for sure—candles, for celeb's sake! He remembered a campaign in the Polis led by the Pre-Intellectuals (or Throwbacks as the Authorities called them) who wanted to send some sort of aid to the Estates, and the Leaderene (may her name celeb forever) making it clear that wolves and machines without off-buttons couldn't really be helped, well, surely the candles proved the point.

Clodrone 1640 suddenly pulled the wheel of the car to the right and Maxo slewed violently with the change of direction. "What . . . !"

Without warning someone had just walked off a pavement. Maxo wouldn't have used the word *packs,* he would have used *swarms.* Dense hundreds of people spilling off the pavements straight into and across busy roads. And the junctions! There were traffic lights, of course, but only about half of them were working, so every crossroad was a life-in-your-hands opportunity with cars and pedestrians hooting and shouting for right of way. And that wasn't the only noise. There were sirens, a high-pitched, panicked sort of sound, and the churning of out-of-sight heavy machinery and sudden, random shatterings as though, every so often, someone was taking a demolition ball to a huge sheet of glass. There were also screams. Human screams. Maxo had only heard such sounds before on The LateNight HorrorChannel. He turned up the music in the car, but the wail of electronic violins did not obliterate the wail of the Dreggies.

"Are we nearly there?" he asked a little plaintively.

Clodrone 1640 checked the Navigator. "One right, two lefts," he announced.

It was then that the first missile landed. It was difficult to see exactly what it was, a piece of brick probably, about the size of a fist—and quite impossible to guess who had thrown it. It bounced off the HardenedShell hood.

"What was that!" Maxo's voice sounded tight.

"Low-level nonspecific accident," said 1640 calmly. "Probably."

"Probably not. Probably some deliberately aimed, high-level aggression," riposted Maxo. "What's wrong with these people, 1640?"

1640 didn't seem to have an answer to that.

"Can we go any faster?" Maxo asked.

1640 swerved his best and within minutes they arrived at the entrance to Block 213. Clodrone 1640 pulled the car to a stop. In the Polis, apartment entrances were Hygeni-Cleaned every forty minutes. This apartment entrance didn't look as if it had ever been cleaned. There was debris—human of sorts—pushed up against the smashed glass doors. Gargoyles with bottles of cheap mescat. But Maxo wasn't looking at the gargoyles, he didn't care what the gargoyles were doing, he only cared about finding his girl.

"Around the back," he ordered 1640. That's where he'd lost sight of the girl, so that's where she'd be.

1640 obediently pulled the car right.

They were so close now, so close. And—she wasn't there. He looked again. She still wasn't there. He scanned all the gargoyles in the street—nothing, no one. He didn't believe it, he'd come all this way and she wasn't there! Then a feeling he didn't recognize jabbed him beneath the rib cage. It was like a knife on bone. He clutched at his chest and a noise like a howl came out of his throat.

"Are you all right, sir?" asked 1640.

This knife feeling was hideous, it was frightening. It hurt. But, inexplicably, he didn't want it to stop because it was about the Girl. The totally, wonderfully, bone-knifing girl! He felt wild, he felt extraordinary, he felt—how could he put it? Extreme! And she wasn't even there. How would he feel when he found her?

That's when the second missile landed. Of a similar size to the first missile but slightly heavier, it smashed into the back passenger window right next to where Maxo was sitting. The glass was reinforced, but not reinforced enough. Where the item (broken paving slab?) landed, it left a small indentation and a series of tiny radiating lines. As Maxo looked at the indentation and the glittery thin lines, reality asserted itself in his superior GemX mind. He put his hand up to his right temple where the Body-Sculpt was.

"Take me away," he roared.

"Where to?" asked Clodrone 1640 reasonably enough.

"Where do you think! To the Lab!" Maxo needed to see his GenPap. His GenPap could take away these hideous lines beneath the BodySculpt, he could stop the hideous extreme feelings, prevent Maxo from falling into the abyss. Because it was an abyss he was facing, wasn't it? A Dreggie abyss!

"Right you are, sir," said Clodrone 1640 amenably.

"1640," came the brusque voice of Igo Strang over the car 'CatorSys, "change of directive. I have an urgent meeting with Llublo Quells. When Maxo appears take him straight to the Orb Gallery. I'll meet him and Glora there as soon as I can."

10

Perle Lorrell was floating. A few inches above her mattress was a pillow of pain and Perle was lying on that pillow. There were clouds in her brain. If Perle wanted less pain she could ask her daughter for a sip of the medicine in the dark bottle Gala had concealed beneath her own pillow. But Perle was not going to ask and Gala was not going to offer. Not yet anyway. They both knew what the medicine meant, it killed pain but it also killed life, which is why the doctor had only prescribed one bottle. Perle would not need a second.

So Perle tried to clear the clouds by thinking, by focusing as hard as she could on things that were important to her. Her missing husband, Finn. Her children, Phylo, Gala, Daz. It made her head ache. Sometimes it felt to her as if ants were marching through her brain, eating as they went. She imagined the ants entering her head through her left ear, marching, marching. When they reached her right ear she would be dead, or at least as good as dead because the ants would have eaten her mind and left her just the floating space.

Finn.

Where was he? Four years and not a word. She

remembered that evening of frantic worry as though it was yesterday. She remembered going, in the middle of the night, to the Donation Hospital and inquiring.

"Oh yes," the night-desk Clodrone had said. "He was one of the lucky ones. He was chosen to donate. Got his money all right. Look, here's his entry. That is his signature?"

It was his signature. Finn Lorrell. He'd obviously signed straight onto the screen with a hospital scriptopen; the swirl of his name was electric yellow. But there was no doubt about his hand, she'd have recognized it anywhere. Her Finn. He'd been paid in TropCredits. Estate money was no good in the inner Polis, to buy anything there you had to have TropCredits.

"We'll do it," Finn had said, so very long ago. "We'll work hard and we'll do it. Get enough to rent some place in the Polis. Our children will leave the Estates, I promise you."

It was a dream, they both knew that, a hopeless, impossible dream. They would never have sufficient money to put a deposit down on a place in the Polis, no matter how hard he worked at the Regeneration Plant or how many reassembled ambisuits she sewed and sold.

Ambisuits. She raised her head a little, which made the ants tip and slew, and looked down at her hands. Useless hands now. Hands which had been so deft with a needle, that had worked seven days a week, because nothing would stop the dream.

Mescat had nearly stopped the dream. But if a man worked the hours Finn had worked and carried the anger Finn carried, he deserved to go, sometimes, to the Mescat House and spend a little of his hard-earned money. If you couldn't—occasionally—forget, then you couldn't go on either. Besides, other men went to the Mescat Houses, went much more frequently than Finn, in fact. And if Finn had once, or twice, been blind drunk, was that so surprising? She wasn't going to deny this little release to the man she loved. She didn't even begrudge Finn the money, but her own money, she spirited that away. She was frugal, she made do (though her children never went short), and if there were a few feligs left over, she hoarded them. She took pleasure in knowing that the money would be there when she needed it. But when would that be?

Finn.

Losing Finn, not knowing where he was, what had happened to him, that was pain. The pain in her body, the ants in her brain, they were as nothing to the loss of Finn. She had first met Finn when she was thirteen and he was just a year older. He had been tall even then, just as Phylo was now, blond and stringy and handsome. She'd adored his face and his strength. He would not be put aside, he refused to be ground down, he was a dreamer and also a worker. She saw that together they might make something of their lives. Other people in the Estates thought long and hard about having children: "It's not a world," they said, "into which to bring children." But Finn had been adamant; their children would not run with the mob, their children would be different, make a difference.

Come to me, Finn.

She said it aloud, as though he might just float into the room to be with her, after all these years. The sound of her calling brought Gala. Hearing her daughter's footsteps in the hall, Perle tried to relax, lay quite still and closed her eyes, composing her face into a mask of calm, contented sleep. The door of her bedroom opened and she felt Gala's gaze upon her. Gala should not be looking after a woman old before her time, Perle thought. She should be spared this. Gala stood and watched a minute and then she left, closing the door softly behind her.

But it was not Gala who Perle really worried about. If she died—when she died—Gala would cope. Gala was practical and had the temperament to make the best of things. But Phylo—Stretch—he was like his father. Thin and clever and explosive. He would get into trouble, she was sure of that. He'd get angry, righteously angry probably, and then he'd lose his temper. It was dangerous to lose one's temper in the Estates—because there were always other people who could lose their tempers harder and faster and more dangerously. But it was also dangerous to lose one's temper in the Polis, where every business and every public building had Clodrone guards and SafetyCells. Sometimes she thought this is what must have happened to Finn—that something that day in the Polis had tripped him up, made him mad, and he'd said something, or done something, and he'd been taken away to "cool off." She imagined him in a SafetyCell, forgotten. When she'd mentioned this at the hospital, the staff had laughed at her, the Poldrone Station staff had laughed at her, the border patrol staff had laughed at her. People didn't "disappear," that was just a myth generated by the Estates' uneducated masses. Everyone was accounted for in the Polis, especially those in the SafetyCells; there were numbers, tags, and checks. If Finn Lorrell had gone missing, then it must have been his choice. He must have wanted not to come home that day. Did he have another woman by any chance?

Finn did not have another woman. Finn had never even looked at another woman. Finn loved Perle, everyone knew that. And he loved his children. He would not have voluntarily gone missing. And yet all the others had come back from donating and Finn hadn't.

"Where's my dad?" Daz had asked. He'd been a wide-eyed nine-year-old.

"He'll come back," Perle had said. "He loves you. I love you. Go to sleep now."

How long was it since Daz last asked about his father? A year? Two years. None of them asked anymore. Phylo tramped about in angry silence, Gala, long-suffering, turned her attentions to her mother, and Daz painted. Painted and painted, mad bold colors as if all was right with the world. Perle loved each of her children with a passion that hurt— but Daz. Why had he been put on the earth? Daz belonged in a different life, a better place.

Perle shifted her weight in the bed. She could feel the movement of her bones beneath her flesh. She was getting thinner and frailer, but she would not give in. Perle Lorrell was going to live. There were still things she had to do. She had to see her husband once again, because he was alive, she knew that, as you do if you're very close to someone. And she also had to ensure her children would be safe. So she refused to die. She refused the pain. She refused the ants.

Perle Lorrell floated on.

Glora Orb stood in the center of Salon 2, the largest of the seven white spaces that made up the Glora Orb Gallery. There were five TropScreens in the room, one on each of the four plasma walls and one suspended (spinning) from the ceiling. The installation was called The Virtually Real Viewer Viewed, a title of genius, Glora thought, much like the work itself.

Only the ceiling TropScreen was real: real in the sense that the images it displayed were those currently being selected by the SecurityServices and beamed into every building up and down the Polis. The four wall screens, by contrast, displayed a kaleidoscope of Trop people and events as seen through the brilliant imagination of Orb artist, Seud Quac. Quac (with the permission of the Authorities—how hard Glora had worked for that!) had installed fifty SpyArt cameras around the Trop and with the aid of some RandomChoiceDeviation software he'd developed himself, was now able to beam into the gallery scenes of the Enhanced going about their daily business. At any given time three of the walls (Walls 1, 2, and 4) would be relaying exterior pictures while Wall 3 concentrated on the interior of the gallery itself. Glora Orb, aware of the precise location of the internal camera, was using the screen as a mirror. She spun around admiring the brightness of her blonde hair, the smoothness of her impeccable skin, the clear shine of her cornflower blue eyes. Not bad for ninety-seven years old! She paid some, but not a lot, of attention to Seud Quac. He was tall, dark, and expectedly handsome.

As Glora spun, the images around her spun, partly because of her movement and partly because of Seud's extraordinary software work with superimposition. The politicos in Leaderene Square suddenly walked in the room with her and Seud, the Dreggie people from the real-life TropScreen were pulled by Compute-Reflect out of their Estate lives and placed in the line outside her gallery. Oh, the charm of it! The skill! What it said about truth and fiction, the genuine and the fake, the possible and the impossible. Or as the catalog put it: "Once again Quac's work challenges the veracity of authenticity itself, the essential, bona fide, honest view of the viewer being constantly subverted and reinterpreted through implicit superimpositions and earnest impossibilities."

Glora trembled with excitement. "It's a triumph," she said to Seud Quac. "An absolutely triumph."

"Your triumph," said Seud graciously, bowing his head just a fraction.

And it was true. Glora had discovered Seud, some people would have said she had "created" him. Without Glora Orb there would be no Seud Quac. Seud Quac existed because Glora had championed his cause, had bought his work, displayed his work, talked up his work, sold his work, and made a mint from his work.

Glora Orb was looking forward to the gallery opening, she was looking forward to the accolades in the *HighArt Review*. She had never had a bad review for a Quac exhibition. In fact, she'd never had a bad review for any of her exhibitions. Her detractors said it was because the *HighArt* reviewer, Fawn Lemming, was a friend of hers. It was jealousy, that was all. Glora was rich, she was successful, she was beautiful, she was . . . in the same room as her GenOff, Maxo.

"Maxo," Glora exclaimed. And then she giggled. The Quac images had fooled her, too! To imagine her own GenOff, here in the gallery. Obviously he was not here. Obviously he was out in the Polis, in Leaderene Square maybe, moving with other Enhanced in and out of the cameras' view, projected onto the walls of the gallery, virtually virtual, but not really real.

"Hello, GenMa," said Maxo.

Glora gasped. He was here. He was real.

"Who let you in?" she squeaked.

Security had been briefed. No one was to be let in. And no one meant *no one*. She hadn't even been taking calls from her own Igo all that day. Igo himself would not have been let in. There were spies everywhere, people who would use any means, any person, to get a sneak preview of a Glora Orb show.

"They do know me," Maxo remarked. "I am your Gen-Off, remember? And GenPap said to meet him here."

"Here? Here! But you can't come here. He can't and you can't. Not now. Not tonight. I—we—Seud and I have things to do."

She looked wild, Maxo thought, she looked frazzled. Her hair stuck out around her face in a mad white blonde frizz. And yet she still did not look more than twenty-five years old. She had no wrinkles.

"It's important," he said. "Really important."

"Nothing is as important as a Glora Orb show," remarked Seud Quac loyally.

"Could we talk in private?" asked Maxo.

"No," said Glora Orb. "You have thirty seconds to explain yourself before I call security."

Which is when Maxo Evangele Strang, who'd had enough for one day, finally lost it. He pulled the BodySculpt from his temple, wrenched it off unceremoniously with one sweep of his right hand. "Look," he said.

The reaction of his GenMa was not unexpected. She screamed. The pitch of her scream was such that one of the four glass faces of the spinning TropScreen shattered into a thousand pieces. Fragments of glass ricocheted about the room. A small slither appeared to get into one of Seud Quac's eyes.

"Aaaarg," he yelled. "My eye!"

Glora Orb dropped to her knees beside her investment.

Which left Maxo walking–unnoticed–out into the Trop night.

11

Dr. Igo Strang took the outside elevator to the 117th floor of GemCorp InterTrop. Access beyond this point was restricted so he exited from the lift and waited in the holding room.

Maxo.

The satellsearch on his GenOff's 'cator had suggested Maxo had gone to the Virtual Date Palace. Surely he wouldn't have gone for a night out if he had been experiencing any of the symptoms being reported to MediAlert? Wrinkles. Three-quarters of the GemXers had mentioned wrinkles, or "cracks" as some of them had described the lines on their faces. That suggested the antiaging module was breaking down—which was serious, not least because GeModify's rival antiagers (the ones responsible for the delightful longevity of his own Glora Orb) had not and were not breaking down. Igo suspected a replication problem in one of the juvenile hormone moderators. He'd need to do some fast research, develop a stabilizer. Or, if Quells wanted a really quick fix, they could try the clean genes approach. Stop the thing in its tracks, as they had for the Clodrones. But Quells liked the money. There was money in stabilizers for the Enhanced. He would suggest it;

Llublo Quells would be impressed at how his chief scientist could turn chief economist.

The emotional disturbance aspect could be more complex. Was it just a side effect of the aging problem, or was it a symptom in its own right? It would need careful investigation. He'd already asked for a breakdown of all the different distresses being reported to MediAlert. There were 6,801 GemXers in the Polis, aged between fifteen and eighteen. At the last count only 3,187 had reported in. Even allowing for statistical variations in reporting and different rates of onset of symptoms, the number of non-reporters was high enough to suggest that not all GemXs were affected. Like Maxo, celeb willing. It sometimes happened that way. Might indicate a cross-referencing problem, a Degrade specific to those with the antiager and some module that Maxo hadn't had, the Huntingdon's Marker, for instance. Nevertheless it was irritating not to be able to contact Maxo directly. Trust him to have his 'cator in the Incommunicado Safe at this critical time. Still, at least Clodrone 1640 was on the job. He'd been instructed to locate Maxo and take him straight to the gallery. Igo himself would go there the minute his meeting with Llublo Quells ended.

"Business?" A Poldrone voice interrupted through a speaker located near the ceiling of the Holding Room. Holding Cell, thought Igo.

"Meeting with Llublo Quells," said Igo, though the Poldrone would have this information on a screen in front of him.

"Name?" inquired the Poldrone politely.

"You know my name," said Igo testily.

"Name," repeated the Poldrone tonelessly.

"Dr. Igo Strang, chief scientist of GemCorp InterTrop."

"Thank you," said the Poldrone. "Iris scan and proceed."

Igo flashed his eye at the cell camera and the steel door of the internal elevator opposite slid open. There were no buttons on the inside of the metal cage, so Igo waited until an unseen hand in the GemCorp control room flicked a switch and decided his destination: Office, Relax, or Penthouse. There were two seconds between floors. Igo counted six. The Penthouse, then.

The door opened straight into the huge, glass-domed room that spanned the entire roof area of the GemCorp building. The first time Igo had been in the room, he had been almost unable to concentrate for the wonder of the view—the panorama—which lay beneath and around him like some distant, imaginary world. The entire Polis, its buildings and roadways and cars, busy and brightly lit but looking slightly smaller than normal, as though the whole Trop was some personal plaything of Llublo's.

"Ah, Strang," shouted Llublo Quells. He was about a hundred yards away, in the BonsaiDom. "Come in."

Igo advanced. He walked through acres of white leather loungers, he passed the huge twenty-seater glass and steel-ite table used for InterTrop meetings and rumored—once—to have been laid for a four-hour SlowFood Feast. He maneuvered his way between the chromite sideboards with their crystal vials of mescat. You drank—if invited—straight from the vial, stoppering it again after each sip, as the aroma and taste of a top-quality mescat was adversely affected by contact with oxygen.

The BonsaiDom was a glasshouse within a glasshouse,

Llublo's personal GrowingSpace surmounted by its own ornamental glass onion dome. As Igo continued his approach the night beyond the glass suddenly whitened. Huge flakes of snow fell from nowhere to land on the onion dome.

"Sudden Onset Snow," cried Igo.

Ice would form on the glass within seconds. Thick, arc-ice. The temperature inside the building would plummet, particularly here, where there was so much glass and so little warmth-exuding Concretia. It could take, Igo calculated, as many as five minutes for the Additional Heating TubeScape to kick in. He was unable to stop his fingers reaching for the thermostat of his ambisuit, touching it, waiting for it to click on and bring instant heat to his inner core. The suit did not click on. But nor did he feel the immediate chill of the weather change. Had the snow stopped as soon as it had begun?

The snow had not stopped. Beyond the glass the flakes still fell and yet, when they touched the glass, far from forming into ice, they simply melted, ran off the surface of the onion dome in cascades of iridescent rain, as though the glass and the weather together were some perfectly designed water feature, a beautiful fountain expressly created to be viewed (with delight) from within.

"Expensive, I grant," Llublo Quells purred, observing his underling's amazed eyes. "But necessary." In his pudgy hands he held a bonsai tree, one fat finger lovingly caressing its tiny, bent trunk.

Out on the streets, certainly in the Estates, Igo thought, there would be people dying because their bodies would not be able to cope with the sudden drop in temperature.

And yet here, Llublo was making stable temperatures a kind of art form.

"Marvelous," burbled Igo, wondering just how far down the building Llublo's cascading rain would become ice. "Glora Orb, my current—well, Glora Orb of the Glora Orb Gallery—the art of it. Oh my . . ."

"Glora Orb," repeated Quells. "A magnificent woman." He licked at his thick red lips. "Or so I've heard. . . . Well . . ." He paused, and then he lifted the exquisitely small tree in its egg-white-colored ceramic dish toward Igo. "What do you think?"

"Charming," said Igo, whose appreciation of art did not run to trees.

"Larch Larix Dumevelt," intoned Llublo. "Easy to grow, but this one was a rescue. I mulched her on her side in a top dressing of sphagnum moss for eighteen months. Then she spent twelve months in recovery rooted over a piece of rock. And that was before I wired a single branch. Do you see what I'm getting at, Strang?"

Strang didn't.

"What I'm getting at, Strang, is, I'm in it for the long-term. I am not interested in things fading before their time. I am a patient man. An extremely patient man. But I don't like mistakes. And I don't like being taken by surprise." He set the miniature larch down with a great deal of care and then he turned the full force of his bulk toward Igo. "Do you see what I'm getting at now, Strang?"

"The GemXs?" volunteered Igo.

As suddenly as it had begun, the snowstorm abated. The rain ceased fountaining. The skies above the dome cleared. Maybe that's why Igo felt suddenly hotter.

"Precisely," said Quells. "The GemXs. I have made a big investment over a long period of time in the AlphaGem program. The GemX model has, like my little tree, been shaped and manipulated and bent to be beautiful, Strang, to be perfect. But now we have a little problem. What are you doing about it?"

"Well," began Igo, "I . . ."

"I said, what are you doing about it!" shrieked Quells.

"I don't see it necessarily as a long-term problem," said Igo, quickly. "And it could be a stabilizers opportunity."

"Stabilizers? Stabilizers! Are you forgetting that we sold the GemX model on the basis of a one-off payment? A very expensive one-off payment, precisely because there would be only the one." He paused. "Strang?"

"But . . . ," said Igo, wrong-footed. "What about the high-blood-pressure stabilizers?" Blood cluster 23 had proved volatile. It happened. There'd been a stabilizer for that. Thousands of GemXs were taking (lucrative) GemCorp blood-pressure stabilizers. Maxo was taking them.

"One mistake, one stabilizer possibility. That was to be expected. That, if you recall, was written into the contract. But two, *two*, Strang. That looks a little careless, it looks . . . greedy."

"Oh," said Igo.

"In fact, Strang, I believe our payment structure was one of the main reasons why the GemX model outsold the GeModify version ten to one. Now, what the celeb is going on?"

"A Degrade," said Igo lightly. "That's the most likely explanation. A Degrade. Similar to what happened to the Clodrones."

"Similar," repeated Llublo Quells, clearly appalled, "to the *Clodrones*?" He wiped his brow and then continued in a low, faintly threatening tone. "Your GenOff, Maxo, he's a GemX, yes?"

"Yes."

"You got him cheap. We cut you a deal. Remember?"

Strang, who was constantly trying to forget the impoverished creature he had been, remembered.

"But the other GemX progenitors," purred Quells, "the ones that paid the price, these GemX progenitors, Strang, they are the Elite. They are the best, the richest, the most powerful group in the Polis. The most intelligent. The most . . . Enhanced." He said this rather deliberately. "Do you get it now, Strang?"

"With some Clean Genes," Igo said quickly, "and a little time—I think I can fix it."

"You don't have time," said Llublo Quells. "We don't have time."

"I need to set up a proper research sample and harvest some eggs, and get Clean Genes, a lot of Clean Genes from the Naturals and . . ." Then there's the emotional disturbance problem, he was going to add.

"In fact, you have less than twenty-four hours," Quells continued. "You don't seem to realize the seriousness of this situation. The Elite do not wish to wait. I do not wish to wait. We want answers. The Leaderene—may her name celeb forever—wants answers. In fact, she has requested a breakfast meeting tomorrow morning. At that meeting I will be advising her of the GemCorp strategy to fix this little problem. Am I making myself clear, Strang?"

Strang nodded.

"Good. We understand each other then." Something resembling a smile larded itself across Quells's face. "Oh . . . and before you go, Strang, bring me a vial of mescat, will you?"

12

Maxo Evangele Strang was lost. He'd turned left out of the Glora Orb Gallery (the snaking line outside parting in amazement to see someone actually exiting from the building) and headed in what he imagined was a southerly direction. He'd stomped down a few vaguely familiar streets without paying more than cursory attention to where he was going. He had, after all, no particular destination in mind, he just wanted to get away from his GenDam.

Glora Orb. Her scream had been precisely what he would have predicted. It confirmed what he already knew, that cracks were bad, that they were repellent, that they were not to be tolerated. So why did he feel slightly let down, as though Glora Orb might have behaved differently, might have said—well, what? That cracks didn't matter? They did matter! Or perhaps that Glora might have . . . touched him. Stomping about the streets, Maxo Strang had a sudden vision of his GenDam leaning across and encircling his shoulder with her perfect arm. He stopped still with the shock of it. HighElites did not touch—not in public anyway. Touching was not on the Eradicated List but it was firmly discouraged—so as to set an example to the young. That's why dating was conducted virtually, so meshes could be strictly controlled, the danger of unregulated GeneTransfer being too horrible to imagine. But the image of his GenDam with her arm about him would not go away and, worse still, nor would the idea that, had she put her arm around him, he wouldn't have felt so bad. Loathsome. Sickening! What was wrong with him, first the Dreggie girl and now this? He must clear his mind, concentrate. On what? On where he was. Where was he?

Apart from the short journey from the door of a Clodrone car to the door of a building, he realized then that he had never actually been anywhere on foot in the Trop before. The Polis grid system, which seemed so simple when one was driven about in a car, became positively labyrinthine when one was actually out on the pavement. The buildings all looked the same, the lefts and rights all looked the same. The sky, by contrast, just looked wrong, the wrong color, or maybe it was in the wrong place.

This street must have a name. He looked about him: The junction where such a name might be was too far away for him to see. However, above the doorway of the municipal building opposite it said, in curly old-fashioned script: Museo. So that's where he was. He was right next to the Museo—whatever that was. If he'd had his 'cator with him, he could have summoned a Clodrone car in an instant. "Come to the Museo," he could have said, and it wouldn't have mattered that he didn't know where the Museo was, because the Clodone driver would have known. But Maxo was unable to summon help, or communicate to anyone in any way, on account of the fact that his hasty exit from the Virtual Date Palace meant that his 'cator was still locked in the Incommunicado Safe. So he was lost: lost geographically, lost physically (because of the repellent thing on his face), and lost, most importantly of all, because he was going soft in the head.

It was then that it began to snow. Not ordinary snow (which probably accounted for the color of the sky) but Sudden Onset Snow. His ambisuit whirled furiously but, within thirty seconds, his hair had frozen into spikes and there was a thin layer of arc-ice on both his hands. He immediately flexed his fingers, as he'd been taught, and the ice cracked a little. Thin, glittery, cracking lines of ice on his hands. Why did everything return him to cracks? More snow fell, more ice formed. With stiff hands Maxo reached for his ambisuit pouch. No ambigloves. No ambihood.

"Not to be prepared," he heard an unseen TropScreen say, *"is an offense against the Germline. All Enhanced must protect themselves and the inheritance of the Polis. Carry your ambihood and ambigloves at all times."*

Maxo crossed the street while he could still move and hammered with his flat icy hands on the door of the Museo. The ice cracked a little more, but did not fall away. The ambisuit was hot around his neck but his teeth still chattered. There was no answer. Maxo beat on the door again. It was the duty of the custodians of all public buildings to open them in the event of any Sudden Onset Weather above a Grade 7. That's why, since the Global Warming Catastrophe, all public buildings had on-site caretaker apartments. This must be Snow 9 at least. Snow 10. Where was the fool who was supposed to caretake this Museo?

A light went on in an upstairs room.

"Come on," shouted Maxo, only he didn't because, when he opened his mouth, the air-chill froze his voice in his throat.

As Maxo closed his mouth, his jaw creaked. He began jumping then—feebly—on the spot; the ambisuit was keeping his heart going and circulation was everything. He knew not to put his frozen hands against his chest. That took heat from the major organs and could prove fatal. He used his hands on the door. He flat-handed it. Why was there no bell? After a full two minutes (which might have been two hours), the door slid open a fraction and a grizzled head appeared.

Maxo had imagined a savior: here was a hideous apparition. The grizzled man (clearly non-Enhanced and well over ninety years old) had a face like a dried-up riverbed. It was a mudflat of cracks. Crack, cracks, cracks. Maxo pushed the old man aside, stumbled into the Museo foyer and collapsed on the floor.

So he never saw how the old man shut and locked the door to the outside world, how he blocked the draft at its foot with a rug. Nor did he see the old man, who didn't have the strength to lift the GemX boy to a place of warmth, go immediately to fetch an electric heater, switch it on, and puff it full blast at the prone body. On the floor, small puddles of water formed where the ice melted around Maxo's feet, his hair, his hands. Gradually, quite fast in fact, Maxo's skin tone returned to normal.

Maxo Strang sat up. "You incompetent idiot," he yelled, "what in celeb's name were you doing? I could have died out there."

The old man stared down at Maxo. His name (it was written on a badge pinned to his custodian's tunic) was Edwin Challice. Edwin Challice, who had for years immersed himself in DefunctReligions and Books (or Manuscripts as they were labeled in the locked glass cases of the Museo), thought of himself as a man dealing with things that had been lost—spirit, soul, history, humanity, pens, pencils, paper, his own memory. Yet here, at his feet, was something found.

"Welcome," said Edwin Challice.

At the same time, in the Estates just a few miles across the Polis, Perle Lorrell was lying in her bed. Beside her lay her daughter, Gala. When the snow had come, Gala had come also. She came uncalled, just slipped under the covers next to her mother and held the frail body close. Perle had cried out with the pain of contact, but then bitten off that pain. She knew what Gala was doing, Gala was saving her life.

A mother, Perle thought, should hold a child, not the other way around. Then Daz came. She did not see him for her eyes were closed with cold and exhaustion, but she smelled him as he came through the door: oil paint and turps. At once, her head reeled as if someone was flinging a ball about inside her brain. Her body jerked in Gala's arms.

"It's okay," Gala said, "I've got her." Perle felt Gala motioning to her brother to go.

"No," said Perle. "Let him stay. Let him come, too."

"But the nausea . . . ," began Gala.

"Please," said Perle.

So Daz, too, got into the bed he had been born in, Perle

and Finn Lorrell's bed. He did not twine himself about his mother, just lay stiffly. The paint was in his hair. It made her giddy, the smell of her own child, but she was so glad of him. She lifted her hand and found his, it was unaccountably warm and he didn't pull away.

Less than two minutes later, Stretch arrived. Now Perle opened her eyes; there was no room for a fourth person in the bed. Stretch was wearing gloves, a coat, and two woolen hats, one on top of the other. In his arms he carried his bedding, sheets, blankets, a thin eiderdown, all of which he laid carefully down over the bodies in the bed, tucking them all in.

"We're all right," said Perle. The balls in her head collided.

Stretch then went to stand at the foot of the bed, near the window. Just stood there, saying nothing. She felt comforted but didn't know why. And then she realized: He was blocking the draft from the broken window, he was taking the icy chill on his own back.

Finn should see them now, thought Perle Lorrell. Good children. His children. Finn.

Finn?

In yet another part of the Polis, Heights Hospital 1 (the Trop's premier hospital), Glora Orb sat by her investment in the Optic Room. The walls of the hospital were made of Advanced WeatherShell, with inbuilt top-of-the-range Weather React. If there was Sudden Onset Snow, the building's Thermals and Heating Gullies could all be activated within twenty-two seconds—guaranteed. Which is why

Glora Orb, in the dark confines of the Optic Room, had no notion at all that it was even snowing.

"Well?" she inquired of top surgeon Bud Braddleman.

Braddleman lifted his face, with its steel digi-optical enhancement mask, from its contact with the left eye of Seud Quac.

"Minor abrasions to the cornea," he pronounced. "A little antibiotic cream twice a day. Should be healed in no time."

"Oh," said Glora Orb, disappointed. "Not an eye patch, then?"

"Not an eye patch, no." said Braddleman.

"I rather hoped for an eye patch," said Glora. She leaned down toward her charge who was still lying on his back worn out with the whole ghastly experience. "You see, Seud, I thought, if we had an eye patch, an attractive old-fashioned black one, we might—I mean you might—attach to it the image of an eye. A little holograph, or a mini, mini digi-screen. An eye, covering an eye. Do you see what I'm getting at, Seud?"

"An eye for an eye?" said Seud weakly.

"The veracity of authenticity," said Glora. "What is seen and what is not seen. The blind eye and the eye that sees. Which is which? How do we know?"

"Oh," said Quac, who went queasy at the mention of the word *hospital*, let alone the experience of one.

"It would be wonderful publicity. Fawn Lemming would die for it. A huge picture of you—Seud Quac with three eyes: the good eye, the bad eye, the eye covered by an eye. The artist whose life imitates art, whose art is his life. Have you got an eye patch by chance, Dr. Braddleman?"

It was then that Glora's 'cator rang.

"Excuse me." Igo's face appeared on the screen. "Yes?"

Her mesh burbled something about being at the gallery, and Glora not being there and Maxo not being there, and was Maxo all right?

"Of course Maxo's all right," said Glora Orb sharply. "Why wouldn't he be?"

"Wrinkles," came Igo's voice over the system. "Has he got wrinkles?"

"What a preposterous man you are," said Glora Orb. "Our GenOff is a GemX. He is perfect." As she said the word *perfect*, Glora Orb's brain rearranged a certain visual image in her mind. "How could Maxo have wrinkles? Now, I'm busy. In fact, I'm in crisis artistic talks. Shall we call later?" She smiled a glittering, perfect smile, and switched off the 'cator.

From his prone position, Seud Quac said: "I thought Maxo did have a wrinkle. I thought that's why you screamed. Why the TropScreen broke. Why I got this thing in my eye."

"Seud," said Glora very softly, "you so perfectly prove my point. What we see and what we don't see . . . you've got it all in a muddle. It's the Stress. It's your irrational fear of hospitals. And your amazing Artistic Temperament. You see things that simply don't exist. That is the genius of you."

"Oh," said Seud, settling back into the leather couch.

"That's why I think a patch would be so useful, Dr. Braddleman," continued Glora Orb, "if not for the soothing of Seud's eye, then to let everyone see how much Seud suffers, suffers for his art, an outward sign, much as a sling tells you an arm is broken. Dr. Braddleman?"

Dr. Braddleman handed Glora Orb a very old-fashioned black eye patch.

"Perfect," she said. "Perfect, perfect, perfect." Which is probably when the lingering traces of Maxo disappeared from her mind.

13

Gala Lorrell left Block 213 at dawn for the long walk to the Regeneration Plant. She hadn't been going ten minutes when she saw her first corpse—an old man lying in the middle of the road. A few streets further on was a middle-aged woman, her ice-darkened body curled around some garbage cans. The Sudden Onset Snow had only lasted six minutes, forty-five seconds according to the TropScreen announcer, but people hadn't taken sufficient precautions, people had been profligate with their lives. Those caught outside, Gala thought, would have had less than one minute to have found shelter. The old man obviously hadn't had the time to cross the road. The woman perhaps thought to climb into one of the garbage cans. Both of them would have been frozen solid within two minutes, their bodies thawing gradually overnight in the ironic heat rise that always followed a Sudden Onset. You might have thought they were just asleep if it hadn't been for their blackened skin. They looked as if they had been charred, not frozen, but that's what the ice did, it burned you.

Gala passed on by. There was nothing she could do for these people and her pity didn't help. The white vans would come—she could hear the jingle of one now—and shovel the dead away. Garbage might remain on the street of the Estates for months, but the dead were picked up soon enough; they were taken to CentralCrem 2 and burned a second and final time. There was money in the dead. Families were required to pay funeral expenses; retrieving a plastic bag of ashes cost more than a week's Estates wages. But it was a very rare family, no matter how poor, that didn't reclaim its dead from the Polis.

Beside these deaths, the possible death of Gala's Agaricus Blazei shouldn't have mattered at all. But it did. Gala was going to the edge of the Regeneration Plant to see if her mushrooms had lived or died. Mushrooms. How Stretch had laughed at her when she had spoken of going to consult Mama Kelp.

"That witch," he'd cried. "You can't believe in that old nonsense."

"What do you suggest, then?" she'd flashed back at him. "Just standing by while our mother dies?"

As hospital treatment had become less and less available to people in the Estates and drugs harder and harder to come by, a flourishing practice in herbals had arisen. People with little experience, but good business sense, set themselves up as purveyors of cures. They didn't call themselves doctors but, for a price, they would mix you a potion. Reputations waxed and waned. Mama Kelp had a better record than most, her cures seemed to work.

"People get better sometimes," Stretch had said, "just with the passage of time."

"No harm in going to ask, is there?" said Gala.

Mama Kelp lived on Floor 20 of Block 157. There was no elevator and, even to be seen, you had to take a gift. There was no point in taking something perishable. The line might be three days long. There was no appointment system and no knowing, before you'd climbed at least fifteen flights of stairs, how long the line was. But the fact that there was always a line must, Gala claimed, mean something.

"It means people are desperate," said Stretch.

But it was Stretch who had gone to the Regeneration Plant and chanced his life among the Scavengers to find the prized pixel unit that was to be Gala's gift. She lined up for thirteen hours, moving upward step-by-step. Once on a step, your place in the line was claimed. But if you fell asleep and a space appeared above you, it was legitimate for someone lower in the line to take that space. After all, people had been known to die in the line.

What sort of experience you had in the line depended on who was above and below you. Gala had been lucky; above her had been a woman with a toddler called Bless, and below her a wheezy but pleasant man called Ramof. Gala and the two adults occupied the time by inventing games for the child who was remarkably cheerful considering she had a septic wound on her right foot. They kept each other's places in the line when one or other of them had to take up the offer of food or toilet facilities from other apartment dwellers they passed on the ascent.

"It's such a scam," Stretch said, unable to stop himself running up the stairs to check on her after a mere five hours. Gala knew why he'd come. Sometimes the gangs made a raid on the line. Not to steal anything, these people had nothing to steal, but for fun, for laughs, because the people were captive.

"It's okay," said Gala. "I'm okay."

Stretch left and Gala continued her slow progress. There was talk in the line about what Mama Kelp looked like, about her witch's cauldron and long fingernails, about how, if she didn't like a patient, she'd just send him or her away, no matter how long that patient had lined up.

It was nine at night when Gala finally came to the head of the line. The time that Mama Kelp shut up shop varied with her mood, but she rarely saw people after 10:00 PM, so Gala felt luck was on her side with this, too.

She was invited into the flat by the wizened old man who seemed to be both Mama Kelp's guardian and her bookkeeper. The reception area was a room with a desk and chair and a watering can. Arranged around the walls of the room were some straggly seedlings and some card-board trays of what looked like sawdust.

"You can go in," said the man.

Gala went through to a small square room with floor to ceiling shelves on which was a huge array of glass bottles and jars. Some of the bottles were tiny, pretty little vials with sparkling liquid inside, some were almost two feet high with things floating inside them that weren't alive but looked as if they might have been once. There was no cauldron.

"Sit down," said Mama Kelp. She didn't look like a witch, she just looked flowing. Her hair was flowing white, halfway down her back. Her garments were flowing blue and so shapeless it was impossible to tell if Mama Kelp was small and fat or big and bunched up in the chair. She smiled.

"So?" she said.

And Gala told her. Told Mama Kelp everything she knew about her mother's disease. Later, she told Stretch that it had been good just saying it all, having someone listen.

"Could you bring her to see me?" asked Mama Kelp.

"No," said Gala. "I don't think she could make the line."

"It may be too late for her, then."

"No," said Gala.

"There is no cure, you know that?"

"Yes. But something . . . to ease her. Something to . . . stave things off."

"One thing, then. It's expensive and there's no guarantee of success."

Gala could almost hear Stretch's laugh.

"I'll try it," said Gala.

It was then that Mama Kelp spoke of the Agaricus Blazei. Spun some wondrous tale of a mushroom first grown in a long-gone country called Brazil. A magical, medicinal mushroom that activated the natural defenses of the body.

"Do you know what killer cells are?"

Gala didn't.

"They're part of your body's immune system, they attack cancer cells. Agaricus Blazei have been proved to enhance a person's killer cells by 3,000 percent."

The problem was that the mushrooms were both delicate and particular. They liked very hot days, damp evenings, and warmish nights. Mama Kelp had spores available at a price (a second pixel unit and eight flashlight batteries— more than Gala's entire supply) but, she warned, even with the right environment, the mushrooms would not be ready to harvest for six months.

"Is it worth it to you?" she asked Gala.

"Yes," said Gala.

That had been five months previously. Gala had begged the additional batteries and Stretch had scavenged a second pixel unit. Four times he'd had to return to the Regeneration Plant before he'd struck lucky. For these prize possessions they received from Mama Kelp a small plastic bag of what she called spawn and a small cardboard box.

"What's in there?" asked Daz.

"Substrate," said Gala confidently.

Daz peered in. "It's sawdust," he said.

"Sawdust substrate," admitted Gala. "To grow the mushrooms in."

Agaricus Blazei, unlike other mushrooms, did not like shaded places, but open spaces. Gala knew that, like any wild food in the Estates, the mushrooms would not last a moment if spotted by another Estate dweller. She needed to put the spores in a place where no one would look for them, no one would see. What better place than the edge of the Regeneration Plant where everything looked like waste, and where such people as came were looking for recyclable hardware, not soft, living things? But it had been Daz who had suggested they place the sawdusted spawn at the foot of the Plant's TropScreen. Daz—Daz with his strangely connected brain and his extraordinary hands—knew a thing or two about electricity. He'd noticed that even when the power was down in the Estates, the TropScreens never blacked out: They were powered from a supply from the heart of the Polis. Of course, he wasn't the only Estate dweller to notice this, others had tried to reroute some of this electricity, running power wires from the screens into their apartments or businesses. Soon enough, these people—greedy people, according to Daz—had found themselves in Holding Cells from which some of them never emerged. Substantial power loss from the circuit, Daz said, was easy to identify, what he was planning was something much more modest. A small power diversion, just enough to keep the earth at the foot of the TropScreen at a constant temperature. Such a tiny variation, he claimed, would be undetectable from the normal ebb and flow of the circuit.

"Are you sure?" asked Gala.

"Sure," said Daz, adding an override switch and a small can to catch rainwater.

"What's that for?" asked Gala.

"Timed evening dampening," Daz said proudly.

Even Stretch had been impressed. "Maybe," he'd confided to his sister, "that boy will be able to make a life for himself after all."

Gala was walking briskly, remembering Mama Kelp's warning: *Even a frost will kill the mushrooms.* What hope then that the mushrooms (which were so close to fruition now) had survived a Sudden Onset Snow? No chance. No chance at all. Yet Gala kept on walking.

As she drew close to the place, she heard the blare of the TropScreen Announcer. The number of dead in the Polis was currently running at 127. Irresponsible people had apparently been found without their ambihoods and ambigloves. These people were a drain on the resources of the Polis and danger to themselves and others. Figures from the Estates were still being compiled. First estimates suggested a figure of more than four thousand dead. There was a central number to call if you suspected any of these were your relatives. Calls would be charged at four feligs a minute.

Gala had arrived; she scanned her surroundings to check that she was not being observed and then she dropped to her knees. Last time she'd come to check on her precious Blazei, there had been the small caps of maybe sixteen mushrooms. She'd had to force herself to leave them alone, not to pluck just one and take it back as a start, as a promise to her mother. If she waited there would be more, they would be bigger, it would be a waste to pick them now, she must wait. So she had waited; and now?

Now there were sixteen limp, wet stalks and sixteen small piles of brown mush. Gala couldn't help crying out, as though she'd been struck. Then she crouched down and lifted the cold, dead things into the palm of her hands.

"I'm sorry." That was Stretch, standing suddenly behind her. She didn't even jump. He would have discovered her missing and known immediately where to find her.

"That's it, then," said Gala bleakly. "It's over."

It was then that the TropScreen flashed, the pulsating image of Leaderene Clore filling the screen as it always did before an important announcement. *"Clean Gene Appeal,"* called the Announcer. *"Clean Gene Appeal. Leaderene Clore, may her name celeb forever, calls upon citizens of the Estates to do their duty by the Polis and present themselves at Hospital 1 this afternoon, Day of Our Leaderene 3,571. This Appeal is, of course, for the benefit of the whole Tropolis. Payment for skin cell donators will be made in TropCredits. Payment for Estate women donating eggs will be made in HighTropCredits. Donation lines will open from 1:00 PM today . . ."*

"How dare they!" shouted Stretch. "After what happened last time. How dare they! And what do they want our genes for anyway? They never say. Do you realize that? They never say."

Gala rose from her knees.

"I'm going to donate," she said.

"What!" screamed Stretch.

"Well, it's obvious, isn't it? I'm fifteen. I ovulate. I can donate eggs. I'll get paid in TropCredits. With TropsCredits, I can buy Polis medicine."

"No!"

"Hospital 1 is close to here. If I go now, I could be first in the line. Or near first."

"You don't know what you're saying."

"Of course I do."

"You might never come back, like Dad. Like our father, Gala."

"You might never have come back from trying to get that pixel unit. But it didn't stop you going, did it? Didn't stop you trying?"

"But that was just for Mom, this is for them, for those self-righteous Plastic . . ."

"And also for Mom," she interrupted him. "And that's all I care about."

"Right," said Stretch, and his mouth was a grim line. She thought he would take her arms, frog-march her back to Block 213. "Right," he repeated. "Then I'm coming with you."

14

Llublo Quells arrived at the PoliticoPalace twenty minutes early for his breakfast meeting with the Leaderene. Euphony Clore did not tolerate lateness. Quite right, too, Llublo Quells did not tolerate lateness either. That's why the Leaderene and the Head of GemCorp InterTrop got on so well, they understood each other. The fact that Llublo had his sober gray ambisuit turned up to AntiSweat was merely a precaution. He was calm. Euphony Clore was a major shareholder in GemCorp InterTrop and thus, he had suggested in a confidential TextTransfer sent to the Leaderene's office late the previous night, it was in both their interests to allow Dr. Igo Strang the short amount of time he needed to sort the GemX problem. Time spent now, Llublo had argued with some passion, would be money saved in the future. A great deal of money. In the meantime, he proposed a holding operation, to dampen panic. The fact that the plans had been sent in advance to the Leaderene and she had not 'catored him immediately (bad news always traveled fastest with the Leaderene) meant, Llublo was sure, that things were going to be all right.

Which is why he was calm.

To prove how calm he was he allowed himself to meander into the public part of the building and take a seat for a minute in the old ParliChamber. Despite the hour, a PodMaster was already instructing a group of about twenty young Clodrones. Dressed identically in their brown ambisuits, the Clos couldn't be more than ten years old. A new generation, Llublo thought proudly, and yet another reason why the Leaderene would need to treat him with respect. Llublo Quells was instrumental to TropVision, to GrandVision indeed. Where, for instance, would Euphony's idea of a gradual reduction in the numbers of Naturals be if it wasn't for his Clodrone Replacement program? Someone had to do the menial jobs. No, it was no good having grand ideas if you couldn't carry them through. The Leaderene might be good at blue-sky thinking, but it was Llublo Quells who was actually the Trop's director of operations, the person who could turn the dreams into reality.

Feeling somewhat expansive all of a sudden, Llublo leaned his large frame over the old-fashioned brass balustrade. It wobbled slightly under his weight. "You owe your existence to me, you know," he considered calling out to the Clodrones below. But, of course, they would know that: in their Limited Schooling Program he was listed as an Authority Figure, one of the key people they would need to learn to identify and respect. Leaderene Clore was obviously another. Understanding and obeying authority figures was a central Clodrone concept. This must be an Unquestion-Obey lesson. Shifting his weight with care, Llublo Quells leaned forward to listen to what the PodMaster was saying.

"In the OldenDays," the Master was intoning, "this chamber would have housed 675 representatives of the Polis."

There was a collective gasp of astonishment.

"Well done indeed, class, you clearly see the waste of resources and energy such a large ruling body implies."

Lots of nodding heads.

"Now, of course, our beloved Trop is run with great efficiency by just one person. And who precisely is that?"

"Leaderene Euphony Clore," the students called out without pause or exception.

"May her name celeb forever," the students added immediately, although one particularly eager fresh-faced boy was just ahead of the others in this.

"Excellent," said the PodMaster, nodding indulgently. "Now Leaderene Clore . . ."

"May her name celeb forever!" they called.

"Yes, yes," said the Master, "is responsible for the stability of the Polis. It is she who decides what is in the best interests of us all. She who knows better than any of us . . ."

"Including you, PodMaster?" cried the fresh-faced boy.

There was a second gasp among the other students, this time of horror.

"25,400," said the Master sharply, "what is Clodrone Lesson 2, Year 2, Rule 1?"

"Asking questions is impolite. The role and responsibility of the Clodrone does not include asking questions." The Clodrone boy's face had fallen, his head hung.

"Correct. You will spend your evening in isolation to better remember this lesson."

"Yes, sir," he said. "Sorry, sir." He moved forward extending both his hands as fists toward the Master. The Master extracted a steelite ruler from a thigh-length ambisuit pocket and smacked the child sharply across the knuckles. "Now, where was I . . ."

People called Llublo's Clodrone Induction Training simple, they called it old-fashioned, but there was no doubt it worked. If his meeting with the Leaderene went well (it was definitely going to go well) then perhaps Llublo might suggest an expansion of the scheme? While they waited for sufficient Clodrones to be bred up to CivicDuty status, perhaps they could call all ten-year-old Naturals for Training? Five-year-olds, maybe? Instilling respect for Authority was what made a society strong, that's what Leaderene Clore always said.

Llublo began walking again. Two iris-scans, a Holding Room, and a digi-check later he was in the inner sanctum of the Palace. He took a seat in the reception area beside a towering—and new—stack of broken mirrors. A Seud Quac, if he wasn't mistaken. Llublo leaned down to inspect the artist's plaque. Seud Quac indeed. *The Divided Self,* he read. The Leaderene was a noted supporter of ProgressiveArt. Indeed, it was she who had ordered all paintings to be removed from the walls of Trop art museums to make way for more contemporary work. Work that, she said, celebrated TropVision, which was, of course, part of Grand-Vision. Llublo looked at himself in the oddly angled mirror strips. His fat nose seemed on a different plane from his beady eyes; his thick neck was separated from his bullish shoulders; his pudgy hand had no relationship with his tree trunk arm. He was generally broken apart and reflected back to himself in fat pieces. He did not like what he saw.

Behind Llublo, the DoorScreen flickered into life and he

quickly pulled himself upright. The Leaderene's face appeared.

"On loan from the Glora Orb Archive," said Leaderene Clore. "What do you think?" She'd obviously had the OneWay switched on and had been observing him.

"Intriguing," said Llublo carefully.

"Makes one think about the importance of seeing the whole person, the whole project. Yes?"

"Yes," said Llublo, who had been thinking more about being fat in an increasingly thin universe.

"Do come in." The screen flicked off and the double doors to Euphony Clore's private office slid open. The mood-sensor walls were lavender.

Normally the Leaderene sat on a tall chair on a raised dais behind a huge desk. Normally a single, low, chair was placed opposite her. There was a pale pink sofa and a pale pink chair in the office but no one, to Llublo's knowledge, had ever been invited to sit there.

"Sit," said Euphony Clore. She indicated the pale pink chair. She herself was reclining her perfectly formed—thin—body on the pale pink sofa.

"Euphony," said Llublo, and negotiated his large behind between the (narrow) arms of the chair.

Leaderene Clore watched but said nothing. She was wearing a violet ambisuit with a black belt cinched about her waist. Her tight blonde curls were in little corkscrews around her face, like some cherubic vision from BannedArt. Her eyes, in keeping with the best gene-pool models, were huge and—today—a matching violet. Euphony changed her eye lenses according to her mood. When she put in her black contacts, you knew there was trouble ahead.

Llublo Quells was aware of a small click down in his ambisuit sweat control. Violet lenses were a good sign, his calmness was justified.

"Eat." Euphony waved at the table to his left on which sat a small silver dish proffering three PoppaPills. The pills were about the size of his little fingernail but perfectly round. There were three different colors: polka dot pink (Long-AgoStrawberry flavor—exceedingly expensive and considered a delicacy); black-and-yellow striped (the BeeSting, a sharp outer pill with a succulent honey center, favored by the HighElites and his own personal favorite); and a white opalescent pill, rather like a pearl, that he didn't recognize.

"It's an OpalMilk," she said delightedly, watching his eyes. "Floods the body with nutrients but has the advantage of filling one up immediately, so there's no need to . . . overindulge," she finished slightly pointedly.

"Aah," said Llublo Quells.

"Go ahead, please."

A FullFlavorSpoon had been placed on the side of the dish. This delicate, tweezerlike implement was only used in the highest society. You used it to pick up your pill (the flavor of top-quality Poppas was detrimentally influenced by even minimal contact with skin) and lodged the pill end of the spoon under your tongue while allowing the handle end to protrude from your mouth. The spoon curve was drilled with very small holes, which meant the pills could not be chewed but had to be sucked out very gradually. Far too gradually for Llublo's liking. He dithered, both with the spoon and the choice of pill. If three pills were on offer it would be polite to eat only two. But which two? His preferred choice did not include the OpalMilk. From what the Leaderene had said, the OpalMilk choice could limit his pill consumption to one. And the BeeSting Poppa was very, very good.

"I suggest the OpalMilk," said Euphony Clore.

Llublo Quells, who had the FullFlavorSpoon poised, grimaced, but it was the white pill that he pincered and placed under his tongue.

"Delicious, yes?"

The pill leaked something sweet and sickly and babyish into Llublo's mouth.

"I asked PoppaPillCo to create me something unique. I asked them to try and find a flavor that no Enhanced person had ever tasted before. I asked for OldTime human breast milk."

Llublo spluttered, he choked, but he could not spit. Spitting out a PoppaPill was the height of incivility.

"Now," continued the Leaderene genially, "I am not a happy bunny. In fact, Llublo, I am very angry indeed." She crossed and recrossed her legs on the couch.

Llublo sucked and gurgled and attempted to swallow, though his gorge rose.

"Your time-delay plans in no way reflect the seriousness of the situation we are facing."

"But . . . ," began Llublo, which allowed the spoon to bounce some more breast milk flavor into his mouth, "we have to proceed with caution, there is so much at stake, so much money . . ."

"Money? Pah!" snapped Euphony Clore. "The continuance of the Trop germline is at stake. If there are defects in the system, or in the people who are the system, then the whole TropProject fails. Which is why, Quells, it is important to look at the whole and not just at the parts."

Quells. Quells!

"I had high hopes of the GemXs, as you know, but if they are flawed, if they are prone to . . . to . . ." She appeared unable to say the word *Degrade,* it was so distasteful to her, ". . . then they must on no account be allowed to breed. They must be lost before the age of GeneTransfer. Lost, that is, now. That is all there is to it."

"Lost?" Llublo managed to repeat.

"Yes. Lost." She smiled at him. She popped a delicious looking BeeSting into her mouth.

"Lost, how?" asked Llublo. "Exactly?"

The Leaderene sighed, as if she found it an effort to be in a room with anyone quite so dim. "Do you know how long it is since the last Atrocity?" she inquired.

Llublo didn't.

"A hundred and eighteen days," said the Leaderene, answering her own question. "I think it's highly likely there will be another one very soon, don't you?"

Llublo's eyes widened. "You think some Dreggie terrorist is going to accidentally wipe out all 6,801 GemXs in the Polis?"

"Accidentally?" repeated Euphony. "Who said anything about *accidentally*? We can't afford any more accidents. I'm talking deliberate targeting. You know what these Dreggies are like. Just like them to plot on wiping out a whole generation of the Enhanced!"

Llublo swallowed, waited.

"It's all a lot simpler than you seem to imagine, my dear

Llublo." Another smile—sadder this time. "I will put out a Mass Call, ask our much valued Naturals to assemble at Hospital 1 on the Clean Gene donation program. Nothing unusual, and not as if the Trop hasn't asked before, and, of course, to ensure the right response—the *largest* response— we'll offer payment in TropCredits. Meantime, you, on behalf of GemCorp, will announce a Trop-wide routine GemX stabilizer check. You will suggest the current problems are minimal and offer a free OnceOnly AddoPill designed to sort the symptoms immediately."

"Free?" Llublo trembled.

"I haven't finished," said the Leaderene testily. "Your announcement will suggest that time is of the essence, a HighPriority call. All GemXs to report in immediately to receive their pill. You'll ask them to come to . . . Hospital 1. The GemXs will be gathering around the front of the building, the Dreggies—coming to donate—around the back. And then . . . oh, dear. A large explosion out front. Dreadful, dreadful what these Naturals are capable of."

The spoon actually fell out of Llublo Quells's open mouth.

"Manners, manners," said Leaderene Clore mildly.

"There'll be outrage! The Elite will be baying for blood!"

"Of course. That is the genius of it. There will be calls for ExtraVigilance. Possibly even a ClampDown. TotalRetribution. A Raze! The idea, as you are beginning to see, serves many purposes."

"And the hospital . . . ," said Llublo, slowly getting to grips with the horrific scenario.

"We have other hospitals."

"The doctors, the nursing staff . . ."

"Collateral damage. You have to expect that."

"Then"—Llublo took a breath—"the GemXs themselves . . ."

"Regrettable, but, as I've said, they cannot be allowed to procreate. Any GemX GenOff would carry the faulty gene. It's too much of a risk."

"What about those who come after them, the younger ones, the GemZs, what if the rogue gene's in their Spec, too?"

"Well, there is that unpleasant possibility. However, with the younger ones, time is on our side. They are not yet near GeneTransfer. So, no doubt Dr. Strang and his research team can get something in place for them."

"But the cost . . ." said Llublo faintly. "As a much-valued shareholder in GemCorp InterTrop, I'm sure . . ."

"Don't worry," said the Leaderene. "I have that covered. I'll call an ImmunizationProgram. Blame some outside influencer from another sector. Some airborne germ perhaps. Absolutely nothing to do with GemCorp at all. People will be more than happy to pay up." She smiled. "Don't say I don't look after the details."

"Which returns us . . . ," began Llublo nervously.

"To the Elite. To the hapless GemX GenParents."

"Exactly," said Llublo. "Some of the most influential people in the Polis . . ."

"Rather too influential, in my view," said Euphony pointedly. "Have you heard the latest from the Throwback-Intellectuals? Some of them are actually using their so-called Enhanced brains to suggest that we impose fewer—rather than more—restrictions on the Estates. Freedom of movement, indeed! People who genuinely believe that if we treat the Dreggies with civility they will return the favor. So, so muddleheaded, don't you think, Quells?"

Quells didn't know quite what he thought.

"Do pick up your spoon," mentioned the Leaderene. "I won't mind if you pop that pill back in your mouth. The floor is HygeniCleaned every five hours, as I'm sure you know. So help yourself, dear Llublo."

Llublo picked the FullFlavorSpoon from the floor and placed it in his mouth once again.

"Good man," said Leaderene Clore. "Now where were we? Oh yes, if these rather out-of-order Elitists see just how bad the Naturals can be, well, they'll all come on side again, won't they? In fact, as you so rightly say, they'll be screaming for revenge. So as well as the Dreggies who are caught in the explosion, there are the others who will go in reprisals, both of which things, of course, advance Grand-Vision. You do remember the GrandVision strategy, don't you, Quells?"

"To make things perfect," intoned Llublo. "To fashion a place where everyone is of equal intelligence, equal beauty"—was she looking with distaste at his fleshy face or was that just his imagination?—"a world without division or poverty . . ."

"Yes, yes," said Leaderene Clore. "So you see it's only a matter of time before the Estates, and all those who live there, have to go."

"All?" repeated Llublo.

"Naturally all." Leaderene Clore laughed at her own delicious wordplay. "Didn't I mention 'all' before? I think I did. You just weren't paying attention. Of course, for the time being, it will remain our little secret. The time for the announcement is not yet. The Clodrone Program is not advanced enough as yet. We do not have quite enough replacements coming through. But it's only a matter of time, yes, Llublo?"

"Yes," said Llublo.

"And, in the meanwhile, the Estates do serve a purpose. Fear, especially fear of attack, is no bad thing. It keeps people in line. After the Hospital 1 attack—well, you can see what a difficult position the ThrowbackIntellectuals will be in! Their argument that we need to give more freedom to the Estates will be in tatters. The Estate dwellers will be seen for what they are—vicious little vermin, which need controlling and—occasionally—culling. I see the explosion as an excellent device to keep everyone marching in the same direction toward the same objective. Progress. Perfection."

"Progress," repeated Llublo. "Perfection." He felt suddenly very full. The pill was finished, he realized. As he took the spoon out of his mouth, he had a horrible feeling that he was going to burp—but he sucked it down.

The Leaderene rose from the sofa, went to her desk, and depressed a small white button. "Go ahead with the Mass Call," she said, "as previously discussed." She listened. "Yes. Immediately." She released the button. "And now, I think we've something to celebrate, don't you?"

She took two vials of mescat from her desk drawer and almost floated back toward Llublo to present him with one of them.

Llublo, who thought it was rather early in the day for mescat, unstoppered his vial and took a long draft.

"May you celeb forever," he said. "Your Leadereneship." He was thinking of Igo Strang and Strang's GenOff, Maxo. Maxo would die. He'd be one of those who would die. But then, Llublo reasoned, it was really all Strang's fault anyway. If Strang had done his work better, there would be no Degrade. A Degrade in the GemX genome was a disgrace, it was not to be tolerated. Strang deserved whatever was coming his way. His inadequacies had nearly cost Llublo dear. Just imagine all those angry GenParents converging on the GemCorp office (the AntiSweat control whirled briefly) but if the GemXs were just to be blown up by Dreggie terrorists—bingo! Case closed. What a woman the Leaderene was! Her strategy advanced GrandVision, saved the germline, and cost him nothing.

He took another swig of mescat. Strong stuff—whatever vintage this was. He looked over Euphony Clore's reclining body, her luscious, curved lips, her swimming violet eyes. He humphed himself in his small chair.

"You know I could really mesh with you," he said.

"Don't be ridiculous," said Leaderene Euphony Clore.

15

Delayed at the Crossing Point for well over an hour, Gala and Stretch still managed to arrive at Hospital 1 by 10:00 AM, two hours in advance of the specified noon donation time. But they were far from first. Harassed hospital officials were already redirecting people from the front of the hospital, with its huge sweeping front steps and gracious half-moon shaped piazza, to the smaller square around the back. As Gala turned the corner of the building, she saw immediately that the line was already hundreds of people long and, unlike the resigned orderliness of Mama Kelp's stairs, this press of people were already jostling, pushing for space and advantage.

"Keep close to me," said Stretch.

He'd take my hand, thought Gala, if he could. But she kept close to him anyway. She was glad of her brother's company and she admired him for being able to lay aside his own agenda to come with her. Though, looking at the numbers gathered already, it seemed they might have had a wasted journey. How many people would the hospital need?

Stretch led her to where the end of the line seemed to be, but the snake of people suddenly changed shape and it looked as though they were line-barging.

"Oi!" shouted a squat, bald man, with a pumping sort of body. "What you think yer doing?"

"Sorry," said Gala immediately, and now she took Stretch's arm, because her brother was already tensing. "We thought this was the end of the line."

"Nah," said the man gruffly, "that's a long way off." He pointed back about a hundred yards, where the beginning of the pedestrian walkway was marked with two square posts.

They turned back. Before they reached the official end of the line, other people had joined it, forcing them back further. Gala stared at this mass of humanity. Could they all need the TropCredits as much as she did? Walking in the Estates, these people looked ordinary, unremarkable. But here, in this clean, geometrically concretiaed square, they looked a ragged, ill-assorted lot. All of their lives would probably be improved with some TropCredits. Gala felt something slip away from her then.

"Clean Gene Appeal. Leaderene Clore, may her name celeb forever, calls upon the citizens of the Estates to do their duty by the Polis and present themselves . . . ," blared the Trop Announcer from a screen just to their right.

"Another few hundred here and we'll all be crushed to death," grumbled an elderly man who was trying to keep his place in the line with a thin, whippy branch of a tree he'd obviously cut for a walking stick. "They should stop the announcements. They should close the Crossing Points. They should . . ."

"They?" questioned Stretch.

"Yes," said the man. "They. The Enhanced. The ones with the big brains."

118

"No," said Stretch suddenly. "No, we should do something about it. We should do something about all of it." And he jumped on one of the posts.

"Stretch," cried Gala. He was going to make a speech, he had that face on, hard and passionate. "Please!"

"People of the Polis," shouted Stretch, his own vehemence making him wobble a little on the post, "people of the Polis, why are we here?"

"To get the money," someone shouted and there was a relieving laugh all round.

"But why are we needed?" continued Stretch undeterred. "What is it that the Enhanced with their 'big brains' want of us? What is it about our Clean Genes that they need?"

"Who cares?" shouted back a pinched-looking woman. "If we get the money."

"Stretch!" Gala looked to right and left, surely it would only be moments before the Poldrones arrived. But there was a tolerant mood among the people nearest Stretch. There wasn't much to do in the line but wait. Here was entertainment.

"What exactly do we have that the Plastics need?" shouted Stretch. "Our own unique 'clean' cells, our own identity . . ."

Did he plan this? thought Gala. Is that why he'd been so willing to come? What an innocent she could be.

"And what do we do it for?" continued Stretch. "A few feligs, that's what."

"TropCredits!" corrected four or five voices simultaneously.

"HighTropCredits if you're lucky enough to be a woman!" riposted a young man in a badly stitched ex-ambisuit.

"But if we really have something they need," said Stretch, "something they can't get from their own people, then we're powerful, right?"

This sounded, to Gala, like TropTreason; if you spoke out, if you attacked the Polis or questioned the Leaderene in any way there were serious consequences.

"Please," she said, putting a steadying hand on Stretch's leg. "Please get down."

"No, let him speak," shouted the squat, pumping man who'd sent them backward in the line. "I wanna hear what he has to say."

In the underground SecuritySuite of the PoliticoPalace, known affectionately as "The Bunker," Leaderene Euphony Clore was speaking with Burton Chavit, the head of InternalPolice. He was briefing her on the finer details of the coming Atrocity when his attention was caught by the image of a thin young man on SecuriScreen 22. There were over a hundred roving security cameras beaming information into The Bunker at any one time, but Chavit had always had an unerring habit of being able to pick out the one screen where the action really was.

"Look," he said to Leaderene Clore, indicating the young man who, in less than nine SecuriAlert minutes, he would be able to identify as Phylo Lorrell. "A rabble-rouser."

"Oh, how perfectly perfect," said the Leaderene. "You won't send the Poldrones, will you?"

"Of course not. Well, not yet."

"Marvelous," said the Leaderene. "Our very own radical bomber."

Chavit played around with some buttons on his Security-Console. "There—footage being saved. How long now until the GemX call goes out?"

"Four minutes and nineteen seconds," said Leaderene Clore, who'd always liked accuracy.

"Well, we'll give the GemXs an hour or so to assemble and then . . ."

"Play this footage on the TropScreen," said the Leaderene finishing Chavit's sentence. It was so good to work with people who knew what they were doing.

"And I thought we were going to have to invent a culprit again," said Burton Chavit. He activated the SecuriTalk Link on his desk and spoke to an unseen lieutenant: "Who do we have at the hospital? Right. Use Agent T. He's pretty invisible in a crowd. Get him to stick a HomingChip on our rabble-rouser. If the boy survives, I want to know where he goes. Yes. Thanks."

"I can't wait for twelve o'clock," said Leaderene Clore. "Can you?"

16

Dr. Igo Strang was biting his nails. All five digits of his right hand were down to the quick and he'd just started on his left thumb. Glora Orb said nail-biting was pernicious and ugly and for over a decade Igo had kept his hands in his pockets. But right now, Igo Strang was in a state: There had been no communication from his boss since his early morning meeting with the Leaderene. Yesterday there had been shouting and pressure and urgency and no possibility of taking the time to organize a Clean Gene Appeal. And today? Well, today there was a Tropwide Clean Gene Appeal and Llublo wasn't answering his 'cator. Why? What was going on? All this on top of the fact that Igo's darling mesh, Glora Orb, had her 'cator on VideoPic (though satellsearch proved her to be back in the gallery) and Maxo had been lost by that idiotic Clodrone driver.

Still, Maxo did not have wrinkles. That's what Glora had said and Igo, biting his nails in the Laboratory, was going to hang on to that. No degrading GenOff. Perfect Maxo. So why hadn't the boy gone back to the Virtual Date Palace to pick up his 'cator? Why had he left it there in the first place? So many questions. So few answers. Most importantly, why was Clodrone 1640 such an incompetent? How could you be waiting outside the gallery with a car and not notice when your charge emerged? And that's really why Igo was biting his nails. Not because of Llublo, not because of the mystery of the Clean Gene Appeal—but because of Maxo and the fact that he hadn't heard from his GenOff since the previous night, since the Sudden Onset Snow. Had Maxo been out in that snow? It wasn't possible. Igo didn't want to think about it. He kept trying to focus on anything—Llublo's face, the crescents of bitten nail falling to the Lab floor—rather than that. Rather than Maxo being out in that snow. Because Maxo had left the gallery. Even Glora had noticed that.

"Dr. Strang?"

"Mm?" One of the younger Lab workers in his white ambisuit was standing in front of Igo. "What?"

"We're on standby," said the man apologetically. "You put us on standby. To be ready for the urgent work . . ." He trailed off, but it was obvious what he meant. No work was being done down in the Lab because everyone was on standby, everyone was waiting, waiting for Igo Strang to decide who should be doing what to save the Polis.

"Just get on," snapped Igo.

"With what?" inquired the man delicately.

"Work," said Igo. "Your work."

It was then that Llublo Quells's face appeared. Not discreetly on Igo's 'cator, but hugely, on the workplace Trop-Screen.

"Germline GemXs," said Llublo, his pale blue eyes somehow lost in his blubbery cheeks, "this is a PriorityOne call for you to attend Heights Hospital 1 to receive your AddoPill. This is a OnceOnly—and totally free—AfterCare gift from GemCorp InterTrop. As you know, GemCorp has the highest standard of germline engineering and our teams are working constantly to predict the unpredictable. Some months ago, our chief scientist, Dr. Igo Strang, with enormous foresight, anticipated the possibility of the—minor—inconveniences some GemXs are currently experiencing, giving our teams time to respond with this TopoftheRange solution. All GemXs, whether experiencing symptoms or not, are requested to come to Heights Hospital 1 immediately. Clodrone taxis will be available at all MajorBuilding points, and the Leaderene herself—may her name celeb forever—has dictated that no Trop-Credits will be deducted from anyone leaving work or StudyDay to answer this call. Please understand that Gem-Corp InterTrop is working at all times to ensure your best health and safety. Your well-being is our primary and only objective."

Llublo's face dissolved and the huge GemCorp slogan—*GemCorp Works for You*—flashed over the screen. After which the TropScreen Announcer repeated the details of the appeal slowly and with text subtitles.

"Gosh," said the white ambisuited young worker to Igo. "Congratulations, sir. You kept that quiet. Do you want me to facilitate the transfer of the pills from your LabOffice to the Hospital?"

Igo Strang, who had the nail of his little finger so far down his throat he was almost choking, knew then that something was very wrong indeed.

Maxo Evangele Strang did not like the old man. Edwin Challice stared at him, he followed him about. Even when, as was right and proper, the custodian had given up his bed to Maxo and elected to sleep somewhere downstairs on the Museo floor, he still kept returning to the bedroom— peering in on Maxo.

"Push off," Maxo had yelled as Challice had loomed out of the darkness a third time. "Leave me alone."

The old man had retreated, but not without leaving his gaze (or so it felt to Maxo) on Maxo's face. Maxo wished, fervently, that he had not pulled off the BodySculpt; the BodySculpt had afforded him protection, the BodySculpt had allowed him, just for a while, to forget. Now he felt the crack burning at his temple. All night long he tossed, he turned, which is why when he finally fell into an exhausted sleep in the early hours of the morning, he didn't wake again until almost ten o'clock. Bleary-eyed, he staggered to the custodian's bathroom. He would have welcomed a soothing reception, he felt he deserved green mood-sensor walls and BodyDirected light fittings and the comforting feeling that someone was actually paying him some attention. After all, he'd had a tough few days. In fact, thanks to the Sudden Onset Snow, he'd nearly died, hadn't he? But this was a very old-fashioned PublicBuilding and, as far as he could see, the WashFacilities weren't even Voice-Activated.

Maxo stepped out of his ambisuit, ComboEntered his preferred AutoClean option on the suit's control panel, and made for the shower. He never arrived. With his right foot poised between one step and another, he caught sight of his face in a square of mirror.

At his left temple was a second crack.

Maxo's raised leg wobbled, his floor-planted leg wobbled,

he lurched, his head swung to and fro (left temple crack, right temple crack) and then his limbs simply gave way, they buckled. There was a crash as he hit the ground.

It was hardly a moment before there was a knock at the door.

"Can I be of any assistance?" asked Edwin Challice.

"No, you can't," shrieked Maxo from the floor. "Go away!"

There was no sound of retreating footsteps.

"Go away, I said!" screamed Maxo Strang.

Edwin Challice went away, but not very far.

Maxo Strang picked himself off the floor. He stood as close as he could to the mirror, or rather he swayed there, because the pain of focusing on the cracks made him nauseous.

"Right," he said. "Right." He did not shower. He turned off the AutoClean halfway through its cycle (which automatically voided the WashGuarantee), put the ambisuit back on, and headed out of the custodian's bedroom. The custodian was standing in the hall.

"Don't look at me," said Maxo.

He went downstairs into the Museo, Edwin Challice followed. Taking charge of himself like this made Maxo feel stronger. He would call a Clodrone car and go straight to his GenPap's. That was all there was to it.

"Call me a car," he said.

The old fool was still fumbling with his ludicrously antique 'cator when Llublo Quells's fat face reared out of the TropScreen.

"Germline GemXs," said the chairman of GemCorp InterTrop, "this is a PriorityOne call for you to attend

Heights Hospital 1 to receive your AddoPill. This is a OnceOnly—and totally free—AfterCare gift from GemCorp InterTrop. As you know GemCorp has the highest standard of germline . . ."

Maxo listened transfixed to the announcement. It was all thoroughly expected! There was a pill! He was not going to die! In fact, he was saved! Maxo Evangele Strang burst into something wet about the eyes.

"Can I offer you a handkerchief?" asked Edwin Challice, drawing something very clean and square and white from his pocket.

"Why?" sobbed Maxo. "I'm not crying!" But he was; for the first time in his short and privileged life, Maxo Strang was crying, if only for himself.

Oh—his wonderful GenPap! How foolish of him to have not gone straight to his GenPap, but then, hadn't he actually been just about to leave for the Lab, when the announcement came? Igo might have let his GenOff into the secret, though, but that was Igo all over, Maxo supposed, such a fine, modest man. Igo Strang, working for all GemXs equally. GemCorp InterTrop—working for you!!

"Is the Museo a MajorBuilding?" asked Maxo, smearing his nose on the arm of his ambisuit. That's where the texts said the Clodrone cars were gathering to take people to the hospital.

"No," said Edwin Challice, "I don't believe so."

"Give me the 'cator." Edwin Challice did as he was asked. The thing was so out of date, that Maxo barely knew how to work it. "You've really got to get into the Year of our Leaderene 34," he said dismissively. In the absence of VoiceRecognition, he dialed his GenPap's loconumber. The 'cator whirred and buzzed. "Doesn't this thing even have a pixel unit?"

"No," said Edwin.

"Extreme," said Maxo. How did these half-lives live? He thought it was only Dreggies that didn't have pixel units.

Igo Strang picked up. At least Maxo had to imagine it was his GenPap, as there was no OnScreenVid.

"Pap, it's me. Maxo."

"Oh, CelebHigh!" said Igo Strang. "Where are you?"

"Right on my way to Heights Hospital 1, for your little wonder pill. Thanks, Pap. Thanks a million. You know, for a moment, I was almost worried."

"So you have symptoms?"

"One," said Maxo, "or two."

"Maxo." Igo's voice sounded contorted, but it was probably just the poor 'cator reception. "Don't go to the hospital."

"What? Why?"

"Just don't. Trust me. I'll send 1640 to get you. He'll bring you to the Lab. Do it for me, Maxo."

"Oh, I get it. I get the pill at the Lab—save on lining up. Right?"

"Wait—I'm running satellsearch on your 'cator, but there's no response."

"That's cos this 'cator came out of the ark, it doesn't have pictures, let alone a GSP unit. I'm at the Museo."

"Right, stay there. Don't move till 1640 comes—Celeb-Honor?"

CelebHonor! That was what his Pap used to say to him when he was a child, to make him keep his promises.

"CelebHonor, Pap."

He clicked off.

"Breakfast?" said Maxo cheerily.

The old man shuffled into some back room and emerged with two rather dreary looking Poppas in a plastic cup.

"What are they?"

"Fish oil and wheat germ," said Edwin apologetically. "Old bones, you see."

"I think I'll pass," said Maxo. He and Challice were having a conversation, so it was reasonable for the old man to be looking at him, but did he have to look quite so hard? "What is it with you?" Maxo said.

"I'm sorry?"

"The staring. Why do you do it?"

"I'm looking for something," said Edwin Challice, seriously.

"Like what?"

"The key to something that I've lost. Something that's been lost."

"And you think I've got that key?" Maxo said. "Like on my face?"

"I don't know," said Edwin Challice.

"We don't use keys in the real world anymore," said Maxo. "We use iris scans and infrabeams and lococodes."

"Yes," said Edwin Challice. "I know."

"So if you've lost your key, it's probably gone for good."

"That would kill me," said Edwin Challice.

"Oh," said Maxo. "Right." Not that it would matter much, the man was clearly going to die soon anyway. Maxo shuddered. Dying, what a vile concept. Thank celeb for his Gen-Pap and the AddoPill!

He sat himself down in the custodian's chair in the front hall.

"Do you want to look around the Museo while you wait?" asked Edwin. "We're officially open."

"No thanks," said Maxo. "History's never interested me much."

Maxo sat, the old man stood, and the TropScreen moaned on in the background. Maxo was planning ahead: He'd get 1640 to drive to the Lab via the Virtual Date Palace, retrieve his 'cator; he might even book a VDP session for later that night. The AddoPills would make people feel like celebrating. Catspaw would be bound to sign in that evening. She'd be well, he'd be well. Things would be back to normal,

Trop Alert, Trop Alert, Trop Alert," The TropScreen's furious, high-pitched Alert 3 siren sounded. Over the years, Maxo had learned to block out even an Alert 1, but his eyes were drawn to the TropScreen, there was something familiar about the pictures, and about what the TropScreen Announcer was saying: trouble at Hospital 1. Hospital 1! But the pictures weren't of GemXs standing in line for AddoPills, the pictures were of Dreggies, hundred. and hundreds of them all pushing and shoving and a thin boy, standing on a post, addressing them.

"What's more," the boy was shouting, "during the last Clean Genes Appeal, my father came to donate, did his duty by the Polis. And what happened to him?"

"Got rich," someone shouted back.

"He never came home, that's what happened. My father never came home."

"Probably went to a Mescat House. Liked it so much he never left."

There was braying laughter.

"We should all go home," continued the boy. "If we all

refused to donate—if no one donated, then we'd find out some things. Then we'd know what's really going on. I'm asking you, fellow members of the Polis, not to donate. To make a stand. To refuse."

This was all very dramatic, but it was not the boy Maxo was looking at. Maxo was looking at the slight figure of a girl standing close to the post. At first, he couldn't be sure because she had her back to the camera and therefore to him. She was staring up at the boy on the post. And yet—that thin frame, the way she held her body, her dark, slightly wild hair. It was her Maxo was sure it was her. His Dreggie.

He got up from the chair, crossed to the Museo Trop-Screen and put his hand on the plasma surface of the girl, pressed his thumb into her soft back. She reacted as if she felt him, reaching up to touch the post boy's knees: "For Perle," she whispered, "for mother," and then she turned away. But the camera caught her, because although she was turning away from the post boy, she was turning toward him. Him! Maxo Evangele Strang. And so he saw her face—her unbelievably beautiful, lopsided face. Once again, his blood surged.

"Sir," said Clodrone 1640 arriving in the hall.

"Perfect timing," said Maxo. "We have to go to Hospital 1 right away." And, because there would be no time to retrieve his 'cator, he accidentally slipped the old man's one into his ambisuit pocket.

Clodrone 1640 sat in the car, key slot activated. *You are an incompetent,* Igo Strang had said, *you are a disgrace to the Clodrone and the Clodrone project. Listen carefully,* he'd added, *this is an UnquestionObey. I want you to collect Maxo from the Museo and bring him here, to the Lab. Once you have collected Maxo you will, under no circumstances, let him out of your sight. Failure to comply with these instructions could, I warn you, result in your being returned to Training."* No one, as far as 1640 knew, had ever been returned to Training. But just the threat of it, the disgrace of it . . .

"What are we waiting for?" clicked Maxo from the back-seat.

Clodrone 1640 was waiting for Finn to make up his mind. Finn had been quiet for a couple of days, but now 1640 felt him stirring. Finn seemed to be more active when there were conflicts, when there were difficulties, like now. Go to the Lab, said Igo, go to Hospital 1, said Maxo. And Finn, what did Finn say?

"Hurry up! Move," shouted Maxo. "She isn't going to stay there forever!"

"Love," said Finn, "in love." *Love.* Clodrone 1640 tried to process the word. He thought it might come from the HistoroDictionary, something discarded by the Elite but still in use in the Estates. But what did it mean? It meant, apparently, for Finn, something sudden and lurching, which caused Finn—and therefore 1640—to pull the car wheel violently to the right, and then right again, so that the car spun one hundred and eighty degrees. They were facing, it seemed, toward the hospital.

Maxo checked the NavigationSystem screen. "Excellent," he said. "How long will it take?"

"Twenty minutes," gasped Clodrone 1640, trying to take in air.

But 1640 was wrong. As they approached the hospital, the roads became clogged with traffic, and although there were Poldrones redirecting any vehicle not carrying GemXs, there were still far too many cars and far too little space.

It was nine minutes to twelve.

"I'll walk," said Maxo.

"No," said 1640. This was an UnquestionObey. He'd undertaken not to let his charge out of his sight. But then he'd also undertaken to take Maxo directly to the Lab.

"I beg your pardon?" said Maxo.

"Sorry," said 1640. Clodrone 1640 was in a muddle. Finn was destroying everything. Training seemed to be going out of the window. What was he to do? That was a question, questions were not allowed. This was an UnquestionObey. This was a circle. He was going around in circles again. And again.

"Stop the car," said Maxo.

Clodrone 1640 kept the engine running, but the car was pretty much stopped anyway, hemmed in, in front, hemmed in behind. So Maxo Strang simply opened the door and stepped out.

Clodrone 1640 watched his Master's GenOff walk away. He was an incompetent. He wasn't fit to carry the heavy privilege of being a Clodrone. Finn whispered something in his ear that sounded like, "cry." *You can cry if you want to.* But 1640 knew nothing about crying, it wasn't in his *Dictionary of UsefulWords.*

17

"Hey, Maxo!" the boy getting out of the car in front was Bovis Frank, the GemX who lived on SkyFloor 6 of Maxo's building. "Maxo!"

Bovis bounded over to Maxo and then stopped when he saw his friend's face. "Wow," he said. "You're brave." Then he laughed and pulled something off his forehead: a BodySculpt. There was a one inch vertical crack between his eyebrows. "But we can all be brave now, I guess, thanks to your GenPap. What a man, Maxo."

They walked together the few streets to the hospital, following the sound of the noise. Gathered in the piazza in front of Hospital 1 was a multicolored array of ambisuited people.

"Yo," said Bovis. "This is big."

"It's not a party," said Maxo.

But it was. There was a cheery, festival atmosphere. The people, most of whom were obviously still wearing BodySculpt, were perfectly, beautifully, similarly formed. They were all GemXs, they were all smiling.

"Hey, isn't that Lydida Malkin?" said Bovis, pointing. "Didn't you have a thing for her?"

Some way ahead was the back of Lydida's blonde head.

"I've got to go," said Maxo.

"Go?" said Bovis. "Go where? Looks like this is the only place to be right now. Everyone's here. Wow. I haven't seen half these guys since EduCate." Then he spotted someone else. "Hey—Postle, is that you? I don't believe it! Where the celeb have you been!"

And, while Bovis's attention was temporarily engaged elsewhere, Maxo Evangele Strang made for the back of Hospital 1.

Stretch only came to a pause when a man, passing too close to him, accidentally jogged his leg and nearly dislodged him from the post.

"Careful!" said Gala instinctively, but the man had already disappeared into the crowd.

Stretch righted himself. He didn't know how long he'd been speaking, it could have been five minutes, it could have been an hour. His head felt light, which, at first, he'd put down to the general strain of trying to keep his balance on the post. But it wasn't just the lightness in his head, there was lightness around him, too, a kind of floating unreality. The only time Stretch had felt anything similar before was when he'd been outside after a Snow 10 and experienced the dramatic rise in temperature that always followed a Sudden Onset. One minute it had been sub-zero, the next subtropical, it didn't make rational sense, but that's how things were. He had the same sort of feeling now—to speak for so long without the arrival of a single Poldrone, that didn't make sense, and yet that's how things seemed to be. Of course, he was grateful for the lack of Pol-drones. He hadn't planned on making the speech, it had happened spontaneously, as things often did with him; he'd just felt impelled to speak and had spoken, with no thought for the consequences.

But now, as he was forced to pause (how did that man melt away so fast?), he saw the consequences etched into Gala's face. She was afraid. And he should be afraid. And also ashamed, because Gala had come here with the best of intentions and he could have ruined everything for her and for their mother. And had his words served a purpose, had they fired up any one of the waiting Estate dwellers? They had not. Only the pumping man had been really interested and his interest turned out to be purely economic. "You mean we can make more money, then?" he queried. "If they want what we've got then we can up the price, is that what you're saying?" It was not what Stretch was saying. But what was Stretch saying?

He stepped down off the post.

"Oh, thank you," cried Gala. "Thank you." And a smile lit her face, which said, "Everything in the world will be all right now."

Which is when the bomb went off.

Of course, Stretch didn't know it was a bomb then, that information came later. All he knew was that there was a bang loud enough to shake his heart from his chest and that the air became dense and full of flying debris. It all happened very fast but, afterward, Stretch said it felt as if time had almost slowed to a stop because everything seemed to unfold at an impossibly leisurely rate. After the noise came the reverberations. Stretch watched the hospital building behind him sway unhurriedly forward and backward, forward and back. He watched pieces of the building lazily detach themselves, lumps of concrete breaking off to hover over the unmoving mass of people below.

Why aren't they moving? thought Stretch. Why aren't I moving? We should be running!

But nobody ran. It was probably only a few seconds, anyway, and there wasn't time to run before the building began to fall. It fell on one of its majestic forward rolls, collapsing onto its own beautiful, half-moon front piazza. From that side of the hospital there was some screaming and then some silence: a great deal of silence.

At the back of the building, where Stretch was, there was a tiny breath of shock and then choking dust. Stretch couldn't see what had happened to those at the front of the line, or maybe he didn't want to see. There was some screaming there, too, but not much. Stretch clamped his hand over his mouth in order to keep the dust out of his throat. Now he was moving, now he was going to get out, and get Gala out. But where was Gala?

Gala was lying—outstretched—at his feet, blown flat and still. Or hit by something perhaps. He didn't know if she was alive or dead.

"Gala!" he dropped to his knees, put his head to her chest. She was breathing.

"Can I help?" Someone else was kneeling by Gala's prone body and, even through the murk, Stretch could see its perfect features and body-hugging ambisuit. One of the Enhanced, a Piece of Plastic.

"No," said Stretch through his hand, and then he held his breath and used both his arms to lift his sister's head, cradle her. "Gala," he whispered, "Gala, please."

"Gala," repeated the Piece of Plastic, as if savoring the

word. His ambisuit was obviously switched to help him breathe. "Gala."

"Go away," said Stretch. More dust swirled. It caught in Stretch's throat and made him gag. It fell on Gala's closed eyes.

"Do you know who I am?" inquired the Piece of Plastic. Stretch didn't. Nor did he care.

"I," said the Piece of Plastic, "am Maxo Strang, GenOff of Dr. Igo Strang, chief scientist of GemCorp InterTrop."

Something in the haze cleared.

"Right," said Stretch, "you can take her legs."

Clodrone 1640 was in a daze. The car 'CatorSys was barking at him in Igo's voice: *"1640, 1640, answer me, are you there? Where are you? Answer me now!"* But 1640 wasn't entirely sure where he was and so couldn't answer the questions. He had been, so he thought, just a few streets from Hospital 1. But now there seemed to be no Hospital 1, only rubble bouncing down the street and bits of metal whirling and falling, and black, blanketing dust. Some Clodrone drivers had got out of their vehicles to see what was happening. 1640 had seen one mown down by a rogue piece of concrete. 1640 himself had not left his vehicle, he'd listened to the bouncing of building pieces on the car roof. He was very afraid that Igo Strang would not like the damage.

"Maxo," shrieked Igo over the 'CatorSys, *"have you got Maxo?"*

1640 did know the answer to this question. He did not have Maxo. Maxo had left the car and walked toward the front entrance of Hospital 1, the epicenter of the explosion. Given the damage in this street, it was unlikely that Maxo had survived. That's what happened in Atrocities. He'd learned about it in Training. The Naturals, who were wild and dangerous people living on the margins of the Trop, periodically blew up the good and decent people of the Polis. Why they behaved like this 1640 couldn't remember, or maybe he'd never been taught. What he did know was that, in Atrocities, people (normally the Enhanced) died and then there would be a Mass Funeral. And sometimes Reprisals. But he was wandering again. The point was he didn't have Maxo. He should have had Maxo, but he didn't. And now Maxo was probably dead. Definitely dead. 1640 had done something very wrong indeed. WrongDoing Level 10.

"Please," begged Dr. Igo Strang, *"please pick up."*

Finn, no doubt, would have had something to say about the situation. Finn would have known what to do and how to do it. But Finn seemed to have gone very quiet indeed. The dust was settling now, 1640 could see it on the cars in front of his, so he imagined it was also settling on his car. Behind him, other cars were reversing, they were getting out, but 1640 had nowhere to go. So he just sat in the car, waiting for—he didn't know exactly what.

"Please," said Igo Strang, *"Maxo?"*

Clodrone 1640 leaned forward and clicked off the 'CatorSys. Clodrones were not entitled to switch off 'CatorSys, it was an UnquestionObey Infringement (Level 2). But given that he was already running at WrongDoing 10, Clodrone 1640 wasn't sure it would matter.

In the explosion, Gala had lost her right shoe. So when Maxo, instructed by the Post Boy (who said his name was

Stretch, but it didn't seem a likely name to Maxo), lifted Gala's legs he saw her bare right foot, her dusty little toes. Had there ever, he wondered, been a more exquisite foot? He wanted to see more and more clearly, so he blew at the dust, but it still clung to her. So he touched her. Touched her! He slipped his right hand down, over the perfect jutting bone of her ankle, across the arch of her foot, down to the hollow between her big and second toe. When he stroked with his thumb there, to remove the dirt, the shock was electric, his body so shook with the thrill of her that his ambisuit, which had been fanning the lower half of his face to try and drive dust from his mouth and nose, momentarily sent an ice chill to his extremities to try and control the shakes.

"No," shouted Maxo, because he wanted to feel the thrill, he wanted to vibrate with the extraordinary delight of her foot. What a foot! He didn't think he'd ever seen such foot before, much less held one. No, he'd never held a foot. Of course not, it wasn't right, it wasn't proper, it was a danger to the germline. What's more, he had the ludicrous feeling that if he held her foot for more than a second longer he'd want to bend down and put his mouth on it, or, more specifically, his lips—though why anyone would want to put their lips on someone's foot was not in any MeshManual he'd ever read.

"Come on," said Stretch. "This way."

The boy appeared to want to take the girl down the streets leading from the back of the hospital, or ex-hospital.

"No," said Maxo. "I've got a car."

Maxo took his hand from Gala's foot, held her clothed legs in an attempt to compose himself for the ordeal of carrying her (not that she was heavy, she wasn't at all, it was just that he didn't ever remember carrying anything before, that's what one had Clodrones for). Holding her through cloth didn't spark his body quite so much, but he still felt a few unaccustomed prickles and fizzes.

"This way."

Given his poor sense of direction, Maxo had thought to retrace his steps from the front of the hospital back to where 1640 had parked. But, of course, there was no front of the hospital, just bewildering heaps of smoking concrete and broken glass. Among the heaps there were bodies, at least an arm here or a leg there. Protruding from underneath a twisted steelite girder was a flow of very blonde hair. If there was a face attached to the hair, Maxo didn't pause to look. So, when Stretch came to a halt, Gala's body shook between them.

"It's horrible," said Stretch. "We should help."

"No," said Maxo, clinging to Gala's legs.

"These are your people," said Stretch.

"They're dead," said Maxo. And most of them were, though one or two still twitched. A siren sounded. "People will come, deal with it. Come on."

Gala stirred then, moaned a little, but did not open her eyes.

"Gala," said Stretch, "you're okay, you're going to be okay. We're taking you home."

She didn't moan again, but Maxo wanted her to. The sound of her, that yawn of pain, it was extraordinary, he'd never heard that in the Virtual Date Palace.

"This way," said Maxo, trying to concentrate. He followed the line of parked cars backward, away from the devastated piazza. What if 1640 had driven away? But he hadn't, there was the car up ahead, at least he thought it was the car, it was difficult to tell because of the layer of dust on the hood and windshield.

Because his hands were occupied, because both of them were still doing exquisite touching, Maxo used his elbow to knock on the window of the car. "Come on," he shouted, "open up."

From inside the dark car, 1640 heard a voice. The voice sounded like Maxo's. Then I must have died in the explosion, reasoned 1640, I, too, am dead. But he still got out of the car.

"Open the back," ordered Maxo. "We have an injury."

Maxo was alive. He was clearly alive. CelebHigh and Praise the Leaderene forever! Alive and carrying a girl. And more extraordinary that all this was that, at the other end of the girl, the head end, was Finn. Clodrone 1640 reeled, he staggered.

"What's the matter, man," snapped Maxo, "give us a hand here."

Only this real-life Finn was a bit too young, he was just a kid, but it was definitely Finn: that thin, angular body, that set jaw, those fierce blue eyes.

"Finn," burbled Clodrone 1640.

"What did he say?" asked the Finn-boy.

"Nothing," said Maxo. "He's a Clodrone. Get a move on, 1640."

1640 opened the side door and the Finn-boy climbed carefully in, supporting the girl's upper body. Maxo eased in her legs, and then stood stupidly, as though he also wanted to get in the back, but, with the way the girl was lying there wasn't any room.

"It's okay," the Finn-boy said. "I can hold her okay."

"Clear the windshield," Maxo barked at 1640, and climbed into the front seat.

As 1640 scraped away the dust, he peered through the glass at Maxo and, beyond him, to the Finn-boy. The middle-aged Finn inside 1640 didn't stir when he looked at Maxo but, when his eyes caught the Finn-boy's, something huge and shuddering passed through him. *Love.* That word again. 1640 had to hold on to the hood, steady himself. *Love love love.*

"Have you been on the mescat?" shouted Maxo.

The windshield was clear. 1640 got back into the car, taking care not to let his gaze ignite again with the Finn-boy's.

"Where to?" asked Maxo.

"Estate 4, Block 213," said the voice from the back. Even the voice made 1640 jingle. It was the voice he'd heard in his head for so long. He felt as if someone was pulling him inside out.

"Drive on, then," said Maxo.

And despite all the rules of Training, 1640 knew he would.

Stretch had watched Clodrone cars purr past him in the Polis, but he had never been inside one before. It was cool and quiet and swift. He could hear the sound of Gala breathing, steady un-labored breaths. He hadn't lied when he'd told her she would be all right. Gala was strong and this temporary loss of consciousness was probably a blessing. He would not like Gala to have seen what he'd seen at the site of the explosion. Accidental explosion or deliberate bomb? The TropScreen Announcer would no doubt inform them soon enough. He hoped that, if it turned out to be a bomb, that no one from his sector would be blamed. Reprisals were often indiscriminate and always vicious.

He could also hear the sound of his own breathing, which was quicker than Gala's, almost a pant. That was the adrenaline still pumping, he supposed, and also the excitement, because Dr. Igo Strang's GenOff was sitting not one foot from him. He looked at the back of Maxo's shaven head, watched the pulse of blood in his neck. He needed to keep calm, very calm; the plan he had already begun to conceive was daring and dangerous. It would get him to Igo Strang, no doubt about that. And then dues would finally be paid.

At Crossing-Point H the car glided through the checkpoint. They weren't even required to stop, not for one minute, not for one second. By contrast, the line of Naturals trying to get into the Polis was hundreds of stationary yards long.

"Does it ever seem unjust to you?" Stretch couldn't help asking Maxo.

"No," said Maxo. "Security is everything. You saw it. You saw what they do."

"They?" questioned Stretch. He promised to keep calm. He'd promised.

"Dreggies," said Maxo. "You saw it! I could have been killed. The girl nearly was killed."

"The girl?" said Stretch, noting how Maxo hadn't added him to the list of the potential dead.

"Gala."

"My sister," said Stretch.

"Oh," Maxo turned around to face him, "so she's your sister. You didn't say."

"You didn't ask." Maxo's face was like a mask, Stretch thought, glassy and ugly beneath its copybook GemX regularity. Still, at least the guy had a couple of lines on his face, which made him marginally more interesting.

They traveled on awhile in silence; only the Navigation-System whirred quietly. As they got deeper inside the Estates, Stretch watched the street movement carefully. Cars like this could be a target. But there were only a few shaken fists and a couple of rocks, which fell short. There were times when he'd thrown rocks at Polis cars himself, it was a well-recognized sport.

It seemed no time at all before 1640 drew up outside the entrance to Block 213. Maxo leaped out immediately to help lift Gala from the car. He seemed particularly interested in her feet. Stretch wasn't sure he liked the way the Plastic was looking, it was as though he preferred the foot without a shoe, the bare one. Maybe Stretch was imagining things. Maybe it was guilt because he'd left the shoe. Shoes weren't that easy to come by in the Estates; Stretch should have found the shoe and brought it home.

"Where's the elevator?" asked Maxo when they got inside the building.

"Over there," said Stretch, "but it doesn't work."

"What?"

"Don't worry, it's only four floors."

"Four! I'll get 1640 to help."

"I wouldn't. If he leaves the car, there won't be a car when you get down."

Maxo panted as he took Gala's negligible weight. Stretch watched him struggle on the stairs. How could the Estates let such pathetic specimens rule over them?

When they finally got to the fourth floor, the door to Gala's apartment was already open. Standing in the entrance, as if they had been expecting her (which Maxo knew they could not have been) were two figures: a middle-aged woman who looked gray and ill and a young, paint-spattered boy.

"Move aside," ordered Maxo.

But they didn't. The boy looked quizzically at Stretch and the woman remained standing fraily, leaning on him.

"Thank God," the woman blasphemed, "thank God."

"She's all right," said Stretch.

"And you're all right," said the woman, and all the breath seemed to go out of her body for a moment.

"I saw you on the TropScreen," said the boy. "What were you doing?"

"Never mind," said Stretch. "Help me get her in, Daz."

The Daz boy came to take Gala's feet.

"It's okay, I've got her," objected Maxo, but Daz was not to be dissuaded.

The woman shuffled back inside leading the way down a thin, dark corridor. They arrived at a room that felt cramped to Maxo, even though there was nothing in it but a bed. They laid Gala down.

"She'll be all right," Stretch repeated. "I promise you, Mama."

Mama? Wasn't that what Dreggies called their GenMas? The woman took the girl's hand, brought it to her lips, and made a kind of soft smacking noise on Gala's skin. Maxo shuddered—so public, so uncivil! But wasn't that the very same impulse he'd had with Gala's feet?

"You're a good boy," said the mother, and she leaned forward and made the same smacking noise with her lips on Stretch's forehead. There must be a word for this thing, there would be a word, a Dreggie one. He wanted that word, he wanted to do that soft smacking. He was sinking to their level. He must act quickly, take control of the situation.

"Who's your friend?" the woman asked then. "I should thank him, too."

"Maxo Evangele Strang," said Stretch.

Which is when Gala, lying on the bed, opened her eyes. At the mention of his name, Gala opened her eyes. Gala's eyes were brown, she fixed them on his face. It was time.

"Gala," Maxo said, "I perfect you. I, Maxo Evangele Strang, GemX GenOff of Dr. Igo Strang and Ms. Glora Orb, bid you to be my LongtermMesh. You may be a Dreggie, you are a Dreggie, but in my eyes you are syntemec, syntemesh, synthetic. I accept you for rights and roles up to and including GeneTransfer . . ."

He didn't get any further with this speech because Stretch clenched his right hand into a fist and punched the idiot's lights out.

18

The TropScreen was replaying the explosion, over and over again. For the umpteenth time, Igo Strang watched Hospital 1 sway to the ground, he saw the flying debris, he zoomed in with the camera to the severed legs and arms.

Still no word from Maxo. Igo had lost track of how many times he'd called the car's 'CatorSys. If 1640 was driving Maxo to the Lab (of course he was driving Maxo to the Lab) then he should have arrived by now. Why hadn't he arrived? Igo had also 'catored Llublo—no response. He'd 'catored Glora—no response. Llublo. Glora. Llublo. The car. Glora. The car.

"This," intoned the TropScreen Announcer, "is one of the worst Atrocities of ModernTimes. An escalation of evil, a deliberate attempt to wipe out an entire generation of Polis people—the GemXs. It has been reported that more than 95 percent of GemXs perished in the blast. The total collapse of Hospital 1 has impaired efforts to treat the injured. More deaths are expected. Leaderene Clore, may her name celeb forever, will address the Polis after the next TropFreeze. All members of the Polis are urged to seek the perpetrator—an Estate radical known as Phylo Lorrell. This man is highly dangerous, do not approach him. If you see him, call Poldrone ActiveResponse immediately."

A picture came on the screen of a blond boy, who barely, Igo thought, looked old enough to know what the word *radical* meant. Across his thin chest the words *Most Wanted* were flashing.

Igo VoiceActivated Llublo's number for the hundredth time.

"Yes?" Llublo actually picked up. His fat face came smiling—smirking even—onto Igo's screen. Igo pointed him at the WallPlasma, blew him up into a million blubbery pixels.

"What's going on?" screamed Igo.

"I don't know what you mean," said Llublo.

"The pills, the AddoPills I was supposed so presciently to have developed. There are no AddoPills. We only spoke about a possible diagnosis yesterday. And that was very tentative, needed research."

"But there will be AddoPills," said Llublo calmly. "Very soon. I believe that's your next job."

"And the explosion—all those GemXs . . ."

"Yes," said Llublo. "Appalling. The mind-set of those Dreggies. Despicable. Oh—and Maxo; may I offer you my condolences."

"Maxo," shouted Igo, "he was there?"

"Of course he was there," said Llublo sharply. "Wasn't he? I mean they were all there."

"Yes," said Igo suddenly, something icy going down his spine.

"Ah," said Llublo, sounding slightly more relaxed. "Well then. There'll be a nice funeral. The Polis will pay, of course. Leaderene Clore—may her name celeb forever—has made that quite clear. So you'll have no worries on that account."

"No," said Igo. "Thank you for your consideration."

"Think nothing of it," said Llublo Quells, smacking his fat lips and clicking off-screen.

Igo sat in the Lab and put his face in his hands. He felt as though someone had extracted his brains from his head, fried them up in a hot pan, and returned them—still sizzling—to his skull. The 'cator vibrated again. Glora! He blew her up large, too, those bright blue eyes, those perfect teeth in that smiling (smiling?) mouth.

"Is he with you?" cried Igo. "Have you got Maxo?"

"No," said Glora. "Why would I have? Is that why you called?"

"The explosion," said Igo. Possibly Glora didn't know, she was marvelously mono-directed just before a Grand-Opening. Maybe she'd been in the storeroom, well away from a TropScreen.

"Oh that," said Glora. "He'll have gone to the hospital, I suppose. Oh, dear."

"Don't you care?" choked Igo.

"Of course I care," said Glora. "He's my GenOff, isn't he? But I also have other important things to consider at this time like how, with the current traffic chaos, people are going to get to the gallery on time for the opening. You do see, don't you, Synthetico?"

Synthetico wasn't sure he did. In fact, he wasn't sure of anything all of a sudden. He supposed it was because he was only proto-enhanced. If he'd been properly Enhanced—like Llublo, like Glora—it probably would all have made perfect sense to him.

"I told Maxo to come to the Lab," said Igo, trying to establish things. "Not to go to the hospital. To come to the Lab."

"Oh, well then," said Glora. "Probably be all right then. Check in later, meshkin. Bye." She clicked off.

Igo tried the car 'CatorSys once again. It had been switched off. Why—and by whom? Certainly not by 1640, it was against regulations for a Clodrone to switch off a 'CatorSys. Maybe the car been commandeered for ambulance duties—but still, why turn off the system? Nothing was making sense. Igo began to pace. Maybe he should requisition a car, drive to the Polis, find Maxo himself? Wait—what if Maxo had been delayed leaving the Museo? What if he was still at the Museo? Igo scrolled back though LastCalls, found the curator's number, and rang it.

Maxo was still out cold. Stretch was pleased, if a little surprised, at the effectiveness of his punch. He hadn't believed himself to be that strong. The Plastic was now lying on the floor of their small sitting room. He and Daz had dragged him there to get him out of Gala's room. Gala had woken briefly, taken on water, and been declared "safe" by their mother. She was sleeping again now, as was Perle, which is why Stretch, in the sitting room, was getting on with easing Maxo out of his ambisuit. A 'cator rang in the Plastic's pocket. It was rather an old-fashioned ring, but not half as old-fashioned as the 'cator itself. Stretch was amazed that Maxo had such a piece of junk. You could pretty much get this model in the Estates. Stretch found the "receive" button and picked up.

"Yes?"

"Is that the curator?" asked a voice.

"No," said Stretch. "Wrong number."

"Wait—I just wanted to ask, is Maxo there?"

"Oh," said Stretch. "Yes."

"Yes? Yes! Oh, CelebHigh! Yes, yes, YES!"

Stretch waited while the man went mad for minute, shouting and screeching and yes-ing. And then he asked: "Who's calling?"

"Dr. Igo Strang, Maxo's GenPap."

It was Stretch's turn for shouting and screeching, only he never made a sound. He was thinking.

"Can I speak to Maxo," asked Igo joyfully.

"No," said Stretch, looking at Maxo's prone body on the floor.

"Please."

"This is a kidnap," announced Stretch. "My name is Stretch. I have personal business with you, Dr. Strang. If you agree to a meeting and answer in full all the questions I put to you, then Maxo will be freed. If not—not. In fact," Stretch concluded melodramatically, "you'll never see him again." That's what they said in CrimeFliks anyway.

"Who are you?" asked Strang, his voice quite different now, thin and strangulated. "What have you done with my GenOff? How do I know he's all right? How do I know you've really got him?"

"He's all right. He's just . . . sleeping now. I'll bring you something of his. And you can 'cator him when we meet."

"If you harm him . . ."

"Are you at the Lab?" interrupted Stretch.

"Yes."

"I'll meet you there," said Stretch. "Tell no one. My brother will look after Maxo. If I don't return," he said addressing Daz but still speaking into the 'cator, "then kill him, okay?"

"Yes, boss," said Daz, and sniggered.

Stretch cut the line. "This is serious," he said.

"Yes," said Daz. "Sure thing, boss." Daz had also seen his fair share of CrimeFliks.

"Shut up and help me with the suit."

Daz obediently bent down and began prising Maxo from the close-fitting suit.

"You shouldn't have said what you said outside the hospital," said Daz.

"Probably not."

"They'll be after you."

"I think they may have bigger things on their minds now. But don't worry, I'm not taking any chances. Which is why I need this suit."

Once free from Maxo's body the ZircomMat of the suit contracted, it became a tiny scrap of itself, a strange, limp piece of Elastamix with the odd ThreadWire and oversize looking ControlPanel. Maxo himself, in scant ZircomMat briefs, looked white and exposed, like a grub pulled into the sun for the first ever time. Stretch stripped off his own clothes and, with Daz's help, he pulled his T-shirt over Maxo's shaven head and pushed the youth's heavy white arms through the armholes. Together they lifted Maxo's weight to pull on Stretch's trousers and then they zipped and buttoned him. Neither of them noticed the tiny metallized Homing-Chip attached to the trouser seam. The clothes were shabby and ill-fitting; Maxo didn't look so perfect anymore. Stretch almost felt sorry for him.

Stretch had always wondered what it would be like to wear an ambisuit—only the Enhanced were entitled—and could afford—to wear such suits. Naturals wearing ambisuits apparently constituted a threat to the security of the Trop. Stretch found the breast opening of the suit, eased his hands inside and felt the material expanding around his fingers like the magic gloves he'd had when he was a child. He identified the leg openings and began to step inside the suit. It slipped about his body with a strange slickness, seemingly sensing him, calculating his contours, before contracting again to outline him as smoothly and as snuggly as a second skin.

Daz observed his brother.

"Do you think purple's my color?" Stretch asked.

"It's indigo," said Daz. "And you look good. Handsome."

"Not too thin?"

"No. Almost normal." Daz laughed. "I should paint you."

"No time," said Stretch. "I've got a car to catch."

"When will you be back?"

"When the deed's done." Stretch left the sitting room and returned a moment later with his knife.

"Change of plan," said Daz. He wasn't looking at the knife, he hadn't even seen the knife. He was looking out of the window. He pulled his brother to him.

Flashed across the huge TropScreen mounted on the Block opposite was a picture of Stretch with the words *Most Wanted* throbbing on his chest. "All members of the Polis," said the Announcer, "are urged to seek the perpetrator . . ."

"What!" said Stretch.

"... Estate radical, Phylo Lorrell ...," said the Announcer.

"Me?" squawked Stretch.

"You," said Daz. "Definitely you."

"That's absurd."

"When's absurdity stopped anything in the Polis?" asked Daz.

"No," said Stretch with rising anger. "It's not absurd. It's a lie. A sickening, stupid, evil, barefaced lie."

"Correct," said Daz.

"And they know it."

"Do they?"

"Whose side are you on?"

"Yours," said Daz. "You can't go."

"I'm going."

"Stretch—think about it. They bulldozed fourteen Blocks looking for the last 'perpetrator.' When they found him, they took him to an IsolationCell from which he never emerged. He lasted just three days before committing suicide because, presumably, of whatever hideous things they were doing to him."

"Right," said Stretch. "You've persuaded me. They're going to get me anyway. So I might as well go and get Igo first."

"Get him?"

"Get the truth."

"Gala wouldn't let you go. Mama won't let you."

"Daz, I'll be back before they even know I'm gone. But you have to help me. Make me different. Paint me different."

"No."

"Please, Daz, I need you."

"No."

"I'll go anyway. Only without your help it will be more dangerous."

The brothers faced each other, dared each other. Daz held his sullen ground. Stretch went into the bathroom and returned with a razor. "Shave my head, Daz."

Daz said nothing, did nothing, but, when Stretch returned to the bathroom, stood in front of the mirror, Daz followed him. There was water in the tap, it seemed like a sign. Stretch soaped his hair, put the razor up; his first stroke drew blood.

"Give it to me," said Daz then, and took the razor. Stretch bowed his head and Daz, his fingers quick and gentle, completed the task. He washed and dried his brother's scalp.

Stretch smiled. "Now for my face."

The two of them went quietly into their mother's room. Exhausted by her vigil, Perle was sleeping soundly. Daz bent quietly to his mother's one set of drawers and withdrew Perle's most treasured possession, a tiny box of makeup. Good makeup was hard to come by in the Estates and, as Perle said, "Some of us need it more than others nowadays." On special days, she would take the dark from under her eyes, etch color into her cheeks.

"She won't mind," Stretch whispered as Daz hesitated one more time. "It's for Finn, for Dad. You need to make me perfect," said Stretch back in the sitting room.

"Impossible," said Daz. But he was an artist and he shaded and redrew Stretch's features until his brother became like a statue of himself, a piece of fabulously carved marble.

"You're a genius," said Stretch, looking at his reflection in a mirror.

On the floor, Maxo stirred.

"What are we going to do with him?"

"You're going to tie him up," said Stretch.

"I can't do that."

"You can. You have to. At least until I get to the Lab. Igo will need to talk to him. You can let him go after that. After that it won't matter."

"Except he'll know where you live."

"I'm innocent, Daz, remember?"

"I want to go with you," said Daz suddenly.

"You can't. You have to look after things here. Not just the Plastic but Mom and Gala, too."

Stretch left the apartment without saying good-bye. He did, however, tap the ambisuit pocket that ran the length of his right thigh—just to check the blade was still there.

Gala awoke to find her mother sitting on the end of her bed. Perle's face was worn and anxious.

"You shouldn't be up," Gala admonished.

"You shouldn't be down," her mother replied. And then: "How do you feel?"

Gala pulled herself upright with care. All of her limbs moved easily. Had she fallen simply with shock? As she rotated her body, dust fell on her covers. She put her hands up to her head, there was ash in her hair and something hard attached to her scalp, which she thought at first might be scabbed blood but which turned out to be grit.

"I wiped your face," said Perle apologetically, and then shrugged.

There would be no water, of course, or not enough.

"I'm okay," said Gala. "Fine. Alive." She paused. "What happened?"

"A bomb, they say. But the other side of the hospital. The building took most of the blast."

"And Stretch?" said Gala suddenly.

"He's fine, too. Got you home. Phylo and one of the Enhanced, a boy called Maxo, they brought you home in a car. Don't you remember?"

Gala lay back and tried to reassemble the pictures in her mind. She could see Stretch on the post and then him falling, pushed by someone in the crowd, or maybe it was the explosion that had pushed him. No, the explosion was later, she remembered the bang, how it had hit the inside of her head, not once but many times, ricocheting against her skull, like a maddened pinball. Even now, there was a faint echo of that sound in her head. Then there had been nothing. Nothing until a shaven, sculpted head with the piercing eyes of the Enhanced had leaned forward, and said . . . something wild about meshes or mashes or sympathy or synthetics. She hadn't understood the words, though the boy's intensity had been clear. The final image was white and bony and fast. A swinging fist. Her brother's.

"Stretch—Stretch hit him!" Gala cried. "The boy who helped me. Why did he do that?"

Perle sighed. "Finn," she said as if it explained things.

* * *

At the same time, further down the corridor, Maxo woke in a dingy room and was unable, for a moment, to locate where he was. One thing only appeared certain—he was on the floor. He tried to sit up, but it was difficult. He peered down at his feet. His ankles seemed to be bound together.

"What the celeb . . ."

The bindings were strips of white cloth streaked with red. Blood! He was bandaged, he was bleeding! He tried to put his hands down to feel the pain, but it turned out his wrists were bandaged, too. But the cloth here wasn't streaked with red but with yellow. He was leaking yellow blood? Instinctively, he brought his bandaged hands to his face, the smell was oily. He was not bandaged, he was not bleeding. He had been tied up with some filthy, oily painting rags!

"Get these off me," he shrieked.

"Sorry," said a voice nearby. Maxo turned around. The Daz boy was sitting on a chair observing him. "No can do."

Maxo, feeling the anger prick at his neck, waited for his ambisuit to trigger SweatControl. But there was no whirring, no icy calming. And no—he looked down at his body—ambisuit. They hadn't just bound him with rags, they'd denuded him, stripped him, they'd put him in—Dreggie clothes! He concentrated. He was wearing some hideously rough trouser things, which scraped his skin as he moved, and a shirt top that only had half sleeves. His forearms were exposed, the hairs he so rarely saw were standing upright on a series of tiny raised skin bumps. The hairs were rippling; it made him shake, it made him feel a little sick. Or maybe the sickness was in his head where the ache was, yes, his head ached, hurt with the dull throb of a skull that had been punched. That other boy, the Stretch one, had punched him!

"I'll report you," shouted Maxo. "I'll have you locked away!"

"Right," said Daz.

Maxo shuffled about on the floor and, after some minutes, managed to get to his knees. Daz watched as though interested in the changing configurations of Maxo's limbs. Maxo found a chair, hung on to it and grimaced himself upright. He was standing—just.

"I demand that you untie me."

"Sorry," repeated Daz mildly.

"I'll call the Poldrones!"

"With what?" asked Daz, twirling the curator's 'cator in his right hand.

"Help," yelled Maxo. "Help, help, help, help, HELP."

The commotion brought Gala—beautiful, fabulous, soft smacking Gala—and, a step or two behind her, Perle.

Maxo stopped in mid shout. "Galamesh," he said in quite a different tone, "I perfect you, I bid you to be my LongtermMesh..."

"What on earth...," said Perle, taking in the scene, the bound and burbling boy, the absence of her elder son. "What's going on?"

"You are syntemec, syntemesh, synthethic...," continued Maxo.

"Where's Phylo?"

Daz shrugged. "Out."

"He's gone to GemCorp, to the Lab, hasn't he?" Perle appeared to stagger, but it might just have been the effort of getting down the corridor so quickly.

"Mama," cried Gala, and her instinctive arm reached for her swaying mother.

". . . for all rights up to and including GeneTransfer," concluded Maxo.

"Oh, Finn, what have you done?" Perle collapsed into an armchair.

"So, Galamesh," said Maxo, continuing to stand as straight as his bound legs would allow, "Come. Let us go."

Gala turned astonished eyes from her mother to the creature before her. She'd never been so close to one of the Enhanced before. Or perhaps she'd never looked. Maxo's strong shaven head was pale, his skin almost opalescent. His cheekbones were high and masculine and his eyes a shining gray. There was a slight flare to his nostrils, a proud and excited upward turn to his mouth. Perhaps she was used to seeing just conformity among the Enhanced, maybe she'd never looked for anything more, for that spark of individuality that might set one Plastic apart from another. What was it about this face looming toward her? Maybe the slight lines around his eyes, she didn't remember seeing those on any Enhanced before. Maybe it was the little pulse of blood she could see ticking on his scalp, or the slightly larger blemish where her brother's fist had landed. Or perhaps it was just that she'd never seen a member of the inner Polis out of an ambisuit. Ambisuits added to the uniformity of the Enhanced. In these ill-fitting clothes there was something vulnerable about Maxo—and also something that made her want to smile.

"Go where?" she asked.

"Away from here, away from this life of poverty and degradation," said Maxo, lifting his bound hands like a kind of prayer. "I'm offering you a new beginning in the Polis. A GrandVision life of Progress and Perfection fed by PoppaPills and illumined by HighArt."

Gala smiled. "You're very kind," she said, and she went to sit on the arm of Perle's chair. "Are you all right?" she asked her mother.

"I won't report your brothers," continued Maxo. "Not for this," he indicated the bindings, "or for the blow to the head. Everyone knows that Naturals have low reasoning skills and poor AngerManagement. This is not their fault, it's to do with their small brains. Extreme Behavior is a natural consequence of this. You will come to the Polis with me and we will forget everything that has gone before."

Maxo had a strange feeling (maybe because of the look on Gala's face, which he couldn't quite interpret) that his words weren't as well chosen as they might have been. Nevertheless, everything he was saying was true, he'd paid considerable attention in LifeSkills.

"Untie him," said Perle from the chair.

"Stretch said not to," said Daz. "At least not until after he arrived at the Lab."

"Untie him."

"You know who he is?"

"Of course," said Perle. "He's Dr. Strang's GenOff."

"And that of Ms. Glora Orb," said Maxo proudly. "Two of the premier GenParents in the Polis," he added to impress upon them his impeccable genetic credentials.

"He is also," said Perle, "a person."

"Is he?" asked Daz.

"And it's not his fault." Perle was tired and she was worried and she didn't have the energy to fight. "Please, Daz."

Daz looked at Gala, who nodded.

"It could be dangerous," said Daz. "For Stretch. I think we should keep Maxo here till Stretch gets back."

"And what if your brother never comes back?" said Perle.

"Mama!"

"I'm asking you, one more time, to untie our guest," said Perle Lorrell.

So Daz, with his beautiful painter's hands, began to undo the knots. Maxo waited patiently. He could be calm now. They knew who he was; there were great advantages to being a HighElite.

"Thank you," he said when he was free, and he rubbed his wrists, leaned down to push blood back into his ankles. "Now," he said, addressing Daz, "kindly return my ambisuit and Gala and I will be gone."

"Look," said Gala. "I'm sorry about what happened with Stretch. He shouldn't have hit you. And, Daz, I don't know what he was doing, tying you up. And I'm really grateful that you helped bring me back but I'm not going anywhere."

"What?" said Maxo.

"You're free to go," said Perle gently. "With our thanks and our apologies."

Small brains after all. They just hadn't understood! Even Gala.

"I'm not leaving without you, Gala."

Daz moved closer to his sister. "Don't you touch her," he said.

163

"It's okay, Daz," said Gala.

Maxo felt some heaving in his chest. If he'd been wearing his ambisuit, the material would have expanded and contracted with the rise and fall of his breast. But this Dreggie top—this stiff, too small Dreggie top—just tightened like a band of steel about him. He could barely breathe.

"Do you not understand the terms?" he cried. The only thing that delayed a mesh in the Polis was the request for Verification, the GeneticPrintout that confirmed you had the specification you said you had. Was it the cracks again, was she doubting his GemX pedigree? No, she was a Dreggie! "What else can you possibly want?"

"Nothing you could give," said Daz.

"Gala," Maxo repeated, "What do you want?"

"My father," said Gala. "And regular water. And more sensible brothers. And a cure for cancer." She smiled again, that radiant smile. "Not much, you see."

Something in Maxo loosened. It was just a small misunderstanding after all. There was so much these people didn't know, and why should they know? There were so many things he would be able to show and teach his Gala.

"Meshkin," he said, speaking very slowly and clearly, "when you accept the LongTermBond, my GenSire becomes as yours. Water is freely available in the Polis at all times. Your brothers you may leave behind. As for cancer, it's an eradicated disease. No one in the Polis has cancer anymore. You need never worry about cancer again."

"Do you want me to belt him now or later?" asked Daz.

"Go away, Maxo," said Gala. "Just go away."

Maxo leaned forward. "Do you think," he said suddenly and with some urgency, "I could soft-smack your foot?"

19

Clodrone 1640 was glad when he saw an ambisuited figure emerge from the entrance of Block 213. While he'd been waiting for Maxo, interest in his master's car had become increasingly aggressive. People had come too close, they'd stared into the car to see if it was occupied, they'd dragged fingernails across its windows, twisted its mirrors. One boy, a ragged hunched thing, had stood banging the hood with his fist. 1640 had activated the alarm to scare him away, but he wouldn't be scared. He had smiled and banged. He'd only moved on when 1640 had revved the engine, as though he was about to drive off, so 1640 had kept the engine revving, in fact, he'd taken to driving up the street, down the street. But now rescue was at hand. 1640 stopped the car and the ambisuited figure climbed in.

It wasn't (1640 saw in his mirror) Maxo.

"Your master," announced the figure, "instructs you to take me to the GemCorp Lab immediately."

The head of the boy was shaved, his features exquisitely shaped and shaded, and, wearing the ambisuit, he could easily pass for a member of the Enhanced. But he wasn't, he was the Finn-boy, Clodrone 1640 could hear it in his voice.

"At once," repeated Stretch into 1640's hesitation. 1640 keyed the engine. Why the Finn-boy had changed his appearance was probably not something 1640 needed to inquire into. He'd been given an order from Maxo and needed to obey. Besides, the Finn-man inside 1640 said: Help the Finn-boy, you love him, don't you? *Love.* That big lurchy word again.

The car began its journey through the Estates. There was silence for a while and then the Finn-boy said: "Will they stop us at the Crossing Point? I mean, I know they didn't when we entered the Estates, but what's it like the other way?"

"They beam the car number," said 1640, "log the name of the owner, the driver number, and request the names of all passengers."

"Do they iris scan passengers?"

"Not unless they're doing RandomStops."

"Then tell them you have Maxo Evangele Strang in the car," said Stretch.

Something did a flip under 1640's breastbone. "But that's not true," the Finn-man in him blurted out and then, because it was not a Clodrone's place to make challenges, he added, "sir."

"Correct," said Stretch. "But that's what your master asks you to say."

Whatever it was in 1640's chest—his heart, he supposed—stopped turning. "Yes, sir," he said, and when, some thirty minutes later, they reached the CheckZone, Stretch lay against the backseat as though he was sleeping and 1640 obediently keyed in "Maxo Strang" to the question of occupancy. They were waved on through.

"How long now?" asked Stretch, opening his eyes.

"Forty minutes," said 1640. "About. The IntellSystem indicates there are certain roads closed, due to the Atrocity."

During the journey through the Estates, the Finn-boy had seemed quite calm, but now he was fidgeting, drumming his fingers on the seat edge, sucking at his lower lip.

"What sort of security does the Lab have?" Stretch asked.

"Excellent," said 1640. "IrisScanLocking, SecuriScreens, six WorkPlace Poldrones, and its own SecuriCell."

"Do you have water?" Stretch asked suddenly.

"Not in the car," said 1640. "But there's a Mescat House one block from here. Do you want me to stop?"

"Yes," said Stretch.

Back in the Estates, Maxo Evangele Strang stood on the pavement outside Block 213 panting heavily. He had sprinted the four flights of stairs from the Dreggie apartment and now there was something wet and disgusting running down between his shoulder blades and making the short-sleeved shirt-thing stick to his back. He supposed it was sweat. There was more of this vile body-juice soaking his armpits. He could not only feel it, he could smell it—hot and tangy and . . . animal. It was revolting but also—strangely exciting! No, what was he saying?

That's why he'd run, to get away from it all, away from the Dreggie girl before it was too late, before he became no better than them, these people with their filthy animal smells and their filthy animal habits. The defining moment had been when he'd heard himself (Maxo Evangele Strang GemX) actually asking a Dreggie if he could soft-smack her foot! The embarrassment of it, the indignity! More of the body-juice bubbled on his forehead just thinking about it. But he'd got out. He'd escaped. How had he had the self-discipline? Well, when he'd leaned forward and mentioned the soft-smacking thing, something had happened to his outstretched hands; this time he'd actually seen it happening, heard it. It sounded like the creak in the branch of a huge tree in a high wind, an enormous sound (though it appeared that no one else in the room heard it), and then the crack appeared, or cracks, four or five radiating lines on the skin of each of his hands. He was disintegrating in front of his very own eyes. The implication was obvious—when he had Dreggie thoughts his body reacted in Dreggie ways. At this rate of aging, a couple of soft-smacks and he could be dead. Him, a GemX, with a projected life span of a 130 years. He had to get out of temptation's way, he had to return to the Polis will all possible speed.

The panting, Maxo realized, had stopped. He looked for the Clodrone car, but it was nowhere to be seen. He looked again. 1640 could not have possibly driven away, not without orders. Who would have ordered him? Not Igo, Igo had wanted Maxo at the Lab, had made him promise to come to the Lab. *Lab*. Hadn't Gala's Mama-person mentioned the Lab? Maxo began to shiver; a Natural might have thought it was to do with the sweat cooling on his back, Maxo thought it was because of Stretch. Maxo pulled at his memory, tried to recall the conversation in the apartment. *"I think we should keep Maxo here until Stretch gets back,"* that's what Daz had said. And *back* meant back from the Lab, Maxo was almost certain he'd remembered that correctly. But why would Stretch want to go to the Lab?

What business could he possible have there? Maxo couldn't answer that question; what he did know for certain was that Stretch was a maniac—witness that totally unprovoked punch. Was Maxo's GenSire also in danger? Maxo needed to get to the Lab and he needed to get there fast. But there was no car. Maxo was alone in the Estates.

If Maxo had had a 'cator, he could have called Igo, he could have called a car, but his 'cator was still in the VDP Incommunicado Safe and the curator's 'cator was in Daz's pocket. Maxo thought about going back up the four floors and demanding the 'cator from Daz—they owed him that, at least—but if he went up, if he saw Gala again, the terrible urges might come on him again, and the creaks and cracks might start again. Solution? He would stop someone on the street, ask to borrow a 'cator. There were thousands of people all around him (he noticed now that he was looking), one of them would lend him a 'cator.

They were all gargoyles, of course, but if he could look one in the eye long enough, he should be able to make himself clear. He had to stop one of them first, though, and they all seemed to be moving very swiftly, as if it was dangerous to dawdle, some of them were even staring at him as they went past, as though it was him, standing still, who was the freak.

"Excuse me," he said politely to a scurrying old woman (she looked about 152 to him, but he knew he had no experience of estimating Dreggie ages), "could I possibly . . ." But she was away, eyes down, as if the pavement was the most fascinating sight in the world.

"Oi!" he said, but she didn't look back.

"Excuse me," he began again, this time to a bent but

169

younger-looking man with a shock of very ugly black hair. The man showed no sign of stopping, so Maxo, who expected a certain level of civility, simply moved in front of him and blocked his way.

"What?" The man looked up at Maxo, his body clenched and his lower jaw protruding at what Maxo thought was an unusual angle.

"I just wondered if you could possibly lend me your 'cator?" said Maxo.

"You having a laugh?"

"Not at all," said Maxo. "Only . . ."—he paused to be sure of getting his words right—"as you can see, I'm not from this part of the . . . um . . . Trop and I need some help. I need a 'cator, got to make a call."

"Do I look like the sort of Nat who has a 'cator?"

"Well, I mean everyone has a 'cator," said Maxo. "Don't they?"

The man stared at him.

"I've got money," continued Maxo. "If that's the problem. I can pay you."

The man's head swung swiftly then, right and left, apparently judging the moment, the street. Then, without warning, he twisted Maxo's right arm behind his back and said very fiercely into his ear: "Right, gimme everything you got."

"I'm sorry?"

"The money, you Trop rat!"

Maxo felt the man's free hand jab into the pockets of his trousers, then quick fingers tracked up the outside of his shirt, and then under his shirt, searching and prodding. The only time Maxo had ever had a man's hand over his torso was in his MediExam, and those hands were cool and respectful. These were rough-skinned and urgent.

"You ain't got nothing!" the man exclaimed.

It was true. If you were wearing an ambisuit your credit line was sewn into your left breast pocket. Credit could be deducted—or added—with a quick InfraBeamScan. Maxo had never before been without money because he'd never before been without his ambisuit. As for feligs, the currency used in the Estates, of course he didn't have any feligs, what possible use could he have had for feligs? But he didn't have time to explain any of this to the little (but surprisingly strong) black-haired man before another fist landed on him, this time in his stomach.

"You lying little Leaderene-licker!"

Maxo might have riposted "*thief!*," but what had the man stolen? Besides, Maxo was lying doubled up and winded on the pavement and not able to say very much. Nobody came to help him, in fact, pedestrians skirted about him in increasingly wide arcs, as if he was the potentially dangerous one. Maxo spent some time on the ground in a stupefied—and frankly hurt—disbelief. Then he pulled himself together. Animals. That's all there was to it. These people were animals. Everything his LifeSkills Tutor had said was true. The Tutor had even suggested (to the AdvancedClass) that it was possible that some Dreggies were now so extreme that they constituted a different species from the Enhanced. Maxo—who liked to think of himself as broad-minded—had reserved judgment. But now, well, what other explanation could there be?

Maxo pulled himself upright and dusted himself down as best he could. Ambisuits repelled dirt, these clothes seemed to attract it. The trousers, which had started as a dull gray, were now streaked with something black. There was gritty, dusty stuff on Maxo's ankles and something pink and gloopy adhering to the underside of his left shoe. The pink stuff smelled vaguely like SteriFruit—only stronger. The smell was not particularly pleasant, but it had the effect of reminding Maxo that it was at least eight hours since he'd had a PoppaPill. Perhaps, if he had something to eat, he'd feel better. Poppas were not just nutritionally effective, they were designed to lift your mood. Maxo's hand moved instinctively to the ambipocket on his right thigh, where he always kept an extra day's supply.

No pocket.

No ambisuit.

So no pills.

When would he learn no ambisuit! He felt something big and gulping in his chest. A HighElite's ambisuit was like a second skin—they'd not only taken his pills, they'd taken his skin!

On his fleshly skin he felt the pricking of the hair bumps. He was shivering again. What if there was a Sudden Onset now. He'd die! Right here in the Estates, be swept away in one of those white vans. He had to get back to civilization, had to get to the Lab, had to rescue his Gen-Pap. But how?

Walk.

He was going to have to walk. But it was such a long way. And he had no Poppas and no water. Mescat would be better, mescat would set him on his way, but there was no mescat and no money with which to buy mescat and anyway the back of his throat was dry. All this dust in the

Estates, dust on the ground, dust swirling about in the air. Why didn't these people pay for HygeniClean? He began walking. Water. Somewhere along the way would sell water.

No money.

How was he going to get water without money? Well, he didn't have to buy water in a bottle, he could just ask at a PillJoint for a glass of tap water. They did have PillJoints in the Estates, didn't they? Yes, they must, even people who did SlowFood had to eat and drink. He'd stop at the first place he saw. A glass of tap water couldn't be too much to ask even in this celebforsaken place. Maybe he could tell someone how he'd been attacked, maybe beg a lift in one of those funny little welded-together Estate cars.

Maxo did not know precisely where he was going and was not inclined to ask for directions. So he was grateful when he saw a huge sign pointing to Crossing-Point H. It didn't really matter where Maxo crossed into the Polis, because once he was back on his side of the barriers, he would be safe, he would be understood.

He walked for what seemed like a lifetime without seeing a PillJoint of any description. This was a residential area obviously, block upon block of apartments rising out of the blank earth. What did these people do when they wanted a quick EnergyBurst? There was a tightness behind his knees, a ridge of something tense across his shoulders, and a sore spot on the little toe of his right foot, which was, presumably, the effect of this ridiculous walking. He paused on the pavement (sensibly waiting for a moment when there was nobody too close to him) and took off his right shoe. There was a transparent bubble of skin on his toe, with what seemed to be a colorless liquid inside. He'd never seen such a thing before. He touched it carefully, the skin was taut and extremely tender. If he had been at home he would have consulted Sappho, or hit MediAlert, or searched the MediBox for something that would give immediate relief. But he was not at home. He put his shoe back on.

It was almost dusk. There seemed no way of knowing how far away the Crossing Point was, but he knew he must hurry. This place was dangerous in daylight let alone after dark. As well as the stiffness in his limbs, he began to feel a kind of stiffness in his stomach. A hard, hollow feeling that nagged. He'd turn a corner, walk another block, and there it would be again, moaning at him, *Moan, Moan, Poppa, Poppa, Moan*. What the celeb was going on? *Give me a Poppa!* Hunger—was that what this was? Hideous, irritating feeling. Maxo reached his mind back into HistoryData: before Poppas, apparently, people went hungry, they starved. Some of them, it was said, starved to death. Did people in the Estates still starve? He'd rather thought starving was Eradicated, or was that just in the Polis, where the Poppas and the clever people were? He was beginning to find it difficult to think straight, what with the stiffness and the bubble on his toe (which rubbed with every step) and the moaning stomach feeling and the effort of avoiding all the other people on the pavement and the coming darkness and the noise (you couldn't believe the noise), the Crime-Flik shouts, the bangs, the spinning of car wheels, and that explosive glass smashing he'd heard last time when he'd come in the car, only now there was no car, and his ears seemed to be full of a constant crashing, an internal water noise and, speaking of water, where was water?

Water.

Please water.

Gala, feeling stronger, was looking out of her mother's bedroom window.

"We shouldn't have let him go," she said.

"We've been through this," said Daz a little defensively. "Stretch can look after himself."

"I didn't mean Stretch," said Gala. "I meant Maxo."

"Oh," said Daz. "Right. Only we didn't let him go. He bolted, if you remember, ran for his life."

"It's his life I'm worried about," said Gala.

"You worry too much," said her mother.

"But he doesn't know the Estates."

"He doesn't know anything," said Daz.

"He'll get in trouble," continued Gala. "He'll get lost."

"Why should you care?" asked Daz.

"He helped us. He helped me."

And that was the essence of it, really. Ever since her father had left, Gala thought, looking out into the evening gloom, she had been caring for other people—for her mother, for Daz, even for Stretch. She'd given her love freely, gladly, and yet there'd still been something relentless about it, as though what she gave out could never be quite replenished. And here—out of nowhere—had come a man who had chosen to give to her. Yes, to her and to her alone, it seemed, for there had been hundreds of injured at the hosptial, and yet it was Gala that he had scooped from the concrete and brought safely home. She hadn't paid enough attention to this before. Why? Probably because she'd been unconscious, so she hadn't actually felt his hands holding her, lifting her, carrying her. But he had carried her—that's what Daz reported. The Enhanced didn't normally venture into the Estates for their own purposes, let alone to aid someone else. Wrapped up in their elite lives, they were generally oblivious to what went on in the wider Polis, had no idea who lived, who died. So, to bring her to Block 213, Maxo had clearly made a journey, crossed more than just the Border Points. And how had her family responded? They had tied him up, stolen his clothes, knocked him out. She herself had told him (emphatically) to go away. She'd abandoned him to the dangers of the Estates because she couldn't handle his wild declarations. But what exactly had he declared? She couldn't call it love—his words had been insane. And yet he had communicated something. She grappled for the right word. *Sincerity*. In his own way, she felt, he had meant what he said. Then there were his actions. "Actions speak louder than words." That's what her father, Finn, always said. And Maxo's actions had been to bring her home. To make her safe. This was the nugget of truth in the madness. He had cared about her!

In the parched desert that was Gala's heart, an improbable flower bloomed.

20

Oh, CelebHigh! Maxo could see a PillJoint up ahead, or at least a lit place, though it might be a mirage, he was aware of that. But he could smell it, the odor was of BakoPills (a common but wholesome pill) only more intense. Everything seemed more intense in the Estates, why was that? Who cared! Here was a PillJoint, though it seemed to call itself a café, Café Paulo.

Inside the café there were metallic chairs and metallic tables and assorted Dreggies drinking huge dark cups of what looked like Chocoffeine and eating small dumpy lumps of BakoBread. It was probably more than two years since Maxo had tasted SlowFood (they'd had that SlowFood-Feast in HistoryEducate) and he'd been sick for days, but the moaning of his stomach and the thought of water brought him straight inside.

There was a line and Maxo waited and waited. When he finally got to the counter, the scraggy blonde serving girl barely looked at him.

"Yeah?"

"Water," said Maxo, or rather he choked it, on account of his mouth being so dry.

"Where you been?" the girl asked testily.

Maxo raised an eyebrow.

"We ain't had water here for days. Three days, in fact. It's reboil MilkoChoc and rolls. That's it."

"Yes," said Maxo faintly, "please."

The girl ladled a cup of dark liquid from a steaming vat and put the BakoBread, or roll, on a plate.

"Ten feligs," she said.

Maxo hesitated.

"Ten," the girl repeated. "It's gone up. What with the rehydrate for the bread."

"I don't," whispered Maxo, "have any money."

The girl put her hands on her hips. "Oh, not another one."

"Please," said Maxo, "I'm starving."

"Paulo," she shouted.

A big man, clearly the boss, appeared from a back room. "He ain't got no money," the girl said.

"I was robbed," said Maxo, with a semblance of truth.

"I keep telling you, Belle," said Paulo, "we ain't running a charity."

"He's starving," said Belle.

"Starving," repeated Paulo. "You're soft. If he's starving, I'm the Leaderene."

Behind Maxo the line began to grumble and push.

"I can get you money," said Maxo urgently. "Give me these things now and I'll send you money. CelebHonor. More money than you could dream of. TropCredits."

"Oh," said Paulo, "so that's your game. An Enhanced-Licker. I thought so when I saw your shaved head. You're the worst, you know that? Wanting to be like them, dress like them, talk like them, fantasizing about Polis money, believing your own pathetic little lies. Now get out, do you hear me? I've got real customers waiting."

"No, it's true," said Maxo. "I am Enhanced, I'm a GemX."

"Yeah, the only one living in the Estates, the only one that escaped the bombing," shouted a man in the line. "Good thinking. Now get out, like the man said. We don't have all day here."

Maxo thought about taking the roll and running, he thought about taking a sip of the drink and running, then he looked at the man's face.

"Oh, here," said Belle, and she took a scrap of bread from a plate behind the counter (her own presumably) and handed it to him. "Have this."

Maxo almost had his hands on the roll when Paulo lunged. "Yeah, and take this, too!" He rolled something around his mouth and spat ferociously. A gob of something yellow landed on the bread and foamy spray spattered Maxo's hands.

"Thank you," said Maxo, and he took the bread.

He walked out amid jeers and laughter, but he didn't look to right or left, just kept walking. He walked a whole block just holding the morsel of bread, feeling the spit slide off the crusty bit and onto his fingers. He wiped his hands on his shirt and then he wiped the bread on his shirt, too. The hollowness inside him ached and something else did, too. He should have been angry, he should have been mad, but he just felt emptied out and also . . . glad. Glad? Was glad the right word, or was it grateful? It occurred to him that he wasn't exactly sure what these words meant. They were words used in other places about other people. But now he was feeling them, or thought he

179

was, because the girl—a total stranger—had wanted to give him bread. The noise came in his head again, the creaking noise, it was louder (to him) than all the din of crowds and traffic about him, and this time he felt a rift open between his eyes. He didn't even put his hand up to his face. He knew there would be another crack. Did he desire a mesh with the bread girl? No, of course not. But she'd given him something or tried to. Had anyone ever given him anything without wanting something in return before? He didn't think so. Being grateful was obviously a Dreggie emotion, one that seemed to age a person, but what could he do? Maxo Evangele Strang bit into the bread.

It was soft inside, fluffy, like eating clouds. You couldn't suck it like you could a pill, you had to chew, and, despite its soft, airy texture, it tasted harsh and salty and set his teeth on edge. Swallowing was also difficult because his saliva seemed to have dried up and he had no water. But still he chewed, he ate every bit of that bread. Half an hour later, when the tiny bit of bread sat in his stomach like a stone and his guts heaved about it, Maxo Strang thought how the girl was harsh and airy, too. And also thin. Was she starving? Or maybe ill? Or perhaps that's just how she'd been born, skinny. He didn't ever remember being curious about another person's life before. What was it about these Dreggies that got under your skin?

Skin.

The evening air seem to be damp, there was wind and wet on his skin. Wet! He licked at his arms, snuffling up tiny droplets of moisture. Bliss. Then the wind blew harder. The thirst and the moaning stomach had stopped him noticing the cold. What he wouldn't do for an ambisuit now. He hugged his arms to him, carried on.

He had begun to think he would never reach the Crossing Point when he saw BeaconLights up ahead. At last! The Crossing Building had never looked so appealing, a huge dome of glass and brightness and civilization, patrolled by Poldrones. Lines snaked for hundreds of yards to the left of the building, but that was the Naturals' side; where Maxo needed to go, the Enhanced entrance, there was no line. But there were no pedestrian kiosks either, just four channels for car drivers. Of course—why would any member of the Enhanced willingly walk in the Estates? Few drivers seemed to be returning to the Polis either, and as two of the Check-Zone channels were unoccupied, Maxo just made for the nearest. It was manned by Poldrone 6234.

The Poldrone's head, like that of all his peers, was brutish, but today (Maxo thought) how comfortingly solid he looked.

"Around the back," said Poldrone 6234.

"What?" said Maxo.

"This side," said 6234 slowly and clearly, "is for Inner Polis and Enhanced only."

"Good," said Maxo. "Because I am Enhanced. In fact, I am Maxo Evangele Strang, GenOff of Dr. Igo Strang and Ms. Glora Orb." He couldn't blame the Poldrone, he probably wasn't smart enough to see beyond the Dreggie clothes.

"Yeah," said 6234. "Right." He flicked a few switches. "So how come I have a record of a certain Maxo Evangele Strang passing through this very checkpoint not three hours ago. In a car," he added pointedly.

"What!" exclaimed Maxo, and then he realized. "That was my car. And my identity. Stolen by some maniac called Stretch who also stole my ambisuit and tried to beat me up."

"Really," said 6234.

"Look, I have been walking for hours. I am tired, I'm . . . hungry and I don't need this."

"Hungry?" asked 6234. "Thanks to the Leaderene, may her name celeb forever, hunger is Eradicated."

"Not in the Estates." What was he doing, entering into a debate with this half-life? And whose side was he on anyway? "Look. I'm in a hurry. So just quit the questions and do an iris scan."

"We don't iris scan Dreggies," said the Poldrone without emotion. "Dreggies have to show their securipasses."

"I am not a Dreggie," shouted Maxo. "Call my GenPap if you don't believe me. He'll confirm everything. Better still, let me speak to him. I need to speak to him urgently anyway. He could be in danger."

Poldrone 6234 depressed a button on his console. "I think we have an EnhancedLicker, can I have reinforcements, please?"

From out of nowhere, four Poldrones, each one larger than the next, began converging on the kiosk. The first one had just clamped a solid paw around Maxo's neck when there was a bark from 6234's console: "HighInstruction 4: Let him pass."

The Poldrone loosened his grip.

Maxo swallowed hard. He didn't have time for recriminations.

"Thank you so much," he said, and marched on through.

* * *

Burton Chavit, head of InternalPolice, was sitting in The Bunker watching a blue dot track across SecuriScreen 210, otherwise known as Crossing-Point H. There was nothing quite like stalking a quarry who didn't even know he was a quarry. A HomingChip meant you could bide your time, find out what you needed to know, and then swoop upon your prey when he was least expecting it.

This is what the blue dot had told Burton Chavit to date: Phylo Lorrell had survived the explosion and made his way to the Estates by car. The car journey had taken Chavit by surprise: Lorrell must have contacts—Enhanced Contacts— in the Polis. Maybe Lorrell really was an insurgent, maybe he'd hooked up with the ThrowbackIntellectuals? It would be a delicious irony, thought Chavit, to lay the blame for an Atrocity at random on a Dreggie only to find he might not be so innocent after all. Once back in the Estates, Lorrell had then spent some time inside Block 213—a good deal of it motionless and, therefore, presumably asleep (what a cool customer he was), a detail which suggested to Chavit that Block 213 was the boy's home, a useful piece of infor- mation vis-à-vis Reprisals. After such a dreadful Atrocity, the Leaderene would, Chavit imagined, call for Reprisals. As for now, now the suspect was heading back into the Polis.

Why?

Lorrell's face was on all the TropScreens and Chavit had half expected some bounty hunter to have handed him in already. The fact that the boy was still at large demon- strated how clever he was. He'd obviously disguised himself and now, thanks to the Crossing-Point H, Chavit knew what as—a member of the Enhanced. Ingenious. And bold. Lorrell had shaved his head, waltzed into the Enhanced CheckZone and claimed to be Maxo Evangele Strang, who was, if Chavit wasn't much mistaken (and he was rarely mistaken), the GenOff of Dr. Igo Strang. Or *had been* Strang's GenOff, as no doubt the poor youth had perished in the bomb. But how quickly Lorrell had assumed his identity. Clever beyond his years indeed. The Poldrone who challenged Lorrell was to be commended, but it was important for the suspect to be allowed to proceed unhindered. Chavit had made a call. The boy intrigued him. Besides, time had to pass. For InternalPolice to pick up a perpetrator too quickly made it look too easy, less convincing. On top of which, if Lorrell really was an insurgent, it was important to know where he might go and who he might meet.

One of the people he would meet was not in doubt. In the not too distant future, Phylo Lorrell would be coming face-to-face with Burton Chavit. Chavit watched the zig-zags of the little blue dot. He did, he reflected, so like to be in on a kill.

If Maxo Evangele Strang thought his luck would change when he arrived back in the Polis, he was wrong. He tried to flag down cars, but they drove on by. He looked for pedestrians from whom to borrow 'cators. There weren't any. At least, not any Enhanced ones; the Enhanced didn't walk, how had he forgotten that! He could, of course, accost one of the Naturals, but he'd been down that route before and it hadn't proved either congenial or effective. So Maxo Strang, using his Enhanced brain, looked for a sign to a PublicBuilding. In a PublicBuilding there would be a rescue, respite, and a caretaker.

The first building to be signed was the Museo.

Maxo gave a bitter little laugh. He'd have to speak to that old idiot Edwin Challice again, but at least the man knew him.

It was dark now, but here in the Polis all the buildings were illuminated and the streetlights worked. Up ahead there was even a giant TropScreen, which gave out its own comforting glare and blare. As Maxo got nearer, he tuned in to what the Announcer was saying. It was about the Atrocity, of course, and how it had been the fault of the Dreggies. No surprise there. What came next was a surprise, though. It was a huge picture of the Stretch boy. Only his name wasn't Stretch on the screen; it was Phylo Lorrell and he had the words *Most Wanted* flashing across his chest. Maxo stopped with astonishment to listen. There was a huge reward for anyone identifying the perpetrator and handing him in to the Authorities.

"The security of the Polis," said the Announcer, *"and the Germline depends on each and every one of us. Progress and Perfection cannot come into being if we harbor among us unstable and criminal elements . . ."*

Unstable—that was an understatement. Stretch was a maniac, he was totally out of control and—according to the Trop Announcer—he was also a mass murderer.

Well, he, Maxo Strang, knew exactly where the perpetrator was. Phylo Lorrell, otherwise known as Stretch, was heading in a Clodrone car to Dr. Igo Strang's Lab. Or he had been—three hours ago. By now, of course, he would have arrived.

"Oh, GenPap," cried Maxo. And something worse than the thirst tightened in his throat, something that gave him that wet feeling he'd had at the Museo when Edwin had offered him a handkerchief.

The Enhanced brain is calm and rational, Maxo informed himself. Enhanced people don't blub, they think. So, through the tears, Maxo thought, and what he thought was that something wasn't quite right about the TropScreen story. There was something missing, only he didn't know what. He tried to remember the scene at the hospital. Stretch, Gala, the post, himself. The explosion. When the bomb had gone off, he had been standing not five yards from Stretch. He replayed the drama slowly, recreated the way Stretch had been knocked from the post when that man came past, watched how he'd instinctively stuck out his hands to save himself from the fall. And there it was—the hands. There was nothing in the boy's hands! How could you detonate a bomb with nothing in your hands? The sweat stuff was pouring down Maxo's back, but he didn't notice it at all, he was thinking too hard. Of course, Stretch could have had an accomplice, someone around the front to do the dirty work, but then why go to the scene, why put yourself in that amount of danger? But it wasn't even that.

Gala.

Why would Stretch have taken Gala? The boy clearly adored his sister and, after the explosion, he was totally focused on getting her away from the bomb site, getting her to safety. Why would Stretch have brought Gala to the hospital if he was going to detonate a bomb?

On the other hand, Stretch was violent, he punched

without warning, he tied people up—and he was probably, even now, at the Lab.

Maxo began to run. He ran despite his exhaustion and the pain in his foot and his lack of food and water, ran, ran and didn't stop until he got to the Museo.

In the DefunctReligions Room, Edwin Challice was looking at the pictures of gods and goddesses from Roman PastTimes, he was reading the label describing the crucifix, which was the symbol of the dangerous ChristianCult. *Spirit* and *soul* were not, (as far as he knew) BannedWords, but they seemed to have disappeared from this room. Or maybe it was just his memory that had disappeared again.

"Challice . . . Challice!"

Someone was shouting. Edwin Challice stood amazed. There was someone in the Museo running about and shouting his name. Edwin Challice, who was not a big or a bold man, walked steadily out of the DefunctReligions Room toward the noise.

"Challice—where the celeb are you?"

"I'm here," said Edwin. "I'm always here."

An apparition appeared in the corridor. It was wild and disheveled. It had the shaven head and fine cheekbones of the Enhanced, it had strange dark lines around the eyes and over the back of the hands. It was wearing filthy, torn trousers and a too-tight shirt.

"Maxo," said Edwin Challice, "welcome."

Something strange pricked behind Maxo's eyes then. He was recognized, he was known.

"I need to borrow your 'cator," Maxo said urgently.

"I think," said Edwin gently, "that you already borrowed it, last time you were here."

"Then the Museo one. I have to make a call. Without delay."

"Of course," said Edwin, "come with me."

But Maxo couldn't come any further. His legs simply wouldn't work. He slumped and slid to the floor.

"Dear boy," said Edwin, "you are not well. Allow me . . ."

Maxo allowed him. Edwin brought the boy a glass of cool, fresh water, he brought him a facecloth, he found two StrengthoPills. Maxo panted and sipped and choked and swallowed and was grateful.

"Thank you," Maxo said and heard the creak in the back of his brain, but it didn't stop him saying it a second time: "Thank you."

"Now," said Edwin, "I will help you to the office, you will sit and make your call."

And the old man let Maxo lean on him as they walked together down the hallway past Mythologies and Ancient-Rites to the door that led to the office.

They never got there.

Four men burst, running, into the building. They were wearing FlakArmor, carrying HighAccuracy Guns and had the solid physiques of Poldrones. Behind them came a smaller man with electric blue eyes.

"Burton Chavit, chief of InternalPolice," he shouted. "Stop where you are!"

Edwin and Maxo had no option but to stop where they were; there were four HighAccuracy Guns pointing at their heads and four huge beasts standing around them.

"I'm arresting you, Phylo Lorrell, on suspicion of carrying out the Hospital 1 Atrocity," said Chavit.

Maxo was too stupefied to speak.

"You have the wrong man," said Edwin quietly.

"Shut up, old man."

"This," said Edwin, "is Maxo Strang."

"A borrowed identity and impressive disguise," said Chavit. BodySculpt had made the job of SecurityServices so much harder. "But that's all. Now move aside."

"If I let the boy go," said Edwin, "he will fall."

"Then fall he must," said Chavit.

Edwin remained where he was.

"Move away, I say."

"No," said Edwin.

Chavit took a very small pistol from his belt. "You have three seconds. One, two . . ."

"Edwin . . . ," said Maxo, finding his tongue.

Which is when Chavit pulled the trigger.

When the old man crumpled, Maxo went with him. Edwin's arm was still about the boy. There was the smallest hole, edged with blood, on the front of Edwin's pale blue custodian's tunic. Maxo put his hand over the hole as if he could close Edwin up.

"What the celeb have you done?" said Maxo.

"Get up," said Chavit.

"How could you? An innocent old man."

"The Museo's a known meeting place for Throwbacks—did you think we didn't know? We know everything."

"You know nothing. Nothing," Maxo screamed. "You've killed him!"

"Stunned him," said Burton Chavit. "Only a stun dart. Too good for him, I agree. Now get up."

"You're hateful," said Maxo. "You're hateful and you're wrong. Wrong about me, wrong about Edwin Challice, and wrong about Phylo Lorrell!"

"Get up," said Chavit again, and when Maxo wouldn't, two of the Poldrones hauled him up by the armpits.

"Right," said Chavit. "You have an appointment with an IsolationCell."

And, leaving Edwin where he lay on the floor, the five of them marched Maxo away.

21

The Mescat House to which 1640 drove Stretch was called, in neon strobes, *Forget It All*. Stretch stepped out onto the pavement, glad to be outside, glad of the air. Yet he felt himself shiver. The ambisuit controls whirred into action, forcing warmth across his back, around his neck. Did this suit think he was afraid?

He was afraid.

And the closer he'd come to his goal of speaking to Dr. Igo Strang, the more afraid he'd become. Why? He'd planned for this encounter for so long, written and rewritten the speech in his mind, imagined every scene. Maybe that was it—what he'd imagined. He'd made this meeting a kind of movie, a CrimeFlik with himself as the hero. That's why he'd said what he had about a kidnap. But in the real world (was the Polis the real world?) a kidnap was a High-Offense. They put people in SecuriCells and failed to remember to let them out for much less than a kidnap. But that wasn't it either. If you wanted the truth in the Polis you couldn't be afraid of SecuriCells. So maybe it was the truth itself of which Stretch was afraid. He stood quite still. What if he finally got to ask Dr. Strang the question and didn't get an answer, or got an answer he didn't want? What then?

Water. Stretch had to have water.

He walked up the steps to the *Forget It All* entrance. It was labeled Enhanced Only. He had heard that there were segregated bars in the Inner Polis, but he'd never actually seen one before. Stretch felt himself hesitate, instinctively looking for the Naturals sign, which would no doubt point around the back of the building, and then his anger lit. This is why he was pursuing Strang, because of this, because of the inequality, because the Enhanced had sucked up his father and spat him out without a care in the world. So Stretch refused to be afraid. He would go to Strang and discover the truth, whatever that truth was. He'd just have a drink first. Some water definitely. And maybe some mescat. He deserved some, didn't he?

He set his jaw, walked through the Enhanced Only door and then hesitated again. It was madness to go into a public place when his face was all over every TropScreen in the Polis. Why take the risk? But then Daz had painted him well and what safer place could there be than among the Elite when the Trop was looking for a Dreggie? Stretch, alias Phylo Lorrell, Most Wanted, made straight for the bar. He'd expected a Clodrone bartender; this man was an Estate worker.

"Water," he announced, looking the bartender straight in the eye.

"Certainly, sir," said the bartender politely. "Carbonated, spring, pure, fresh, or recycled?"

And Stretch wanted to shout simultaneously *Bless you, Daz,* and *five types of water, how dare you have five types of water here when half the time in the Estates there is no water at all.* What he actually said, very quietly, was: "pure, please."

The bartender put a shining glass under the relevant tap and pressed.

"Anything else?"

"Mescat," said Stretch precipitously.

"Glass or vial?"

Vials, Stretch knew, were more expensive. He felt his hand rising to the ambisuit breast pocket: How much credit would Maxo have? Enough for a vial of mescat, enough for a thousand vials probably. That's how it was. For them.

"Vial."

"We have CurrentSeason or Vintages One to Eight."

"Vintage Six," said Stretch at random.

The bartender selected a crystal tube from a glistening tray of such tubes. Light sparked on the pale gold liquid inside. The bartender ceremoniously passed the vial to Stretch, laid a mat for the water, and then pointed the Bar-Wand at the left breast pocket of the ambisuit. There were a couple of tick-ticks and then the TransactionComplete noise.

Stretch settled himself on a bar stool, where he could sit alone, and unstoppered the vial. Many boys his age in the Estates were heavy mescat drinkers. Stretch had always moderated his drinking. The only mescat available in the Estates was the cheap sort, and, with its thick taste, it was easily adulterated. People in the Estates died of overindulgence in mescat. The odor of this top-quality mescat was quite different—headily sweet and spicy. For a moment Stretch just inhaled it and then he took the tiniest of sips. It was like drinking fire. It was as if all the veins in his body were running with flame. But it was a good feeling. In the mirror behind the bar, Stretch looked at the shape of his shaved skull, observed his own piercing blue eyes. What made him a lesser person than a member of the Enhanced? Nothing. Nothing at all! He was handsome, he was on fire, and he was—quite suddenly—not afraid.

At the other end of the bar, he was aware of another pair of eyes looking at him. Dreggie eyes. The bar was split, Stretch realized then; the curve where he was sitting accessed through the Enhanced door and the other end, where the Dreggie was, presumably accessed from around the back. The Dreggie man (Dreggie—what was he saying—the man was a Natural) was dark and middle-aged, and he held out one of the large schooner glasses that was used for the cheapest mescat. The bartender was coming to serve him, but the man wasn't interested in the bartender, he was staring, via the mirror, at Stretch.

"Do I know you?" he asked.

Handsome, fiery Stretch stoppered the vial. "How could you?"

"I'm sure I know you."

"I'm a HighElite. You . . . ,"—Stretch paused—"are not." The announcement lit a different fire in Stretch's veins. For a moment he blazed with superiority and then, just as suddenly, his whole body flooded with self-disgust.

"Don't bother the gentleman, Jenks," said the bartender.

"I'm not bothering him," said Jenks, "I'm just saying, he looks like someone I know. Or used to know."

Stretch laid the still almost full vial down on the bar and drained his water.

"Only the other guy," continued Jenks, "was nicer . . ."

"Jenks . . . ," warned the bartender.

"And had more hair," finished Jenks.

But Stretch did not hear this last remark, because he had already gone, out of the Mescat House, out to the street, the car; he was on his way again. He had business to attend to.

"Looks like he left the mescat," said Jenks, "d'you think I could have it?"

Igo Strang had the GemCorp Poldrones on HighAlert. He hadn't informed them as to the precise nature of the threat expected, but he had asked them to maintain extra vigilance and suggested that, were he to press the ExtremeRed button beneath his desk, then at least two of them would be required to make an appearance in his office within twenty-five seconds.

Igo had not informed Glora of the situation. Glora was a good Mesh and a miraculous example of all that was best in germline engineering, but she didn't always say the right things to the right people. He would wait, he would inform her of the situation after it had been resolved. And resolved it would be, very shortly. Clodrone 1640 was, even now, coming up in the elevator with the kidnapper. Having 1640 at the meeting would be a security bonus, Igo had decided, Clodrones were encoded to protect their masters. And then there was the glass window behind Igo's desk, which overlooked the Lab below. Despite it being dusk, at least half of Igo's forty-four strong workforce were still poring over their pipettes and their petri dishes. Igo was far from alone. He sat himself down behind his desk. The desk was protection, too, protection and power. The entry-scanner buzzed.

"Come in," said Dr. Igo Strang.

Two figures entered, the unmistakably plodding shape of Clodrone 1640, and, just in front of him, a youth with high cheekbones and piercing blue eyes. The boy with his shaven head and ambisuit would have passed for Enhanced in most quarters of the Polis. He did not pass here. Igo had overseen all the germline specs since before this creature had been born. The boy had a good natural body (if a bit thin), excellent eyes and exceptional face shading, but not exceptional enough to fool Dr. Strang. Besides, he was twitching. GenOffs of the Enhanced had a certain languid ease; this boy's hand kept moving to his ambi-thigh pocket, feeling the outline of something there. A weapon of some sort, Igo supposed. Igo rose but did not move from behind his desk.

"Mr. Stretch," he said, "I am Dr. Strang."

"Not Stretch, not even Mr. Stretch," said the youth, jerking forward a little. "I'm Phylo Lorrell."

Stretch was pleased to see the doctor blanch visibly. "You know who I am, then?"

"Of course," said the doctor, recovering himself and planting his hands firmly on the desk. "You're our insurgent, the Polis's most wanted man. A large reward is on offer for your capture and your face is on every TropScreen in the Polis. But it is not this face I see before me. I congratulate you on getting here undetected, Mr. Lorrell."

Was the man playing with him? "But you know what I want," said Stretch. "Why I've come?"

"Mr. Lorrell, I have no idea. Perhaps you would care to tell me. Why don't you take a seat?"

The chair in front of the desk was considerably smaller than the one behind it.

"I'll stand," said Stretch.

"As you wish," Strang said, settling himself on his side of the desk.

Stretch was sure the decision to remain standing was the right one, but standing while Strang was sitting put him, he felt, at a disadvantage, as if he was a naughty schoolboy sent before a HighMaster.

"It's about my father—Finn Lorrell."

Igo Strang was surprised, though he tried not to show it. Insurgents weren't known for caring about their fathers, they were known for InequalityRants. Even Clodrone 1640, Igo noted, was surprised by the mention of the boy's father. In fact, by the look on 1640's face, he was astounded. "Go on."

"My father—Finn Lorrell," the boy repeated as if he liked the sound of his father's name in his mouth, "came to donate last time there was a call for Clean Genes. He came to the Polis and never returned."

"Ah," said Dr. Strang, this made more sense. "So, let me guess, in a delayed fit of Insurgency temper about your loss, you decided to make the new Clean Gene Appeal grounds for trying to wipe out an entire generation of GemXs, a generation that includes my own GenOff, Maxo."

"What?" said Stretch. "Of course not. I never detonated that bomb. That's all Trop lies, nothing to do with me. Nothing to do with my father."

"Really," said Strang. "Tell it to Burton Chavit." He paused. "Head of InternalSecurity."

"Are you threatening me?" asked Stretch.

"No," said Strang. "I rather think it's the other way around."

"Good," said Stretch. "Because we're not here to talk about the bomb. We're here to talk about my father."

"And my Genoff," said Strang. "You said you'd bring something of Maxo's, so I'd know you were really holding him."

"This suit," said Stretch. "Don't you recognize the color, the line credit symbol?"

Strang stood up, peered across the desk.

"Okay," he said. "It's Maxo's suit. Which proves you have been with him. But not where he is now or if,"–Stretch heard the soft whirr of Strang's ambisuit–"he's still alive."

"He's alive," said Stretch.

"Then give me proof. Let me speak to him."

"Not until you've answered my questions."

Man and boy faced each other across the desk.

"They're not difficult questions, Dr. Strang."

Strang sat down again. "What is it you want to know?"

"Where my father is."

"How could I possibly know that? People come— hundreds of people—they donate. Not here—at the hospital. It's a simple procedure for a man, a matter of a few skin cells. A scrape, nothing more. Their names are logged, they're paid, and then they go their own way. After they leave the hospital, we are not responsible for them. I'm sorry if your father did not return to the Estates, but I fail to see how it could be anything to do with me or the Clean Genes program. That's as much of an answer as I can give, now let me talk to my GenOff."

"I don't believe you."

"Your prerogative, Mr. Lorrell."

"And I don't believe the Leaderene's justifications for the Clean Genes program either."

"That, I believe, Mr. Lorell, is TropTreason."

"Why do you do it, Dr. Strang?" Stretch burst out then. "This Clean Gene program. What do you need the clean cells for?"

"That's no secret. It's all advertised, all above board. For the good of the whole Trop we need to ensure the health of the germline. If we are to progress toward perfection, we must preserve the germline. Everyone knows that."

"So why don't the Enhanced donate cells for themselves? Why do you need Natural cells?"

"Science," said Strang. "You wouldn't understand."

"Try me."

Strang drew in his lips. "Enhanced cells are slightly more unstable, that's all."

"More unstable for what, exactly?"

Igo Strang's hands hovered at the edge of his desk.

"Tell me!" said Stretch. "If you value Maxo's life . . . tell me!"

The hands stopped hovering, interlocked. "Splicing."

"Splicing?"

"Damaged DNA. We remove a faulty gene and splice in a healthy one. That's all. It's called HealthCare."

"HealthCare for who? No one gets spliced in the Estates."

"The health of the entire Tropolis depends on the health of the HighElites. That's the way it is," said Strang.

"And what about my father's health? Doesn't that count

for anything? He's missing but so long as his cells are floating about in some HighElite, that's okay, is it?"

"They're not floating about in some HighElite," said Clodrone 1640. "They're floating about in me."

"Don't be ridiculous," said Strang.

"It's true," said 1640. "And truth is very important."

"You know nothing about truth," said Strang quickly. "You are not encoded for truth. You're encoded to obey. Although you seem to have been derelict in your duty recently. Now—this is an UnquestionObey, be quiet, 1640!"

"No," said the Finn-boy to 1640, "speak."

"Your father's in me," said 1640. "He's growing in there—in here—cell by cell. I see it now. I go in after the Degrade and I don't come out myself. I come out mainly myself but something in me's wrong. Nice wrong but wrong. And not nice wrong, too. For me."

"1640, I'm warning you. You are in serious danger of being sent for TotalRetraining."

"Go on," said Stretch. His face looked white and appalled.

"I think the cells are growing. I think they're multiplying. I think I may be becoming entirely more not myself. But Finn."

"I apologize for my Clodrone," said Strang. "If you understood anything about science you'd know that what he's positing is completely impossible. One does not grow a personality from a single cell."

"But you're not denying you put those cells in him, are you? A Clodrone? What's that got to do with the germ-line?"

"Enhanced, Clodrone, what does it matter?"

"It matters to me, because it proves you've lied. That the Leaderene's lied, that there's something you're hiding."

"Mr. Lorrell, it is possible that 1640 received cells from your father, there was an aging problem we needed to fix. Health for all, you understand."

"An aging problem?"

"That's what I said."

There was a pause while Stretch digested this information. It was coming to him, suddenly it was coming . . . "I think I get it. At last I get it. You can't afford to let them grow old, can you? If they get old, you lose your investment. So you're using our cells to increase their lifespan. That's what you're doing, isn't it? Designing servants . . . whose batteries never run out."

"You're getting a little hysterical, Mr. Lorrell. Everyone expects to live longer these days."

"Not in the Estates. We're not living longer. We're dying like flies. Which is convenient, don't you think, especially when you're developing a huge obedient workforce . . . which, if you can get it right, if you can get them to live long enough, will obviate the need for workers from the Estates. The Estates simply won't be needed. We won't be needed. We'll be surplus to requirements. You can raze us all!"

"Preposterous. Come on, Mr. Lorrell, I thought you wanted to talk about your father."

"I am talking about my father. Because he realized, didn't he, all those years ago, he realized what was going on. Did he complain? I bet he did, I bet he caught you out and then you had to silence him."

"This is not a CrimeFlik, Mr. Lorrell."

"Isn't it?"

"And Finn-boy," said 1640 suddenly, "your father says he loves you."

"What!" cried Stretch, and then he looked at 1640. "What have you done to him, Strang?"

"Look," said Igo. "I can access the records." He twisted a desk screen to face Stretch. "Here are the names of those who donated the last time." He scrolled down page after page. "Here we are . . . Fallow, Jenks, Lorell. Finn Lorell, sign-out time 3:45, there's his scriptopen signature for the money. He took the money and left."

"So where did he go?"

"Probably for a drink. That's what most of them do. They come with friends, they get the money, and then they go and blow it all on a vial or two of mescat."

"That's a filthy lie!" But Jenks. That name—Jenks. Mescat. "You know nothing about my father," shouted Stretch. He bent down and he drew something sharp and glittering from his thigh pocket. "Now tell me the truth!"

Clodrone 1640 saw the sharp and glittering thing. It was a knife. He watched the Finn-boy hold the knife up in the air and step toward his Master, Igo Strang. Clodrone 1640 knew what was right and what was wrong. Stabbing people was wrong. He was encoded to know that and also the Finn-man told him that. The Finn-man (how horrible to think he had Finn Lorrell's cells multiplying inside him) knew all about right and wrong, he was very strong on it and, despite his love for the Finn-boy, right and wrong came first. Clodrone 1640, without any thought for himself, sprang into action. He launched himself at the Finn-boy's legs and knocked him to the ground. Stretch, who had not been expecting attack from this quarter, watched the knife spring from his hand and skitter across the floor. Approximately twenty-five seconds later, two hefty Poldrones arrived. They were barely needed. 1640 had the boy in an armlock.

"Sorry," said 1640, because the boy was crying. The Poldrones had no such compunction, they hauled Stretch to his feet, pulled his hands behind his back, and attached a WristScrew Lock.

"Now," said Dr. Igo Strang, "you can tell me where you're keeping my GenOff, or you can tell Mr. Burton Chavit. You have three seconds to decide."

22

Leaderene Euphony Clore sat at her desk in the High-Council Chamber, console activated. It was fifteen minutes before she was due to receive the delegation of GemX GenParents. There would be sixteen of them, nine men and seven women, all of whom had lost offspring in the Atrocity. Clore consulted her list, two of the delegates were only proto-enhanced; she noted their names: Mortimer Malkin (whose GenGirl Lydida had died) and Broda Frank who'd lost her boy Bovis. She'd have to be wary of those. Some of the proto-enhanced had ThrowbackIntellectual tendencies. But mainly the news was good: The delegation was, apparently, fuming.

The Leaderene moved on, SwiftButtoning Glora Orb's number and watching Glora's astonishingly beautiful face assemble itself on her screen. That's what it was all about, thought Euphony Clore, this sort of perfection. It made all the effort worthwhile.

"How are we doing?" she asked.

"Spectacular, your Leadereneship," purred Glora. "This will undoubtedly be the finest funeral ever seen in the Polis."

"And Seud Quac?"

"Absolutely on track. We prototyped the first hologram in the PolisDome not two hours ago. Each of the dead will have his or her own hologram, which will move individually through the central drag of the assembly. Quac's working on the VidMemory even as we speak. Each hologram will stop in front of his or her family and make a Leaving-Speech, I'm working on the words and Seud is perfecting the voiceprint. The parents won't know it's not their own GenOff speaking."

"You know," said the Leaderene rather brutally, "about Maxo."

"Yes and no," said Glora. "Igo seems to think he may have survived."

"What?" said the Leaderene.

"Only an outside chance, but, of course, we hope. But then again we don't because, well, if he has survived I won't be eligible for one of Quac's Holojars."

"Holojar?" inquired the Leaderene.

"It's perfection itself," said Glora. "The idea. You'll die for it." She laughed. "Each family gets (for a small cost, say two hundred and forty TropCredits) a replica hologram in a jar, to take out whenever they like. A miniature version of their GenOff—Seud's so into miniatures at the moment—who'll smile and wave and (for an extra fifty TropCredits) actually reproduce their funeral speech. Brilliant, don't you think?"

"Indeed," said the Leaderene. "I congratulate you. The Polis is in your debt. Remind me about that sometime."

"May your Leadereneship celeb forever," replied Glora Orb and was smartly clicked off.

Clore depressed another button. "Send in Chavit."

Burton Chavit, who must have been hovering just outside the Holding Room door, made his entrance.

"I gather there may be GemXs who survived," said the Leaderene as if they were in the middle of a conversation about this. "How many, Chavit?"

"We can't be absolutely sure," said Chavit, "but my best guess at this time is fewer than seventy."

"Too many," said the Leaderene. "Can we get at their Verification PrintOuts?"

"Of course."

"Good. Well, lose them."

"What?"

"Lose the PrintOuts. Corrupt the DataSystem. No self-respecting GenParent will agree to a mesh if there are no details. Specifications have to be officially verified, that's the rule. The remaining GemXs are not to breed, Chavit."

"Understood," said Chavit, who was waiting to be asked to sit down.

"Sit down, for celeb's sake," said the Leaderene, watching him dither. "Now what's the news on our perpetrator?"

"Excellent," said Chavit, placing himself in his accustomed HighTable seat to the right of the Leaderene. "We picked him up last night as you know, since when he's been doing a little time in the IsolationCell."

"Thinking time," murmured the Leaderene.

"Precisely. Good to be alone. Though, of course, he might have had the odd visitor overnight, you know, bit of softening up. And I was on my way for the first interview—I so look forward to that—when you called me here, your Leadereneship."

"And I think I should have called him, too," said Euphony.

206

"What?" said Chavit.

"The insurgent. Get him here now. Could be useful. Up the temperature."

"Will the temperature need 'upping,' Leaderene?"

"Possibly not. But we can't afford to take any chances. I'm looking for a groundswell of opinion for a TotalRaze."

"The suspect might not . . . ," said Chavit, ". . . look too good."

"Well, he'll probably look worse," said the Leaderene, "after the delegation have sunk their teeth into him."

"Besides," said Chavit, "he didn't really do it, did he? The Atrocity. And as he hasn't had time to admit it yet . . ."

"Who says he didn't do it?" asked Euphony sweetly.

"He'll say so," said Chavit. "He'll say he's innocent. He'll say we picked him at random, framed him."

"I do so love it," said Euphony, "when they deny things. It makes me go all . . . *shivery.*"

"Besides, you know I like first dibs," said Chavit plaintively, "on the intellectual side."

"Just get him here," said Euphony Clore, losing patience. "And fast."

Burton Chavit made a call.

"Good," said Euphony. "Now, I think we're ready to begin, don't you?"

The delegation were let in through doors at the very far end of the room. As the room had previously been the Trop's OldTimes three-hundred seater debating chamber, the delegates had to walk a fair distance before they arrived at the HighTable. Leaderene Clore watched them all: who was ahead, who hung back, who seemed confident, who uneasy. She recognized at least half of them including

Grando Farque, chiefexec of TropBank and Lilhelm Minx of CorporateImageCo. One man she didn't recognize was wearing black and using a stick to clip his way down the chamber, as if he had a limp. It was disgusting here in the HighChamber, but Euphony Clore wasn't a leader for nothing. She kept herself calm, waited, and when the Gen-Parents were near enough for her not to have to raise her voice, she said: "Welcome. Though I'm sorry to have to receive you under such tragic circumstances."

There were at least sixteen chairs around the HighTable but she did not invite the delegates to sit.

Farque, who had clearly designated himself leader, stepped forward. He was plump (clearly pre-Obesity-Module) but not unattractive, thought Euphony, though his blazing red hair had the effect of making him look angry even when he wasn't.

"On behalf of those gathered here," Farque began, "I'd like to say that the situation in the Estates has become intolerable."

"Absolutely," said the Leaderene.

"And we, the GemX parents, demand TotalRetribution."

This, thought Euphony Clore, is going to be easy.

"Extra Vigilance, a ClampDown, and GrandScale Total-Retribution," put in Lilhelm Minx who was dressed in a fluorescent pink ambisuit with thigh high black military boots.

"And an honorable funeral," said Broda Frank. "Bovis was . . . all I had." She spoke so slowly that she reminded the Leaderene of an OldTime cow.

"Ah," said the Leaderene, with an intonation of pity, "let us begin there. The Polis owes its GemX parents much. You have been—and are—the fount of this Trop. Without you and your contributions to genetic progress we would be far less close to our GrandVision goals than we are. Perfection has its seeds in you and therefore I'm pleased to announce the most prestigious Mass Funeral the Trop has ever seen, a funeral that will be overseen by no lesser persons than Glora Orb and Seud Quac."

There was a suitably impressed gasp. The Leaderene went on to outline the extraordinary plans that were afoot.

"In recognition of your contribution to the germline project," she continued, "the Polis will fund this funeral in its entirety except, of course, for the Holojar replica GenOffs. As you will appreciate, we cannot expect Seud Quac to produce ArtWork of this quality without some recompense. As working members of the Trop, you will all understand that, I'm sure."

There were murmurs of assent.

"And TotalRetribution?" persisted Grando Farque. "What about that?"

"You are pushing at an open door, Mr. Farque. Security of the Polis has, and always will be, my primary concern. In fact, even now, thanks to the good offices of my head of InternalPolice"—she indicated Burton Chavit—"I am able to announce that we have apprehended the primary suspect, Phylo Lorrell."

"Impressively fast," said a voice from the back of the group in a tone that might have been ironic. The Leaderene scanned quickly and identified the man in the black suit carrying the black cane. Now he was nearer she saw that he had the ever-so-slightly lopsided face of the proto-enhanced. Mortimer Malkin, then.

"Mr. Malkin?" the Leaderene questioned, with apparent graciousness.

"I'd just like to ask him why," said the man.

"I'd like to pull his head off," said Broda Frank.

"I mean why did he do it?"

"Who cares why he did it," exploded Farque. "He did it. Killed my GenOff. And yours. That's all we need to know."

"That's not all I need to know," said Mortimer Malkin.

"Do go on," encouraged the Leaderene.

"There have been Atrocities before," said Malkin, stepping forward a little. "Many of them. And there have been Reprisals. Many of them, too. And has it helped? Has it stopped the murdering? No. Reprisals don't work. We need to ask what's going on, at a deeper level. We need to ask and we need to listen."

There was a stunned silence. This was TropTreason surely? Everyone looked to the Leaderene.

"Well, Mr. Malkin," the Leaderene smiled, "I am an enlightened person. And a just one. Let me demonstrate how just." She pressed a button and spoke to an unseen screen. "Has Mr. Lorrell arrived yet? Oh, good. Do send him in." The Leaderene was aware of the look of horror on her InternalPolice chief's face, but she paid no attention to that. "Now, Mr. Malkin, perhaps you would be good enough to conduct the inquiry yourself?"

Among the group, people parted around Mortimer Malkin as if he had a dangerous disease. There was a long moment's pause and then the sound of the far doors of the room being opened. Four Poldrones entered suspending, somewhere between them, the body of a boy. It was difficult to see the boy at first, obscured as he was by the bulk of the men guarding him, but as the fivesome approached, it was clear the suspect was more being dragged than walking down the hall and that his head was hanging as if it was too heavy for him to lift upright. As he got closer to the HighTable his clothes—a dirty, too-tight T-shirt and a pair of Dreggie trousers—became apparent, but still the only thing they could see of his face was his shaven skull.

The Poldrones stopped.

"Leave him," said the Leaderene, "move aside."

The Poldrones moved aside and the suspect was left looking alone and slightly slumped, a limp doll on invisible strings.

"Murderer," shrieked Grando Farque.

"Mr. Malkin?" the Leaderene proposed.

Mortimer Malkin coughed slightly. "Mr. Lorrell . . ." he began.

"Head up when you're being spoken to, Lorrell!" shouted Burton Chavit, unable to contain himself.

The suspect lifted his head.

"I would just—" started Malkin again, and then he stopped. He stared at the face in front of him. The boy had a bruised lip and a swollen eye and cracks about and between his eyes, and yet there was little doubt in Malkin's mind. "Maxo," he said, "it's Maxo, isn't it? Maxo Strang."

"Yes," said Chavit. "A brilliant impersonation. Almost had me fooled, too."

"No," continued Mortimer Malkin, coming ever closer to Maxo. "It is Maxo. He and Lydida were in EduCate together. Maxo?"

"Hello, Mr. Malkin," said Maxo in a kind of whisper.

"I think there must be some kind of mistake," said Mortimer Malkin.

"No mistake," said the Leaderene, thinking fast and rising to her feet even faster. "I've brought Mr. Strang here today for one purpose and one purpose only. To prove to you exactly what kind of foe we are up against. I didn't think you would believe it," she continued, her unflinching gaze on Malkin, "unless you saw it with your own eyes. But what have we here? I'll tell you what. A perpetrator so devious, so clever, that he can even fool my chief of Internal-Police!" Here she paused dramatically before giving Chavit a savage sidelong glare. "We have a perpetrator not only willing to engage in MassKilling but clever enough to fool our SecurityServices. Though not, thankfully, myself."

There were murmurs of stunned appreciation, but Euphony barely drew breath. "A perpetrator," she continued, "who has managed to lay the blame for this Atrocity on one of the few remaining members of the GemX bloodline. Mr. Strang"—she turned to face the battered boy—"please accept the Polis's TotalApology and Gratitude. We are sorry for your incarceration, but we know you will have wanted to play your part in letting the Polis Elite know just what an enemy we face at this time. HighElites, ladies and gentlemen, proto-enhanced, this is the level of evil and cunning we are up against. Do you think," the Leaderene concluded dangerously, "it is a time for talk?"

"Kill them," shouted Lilhelm Minx, "skewer them through."

"Take them before they take us," cried Broda Frank. And then, "Poor Maxo."

"Flatten them. Flatten the Estates!" cried two or three voices in unison.

"RazeMachine them," bawled Grando Farque. "Total-Raze them!"

If Mortimer Malkin wanted to say something different, no one heard him. If he thought something had gone wrong, or something had been snatched away from him, it was all lost in the melee.

Euphony Clore looked down at the baying little mob with satisfaction. She'd have to deal with Chavit, of course, but that would be easy. She'd always found Fikk Powell, Chavit's deputy, an attractively brutal man. As for Mortimer Malkin, he would require a different approach.

23

Dr. Igo Strang almost felt sorry for the boy. The Poldrones did not (Strang believed) have the WristScrew done up particularly tightly, but the boy was still crying. His tears had made discolored runnels down his cheeks. Makeup, Strang realized, Lorrell was wearing makeup! He must want so much to be one of the Enhanced.

"Your three seconds," said Dr. Strang, "are up."

"Give me a 'cator," said Stretch. "I'll call, you'll be able to speak to Maxo."

"Incorrect," said Strang. "You give me the number and I'll call myself."

"The curator's number," said Stretch. "The one you called before. Daz will answer it."

"Daz?" queried Strang, dialing.

"My brother."

Strang listened to the old-fashioned ring tone.

"Yes?" answered a voice not unlike that of the boy's, but even younger.

"This is Dr. Igo Strang," said Igo, putting the 'cator in speaker mode so the whole room could hear the conversation. "You're Phylo Lorrell's brother?"

"Yes."

"Then listen carefully. I have your brother here. He's under Poldrone guard. Unless you put my GenOff Maxo on the line right now, Phylo will be taking a one-way ticket to one of Burton Chavit's IsolationCells."

There was a pause.

"Do you hear me?" shouted Strang.

"Yes," said Daz. "Can I talk to Stretch?"

"No!" thundered Strang. "I said now, put Maxo on NOW."

Another pause, shorter this time. "I would," said Daz, "I really would. But he's not here."

"Not there?" said Strang.

"We let him go."

From where Stretch was there came a kind of strangulated cry.

"Let him go—where? Where is he now?"

"I don't know," said Daz. "He just . . . left."

"You're lying," said Strang. "Nobody kidnaps someone and then just lets them go!"

"Well," said Daz carefully, "it wasn't really a kidnap. He came of his own free will."

Strang began drumming his fingers on his desk. "Right. So you're telling me that my Enhanced GenOff Maxo, having survived probably the worst Atrocity of modern times, willingly drove straight into the Estates, coincidentally managing to light upon the home of the Dreggie perpetrator of that Atrocity?"

"It wasn't quite like that," said Daz.

"And I didn't do it," said Stretch, "the bomb!" Anger finally wiped away the tears that his hands couldn't.

"It was because of Gala," said Daz.

"Gala?" inquired Strang.

A new voice came on the line, intense but mellifluous. A girl. "This is Gala speaking," said the voice, "I'm Daz's sister. Your son—GenOff—he helped me, Dr. Strang. I was injured in the hospital blast and he helped get me out, get me home."

"Ludicrous," said Strang. "You're crazy!"

"It's true," said Stretch.

"Is that you, Stretch?" asked Gala.

"Why in the name of celeb would my GenOff do that?"

"Well," said Stretch, "it's because, well, Maxo has a kind off . . . um . . . a bit of a thing for Gala."

"Maxo—my Maxo in mesh with a Dreggie girl? What do you take me for? The Enhanced do not fall for Dreggies."

"Or Dreggies for the Enhanced," said Gala mildly. "Usually."

There was what sounded like an exasperated exchange and then Daz came back on the line. "That's why Maxo had to go. His protestations were getting wild. They were embarrassing my mother."

Strang felt his ambisuit whirr. None of this made any sense and none of it proved that this mad family had ever held Maxo at all. "Hang on." Igo spun around and faced Clodrone 1640. "You were there! You drove our kidnapper here. So you must have been there. In the Estates. You must have seen what happened!"

"Yes," said 1640.

"So?" yelled Igo Strang. "What happened?"

"What he says," said 1640. "I think."

"You think?"

"Apologies," said 1640. "Thinking is contrary to Training."

"Maxo went willingly to the Estates?"

"He ordered me to take him. To drive him and the girl, Gala."

"And Maxo—and the girl?" said Strang. "Did they . . . were they?"

"I'm not sure," said 1640. "Though I believe my master liked her foot."

"Foot," repeated Igo. "He liked her—*foot*?"

"Yes," said 1640.

Igo Strang took a deep breath. "And then what—what happened when you got to the Estates?"

"My master went into the building—Block 213—and he didn't come out."

"If you've harmed him!" Strang shouted at Stretch.

"We haven't, we never harmed him."

Gala's voice came back into the room. "Dr. Strang, Maxo left here safely. I sincerely hope he's safe now. I'm sure he is. You must believe that, just as I believe you never harmed our father, but you might know where he is. Do you know where he is, Dr. Strang?"

Strang turned the volume up on the Speaker Cate: "Your brother," he said, "is thirty seconds away from an Internal-Security IsolationCell. You are in no position to ask questions, only to answer them. I will ask you this once and once only, where is Maxo now?"

"We told you"—Daz had clearly snatched the 'cator back— "we don't know. He left. Three hours ago, maybe four."

"But he had to walk," said Strang, piecing it together. "Because you took the car, didn't you, Lorrell?" Strang turned on 1640. "And you let him, 1640. Left your master to walk in the Estates while you drove his kidnapper."

"Sorry," said 1640, though he wasn't entirely sure it was his fault.

"Maxo should be in the Polis by now," said Daz. "Even on foot it doesn't take that long. Can I speak to Stretch?"

Igo made a gesture at the Poldrones that looked as if he was screwing the lid on a jar. The Poldrones reacted immediately.

"Ow!" screamed Stretch as the WristScrew tightened.

"No," said Igo, "you cannot speak to your brother. But if you suddenly recall any information previously forgotten, you know where to find me." He clicked off. His brain was whirring more furiously than his ambisuit. 1640's testimony confirmed that Maxo had survived the explosion and that he had gone to the Estates. But not that he was still alive. But Igo Strang wanted Maxo to be alive, he wanted it so much that he believed the story of these brothers, one of whom, it appeared, was a mass murderer. He stared at the boy: with his shaved head and makeup smears he didn't look like a murderer, but then what did murderers look like? Igo was less sure about the story of Maxo and the Dreggie girl's foot. If it was true—*if*—it was intolerable, it was frightening. Poor Maxo! Still, if such horrifying impulses were side-effects of the GemX genotype disintegration, then who better to address the problem than Igo Strang himself? Igo would find a cure, make a pill. Maxo would be well, Strang swore it on the germline. But first things first: Maxo was adrift, presumably still in the Estates, or he would have called. Igo had to find him. And fast.

As for Lorrell, Igo would have to be careful. Handing suspects over to the SecurityServices was not always wise. People had been known to go into one of Burton Chavit's

IsolationCells and fail to come out. And if—despite Daz's protestations—the Lorrells were still holding Maxo, it would be best to hang on to Phylo as a bargaining chip. So, decision: deposit Lorrell in one of GemCorps own Securi-Cells, but keep the threat of Chavit hanging over him. If there was something to say, perhaps a night without food and water would encourage the boy to say it. He gave the relevant orders to the Poldrones and Stretch was taken away.

"Now," said Strang to 1640. "Give me the precise address where you took Maxo in the Estates."

"Do you want me to drive you?" asked 1640.

"No, said Strang. "I do not want you to drive me. In fact, I may never want you to drive me again. When you have given me the directions you will go straight to your pod and stay there until your PodMaster arrives. Your current—aberrant—behavior is not to be tolerated. You think; you ask questions; you drive kidnappers; you disobey; you believe yourself inhabited by multiplying cells. In short, 1640, you are a candidate for ReTraining."

"Oh," cried 1640, the wind going out of him.

"Directions," said Strang threateningly.

1640 gathered himself, gave directions.

"I will see you," said Strang, "if I see you, when you are recovered."

Then, having selected a particularly brutish Poldrone guard to be his driver, Dr. Igo Strang headed out into the Estates.

The Poldrones had gone, the Finn-boy had gone, his Master had gone. Clodrone 1640 was alone in Dr. Igo Strang's office. He sat down in the little chair that faced his Master's huge desk. He felt small in it, but then he felt small anyway. Small and shivery. In his lap his hands were flapping as was something inside his rib cage. He would have thought he had a bird in his chest and wounded birds for hands. But there weren't any birds anymore, he knew that, all the birds had gone in the AvianFlu Pandemic.

ReTraining.

He should go right now, report to his PodMaster, begin at once. He deserved ReTraining. He had indeed done many wrong things. And he couldn't even blame it on Finn anymore. What was it his Master had said? *If you understood anything about science you'd know that what he's positing is completely impossible. One does not grow a personality from a single cell.* And if it wasn't Finn's fault it must be his own. He had Finn's cells, he knew that for certain, he'd seen Finn Lorrell's name on the DegradeDocket. Had he invented everything from there? Maybe he had, or maybe Finn's cells had triggered some reaction in his, made him more the man he might have been if they hadn't spliced him, trained him, bred things out of him. Flutter went 1640's heart, flap went his hands.

If other people did wrong things—1640 struggled a little with this thought—then that didn't matter, did it? Because no one said the Masters had to be good, as far as 1640 knew. Only the Clodrones needed to be good. Which is why it was all right for Dr. Strang to put the Finn-boy in a SecuriCell and deny him food and drink. It would not have been right for 1640 to do this, but it was a perfectly honorable action on Dr. Strang's part. After all, hadn't the boy tried to attack him with a knife?

Boy.

The Finn-boy was barely more than a child. A child who had lost his father. A father who, in some strange way, 1640 felt he might have stolen. That made up 1640's mind. He had done so many wrong things, one more could not matter. He would take the Finn-boy a drink.

There were four types of water in Dr. Strang's office fridge. 1640, who had often been required to pour his master a glass, selected Igo's favorite: Vintage ClearPure2. It came in a beautiful blue glass bottle. 1640 had always liked the color. The sky was that color sometimes, mainly after a SuddenOnset; it was like a promise of things getting better.

1640 undid his ambi-thigh pocket, meaning to conceal the water there, but it was far too bulky, besides there was something in the pocket already, the Finn-boy's knife. 1640 had retrieved the blade when it fell to the floor. It was a sharp knife, 1640 had thought as he picked it up, certainly sharp enough to kill a man. 1640 re-fastened his pocket. He would carry the water; he would make no secret of it; that would be his story, he decided, what he'd tell the Poldrone guards, that Igo had changed his mind. Igo Strang wanted the boy to have water. Besides, having to carry the bottle would stop the flapping of 1640's hands.

There were two Poldrones in the SecurityNerveCell and a bank of screens successively relaying pictures from Gem-Corp front and back entrances, the Lab, Igo's office, the SkyLift and, of course, the doors of GemCorp two Securi-Cells. One of the SecuriCell doors was open, the other one, where the Finn-boy obviously was, was blankly, darkly shut. He would be frightened in there, 1640 thought.

"Change of orders," said 1640 smartly.

"What?" The Poldrones were big, 1640 thought, but slow to grasp things.

"Your Master and mine, Dr. Igo Strang, wants the Finn-boy . . ."–1640 stumbled, regrouped–". . . wants Phylo Lorrell to have water."

The Poldrones didn't seem to notice the stumble.

"We ain't got no orders," said the squarer of the two, Poldrone 11,434, "where's your authorization?"

"As you know," said 1640 quickly, "our Master has left on urgent business in the Estates. He has 'catored me with instructions. That should be good enough for you."

"Well, he never 'catored us," grumbled the second Poldrone. "He's supposed to 'cator us."

"Masters are not supposed to do anything," said 1640. "Masters must always be obeyed, TrainingRule One. The price of noncompliance . . ."

"Yes, yes, all right," said 11, 434. "Put your eye here."

1640 put his eye to the scanner. 11,434 pushed some buttons. "I'm giving you a fifteen-minute access. Stay longer than that and you'll be in for the night, too." He laughed.

"Thank you so much," said 1640.

SecuriCells were always located on the higher floors of BusinessBuildings to deter possible window escapes. 1640 took the SkyLift to GemCorp's twenty-fourth floor and used his ordinary ClodronePass to go through the secure door into the HoldingArea. The two cells were up ahead. They would be watching him, of course, the Poldrones. 1640 presented his eye to the CellScanner and then stood back as the door ground open. The room was small, white, and bare. The window was very high up and it was dark outside, but the cell was unpleasantly brightly lit. 1640 couldn't see the light's source, maybe the whole ceiling was a light. The Finn-boy was crouched in a corner, his head buried in his arms. He did not move as 1640 entered, or as the door ground shut behind his visitor.

1640 stood for a moment not knowing quite where to start, and then he said simply: "I've brought you water."

The Finn-boy uncurled then, looked up. The purple sleeves of the ambisuit he was still wearing were darkly smeared. He must have wiped off the remains of his face makeup with them. You could see his own bones now. He looked sad but also, 1640 struggled for the right word, truthful. 1640 held out the blue glass bottle.

The Finn-boy reached for it, unscrewed the lid and drank deeply, drank without, apparently, pausing for breath. Then finally he lifted his head. "Thank you," he said.

There was a silence, and then the Finn-boy said: "I'm sorry about what they did to you. You know, about the splicing, the cells."

"And I'm sorry," said Clodrone 1640, "about your father, about him not coming home."

The Finn-boy nodded slightly.

"But not about your father's cells," continued 1640. "They were good cells. Better than mine maybe. Your father— a good man." And he realized he didn't mean *good* as in Training.

This time the Finn-boy smiled. Not just with his mouth, which 1640 sometimes saw with Igo, but with his eyes. He looked happy. Then the blue clouded over: "What are they going to do to me?"

"Nothing," said 1640.

"What?"

"Because I'm going to let you out," continued 1640 precipitously. "You're going to go free." This was wrong, very wrong indeed. The Finn-boy was a mass murderer, the Finn-boy had tried to attack his Master with a knife. But that smile—1640 wanted to see it again.

"I don't understand," the Finn-boy said.

"I will be you and you will be me," said 1640. He began pulling at his Clodrone brown ambisuit. "You take my suit, I'll take yours. We have fifteen minutes. Maybe only ten now. That's how long my iris scan will open the door. If you're out by then, you can walk away."

"And leave you here?"

"Yes."

"They won't like that. Things will get very bad for you."

"No," said 1640, "I'm being sent for ReTraining anyway. Things don't get worse than that. Not for Clodrones."

"I don't think you need ReTraining," said Stretch. "I think you're fine just the way you are."

"I love you, Finn-boy," said 1640 suddenly, and he meant it. It was nothing to do with Finn or any cell splicing; he, Clodrone 1640, loved this boy. He'd never loved anyone before in his whole life. It was a lurchy feeling, but wonderful, ecstatic. The boy was smiling.

"Are you sure, are you really sure?" the Finn-boy asked.

"Of course. Hurry. We don't have much time."

The boy and the Clodrone exchanged clothes. "Only keep this." 1640 pulled the TropCredit console from the breast pocket of Maxo's ambisuit. "You'll need it. And this also. . . ." He unfastened the thigh pocket on what was now Stretch's suit and took out the knife.

Stretch felt the knife's weight, slid it away. "Thank you," he said.

"Now, let me see." 1640 narrowed his eyes, studied Stretch.

"Do I look okay?"

"Yes."

"No," Stretch cried out, suddenly putting his hand up to his shaved skull. "What about this! They'll see it on the way out. They'll know what we've done."

1640 should have thought of that. He felt defeated.

"What about a Clodrone cap?" asked Stretch. "Don't you have one?"

1640 shook his head. Some Masters liked their Clodrones to wear caps when they were on duty, especially when they were driving, but Igo had never minded, so 1640's cap had stayed, unused, in his pocket.

"Pocket!" burbled 1640.

"What?"

"Pocket!" 1640 scrabbled at the Finn-boy's upper arm. And there it was, in the PectoralPoc, a neatly folded unused brown cap. Stretch pulled it on.

"How do I look now?"

"Perfect," said 1640. He had often heard his Masters use this word but he'd never really felt what it meant before. Now he knew. It was a beautiful thing—like the boy's smile.

"Go," he said, "go now."

"I won't forget this," said Stretch.

1640 iris-scanned the lock and the door ratcheted open

again. He kept out of the line of the cameras as the Finn-boy exited. Within a moment the door shut once more and 1640 was alone.

He sat on the floor. He chose the corner in which the Finn-boy had sat, but he did not put his head in his arms. His hands had stopped flapping. His heart had stopped flapping. He took the empty blue glass water bottle and smashed it against the wall. It broke into three pieces, one of which was large, triangular, and vicious-looking. He'd done some terrible things and if you did terrible things there was always a price to pay. Or that's what he'd been taught. He could wait until they came to get him or he could administer retribution himself. He certainly deserved it, because he'd done wrong and, what's more, he knew he'd done wrong. And then there was ReTraining itself. If they ReTrained him (1640 couldn't suppress an involuntary shudder) he'd forget about the Finn-triggered part of him, wouldn't he? He'd go back to not understanding smiles, not laughing, not ever feeling the lurchy love thing, and 1640 didn't think he could bear that. Which is why he put the glass shard against his left wrist and pressed. When he saw the blood, he began to carve, right and left, right and left. It was the correct thing to do, this carving, he thought, it was the price, and it also allowed Finn and him to remain together, and so he continued, time and again until, finally, he severed a main vein and the piece of glass fell from his lifeless hand.

24

Maxo Evangele Strang was taken back to his apartment in one of the Leaderene's PriorityCars. He was to have unlimited use of the car, the Leaderene said, just as he was to have Compensation and a free MedicalAssess and a place in the Polis GratitudeHonor List; did he understand the distinction being bestowed on him?

Maxo Strang didn't understand much, only the need to be at home, to be somewhere safe. The PriorityCar driver, Clodrone 2204, asked him if he wanted to be accompanied to his front door. Maxo didn't. Maxo wanted to be alone. As he ascended the SkyLift he remembered Bovis. He remembered Lydida. Dead, both of them, like hundreds, thousands of other GemXs. Maxo tried to put his mind around what that meant, he should have had a reaction, he should have known what to think or do. But he didn't. And then there was Edwin Challice. An old man tranquillized as if he was an animal. Why? For what? Maxo felt something large at the back of his throat, a lump he felt he ought to be able to swallow down but he couldn't even do that.

He iris-scanned himself into the apartment. He had to use his left eye because the right one didn't open very well because of the swelling. They'd come to him in the night (who it was who had come, he didn't know) and asked his name. When he said his name was Maxo Strang, they'd hit him. Sometimes it had been with their fists, sometimes with what he thought was wire of some kind. As well as the marks on his face, there were welts across his spine, bruises on the back of his thighs. After awhile he learned not to say his name was Maxo Strang, but as he didn't know what other name to offer, they hit him still. He slept, of course, between the beatings, but only lightly, waiting for the cell door to open again.

Maxo passed through Living Space 1; it looked foreign, it all looked a lifetime away. Maxo was half afraid there were people behind him, but there were no people behind him. The walls changed from neutral to pink. They were trying to enliven him.

There was only one place Maxo wanted to be, his Wash-Space. He wanted to be clean. As he approached his basin mirror, the lights swiveled to give him the best view of himself. He didn't look, just stripped away the Dreggie clothes, stepped into the shower, and pressed the water on. It flowed and flooded over him. The water that fell from his hands was red. The force of the jet when it struck his bruises made him gasp, but he didn't move from the stream. Only when he was clean, when the water had washed over every part of his body, did he stand away, look at his face. His right eye was purple and partially closed. There were cuts to his forehead and swelling to his lower left cheek. And there were also cracks, many, many cracks. Lines that ran into the bruises between his eyes, lines that curved from his nose to his mouth, myriads of tiny lines radiating from his lips. Maxo Evangele Strang looked and looked and he didn't care a bit.

Gala stood on the bottom step of GemCorp InterTrop. Why was she here? It was insane to have left Daz to cope alone in the Estates. Since the TropScreen had announced that Phylo was the Atrocity perpetrator, the bounty hunters had already started banging at their door. And then there were the last batteries and the promise of a pixel unit she'd had to trade for a lift into the Polis. But it had been unbearable to sit in the apartment and think of Stretch in a Gem-Corp SecurityCell. She needed to speak to Dr. Strang in person, speak to him quietly, negotiate her brother's release. And . . .

And . . . had she also come because this is where Maxo would come, to the Lab, to his father? Maxo had cared about her safety, wasn't it right that she should care about his, ensure that he had got home unharmed? Perhaps she needed to say "sorry," too, or "thank you." Or maybe she just needed to look at him again. If you looked at people, not superficially, but right into them, then you knew what they meant. Insanity. Love. His eyes might tell her things; then she could be more sure.

She shook the thoughts from her; right now she had a job to do. She concentrated on the GemCorp entrance. There was a Clodrone coming down the steps and Pol-drones, four of them—just as Stretch had said—patrolling the main doors. She would not be allowed in unhindered. She would have to state her business, say why she'd come and . . . The Clodrone was coming closer, a male, his head down.

"Gala?"

She wheeled in fright—who could know her here?

"Gala," repeated the voice, softer now, amazed. It was coming from beneath the Clodrone cap, from out of the Clodrone mouth, but it wasn't a Clodrone voice, it was her brother's.

"Stretch!" She flung herself around him. "What on earth . . ."

He pushed her roughly away. "Clodrones don't hug," he hissed. And, with a quick backward glance at the Poldrones, who seemed too blind or too stupid to have noticed anything unusual, he whispered: "Quick." Putting his fingers to his lips to silence her, he motioned for her to follow him.

She followed, a welter of conflicting emotions: She was elated because he was clearly free; furious because she'd abandoned Daz when Stretch had so obviously been able to look after himself; agitated and afraid because of his Clodrone disguise and his urgency—where was he taking her? Stretch marched on ahead, saying nothing and not breaking his stride for what seemed like hours as they right-angled their way street after street away from the Lab. He finally stopped in a busy road by a Mescat House.

"Thank you," he said at last, perhaps because she'd kept quiet or perhaps because he knew what it must have cost her to come for him.

"What's going on?" she asked. "What's happened?" He told her everything, about the interview with Strang and the information about Jenks, about the SecuriCell and about Clodrone 1640 bringing him water and letting him go. It all flooded out of him. But there was one question he didn't answer.

"And Maxo?" she asked at last.

"What about him?"

"Is he . . . found?"

"Don't know. Don't care." He looked at his sister. "Do you?"

His tone—his incredulity—stung her. To imagine that Maxo had any real feelings for her was clearly as ludicrous as her having any real feelings for him. She was obviously just hanging on to the idea as you might hang on to a piece of string if you didn't have any rope in your life. "No," she said, "of course not."

"Good, let's get in the Mescat House."

"What—why?"

"It's where Jenks will be. The man who donated next in line to Dad. I told you I saw him here. This is the Mescat House he was in."

But that was hours ago, thought Gala, and he might not even be the same Jenks, but she said nothing, for she saw the fire in Stretch's eyes. This was obviously Stretch's little piece of string, and she knew what it was to be denied.

Stretch led Gala to the segregated Naturals' entrance of the Mescat House.

"Don't," said Stretch, looking at her face. "Just go in."

It was difficult to get in for the press of people. The air was hazy and the mood upbeat. Be here, Jenks. Please be here. Stretch edged his way in, clearing a way for Gala behind him. There were enough Clodrones here for him not to feel out of place, but most of the people were Naturals, workers from the PodEstates, Stretch supposed, men and women who preferred to pay sky-high rents for minuscule spaces in the Polis during the week to save on the hassle of having to line at the Borders on a daily basis.

Stretch scanned the room. There were many fewer tables this side of the bar; it was fine for Naturals to stand, he supposed bitterly, you could pack more of them in that way. But it was only a moment before he was glad of the tables because it allowed him to spot, in the far corner, the unmistakable outline of Jenks. He and his male companion had obviously been in the bar long enough to get seats.

"That's him. I knew he'd still be here. I knew it." Stretch pushed his way through the throng. "Let me do the talking." That wasn't to say he wasn't grateful to have Gala by him. More than grateful—she'd used the last of her hoarded treasures to be here. But he couldn't dwell on that now, it would choke him up.

"Excuse me," he began with Clodrone politeness, when they arrived at the table, "Mr. Jenks, isn't it?"

The man lifted a rather sodden face. "What?"

"It's Mr. Jenks, isn't it?" repeated Stretch.

"Is it?" asked Jenks. The colored part of his eyes looked hard and glassy, a characteristic of the long-term mescat drinker.

"Do I know you?" asked Jenks.

"No," said Stretch quickly.

"I'm sure I do," said Jenks.

"You know everybody when you've had a few," said his companion amiably.

"Shut up, Pavel," said Jenks. "The man's talking."

"The Clodrone's talking," said Pavel.

"Don't mind my friend," said Jenks, "he's a little . . ." Jenks poked a slightly shaky finger at his temple and nodded conspiratorially. "What can I do for you?"

"It's about a friend of mine," said Stretch, "I mean, a friend of Gala here's." He indicated his sister.

"Doesn't the doll speak?" asked Jenks.

"Why keep a dog and bark yourself?" said Gala quickly. Stretch looked aghast—too aghast for a Clodrone—but the men were well oiled so they just laughed.

"Finn," said Gala, "Finn Lorrell, do you know him?"

"Nope," said Jenks, "can't say I do."

"Not now," said Stretch, "four years ago, when there was the last Clean Gene Appeal?"

"He can't remember what he had for breakfast," said Pavel, "let alone what happened four years ago."

"Hang on, hang on," said Jenks. "Four years ago, you say. And I knew him, did I?"

"Yes," said Stretch. "At least I think so, if you were the Jenks that went to donate that afternoon."

"Yeah. I donated."

"Okay"—Stretch breathed in—"according to the records you both arrived at the hospital at roughly the same time, must have lined up together, were signed out at the same time."

"What name did you say?"

"Finn. Finn Lorrell."

"Oh, Finn." Jenks banged a feeble fist on the table. "Course I remember. What's to forget! Best night of my life, that was. Finn Lorrell—what a man!"

"Tell us," Gala couldn't help crying out.

"Well, we donated, like you said, took the money, like you do, and well, had a few."

"Finn Lorrell," said Stretch tightly, "spent the money on drink?"

"I should say. Yeah. He had a few. Had a few more. We all did. Then we went to the Spinning Wheel."

"The Spinning Wheel?"

"You know, the really glitzy GamblaDome, where they have that giant four-tier roulette table and you can win a million. Not feligs, TropCredits. One million smackeroonies."

"Only no one does," said Pavel.

"Lorrell did," said Jenks.

"What—won a million!" Stretch asked.

"Quarter of a million. He got a quarter of the big one."

"And what then?" cried Gala.

"Then we all had a few more drinks." Jenks laughed.

"Quite a few," added Pavel.

"You were there, too?" asked Stretch.

"I think so."

"You think so?"

"None of us remembered very much in the morning."

"Morning!" Jenks scoffed. "You didn't have a morning. You was passed out for forty-eight hours afterward."

"So?" riposted Pavel. "At least I walked out the Spinning Wheel."

"Staggered," corrected Jenks.

"Whereas you, you were thrown out. You left head first!"

"But what happened to our . . . my . . ." Gala's head seemed to be rolling. "What happened to Finn Lorrell?"

"Don't rightly know," said Jenks. "He wasn't thrown out.

Don't think. But I never saw him after. Mind you I never saw 'im before that day either."

"I reckon he took the money and ran," said Pavel. "The ones that have the most, they're always the tightest."

Jenks waved his empty glass somewhere between Gala and Stretch, "D'you think you could, you know, see us right?"

Gala looked alarmed, but Stretch immediately put his hand up to 1640's ambisuit breast pocket and felt the slim outline of the CreditLog. Bless the man, he had left Stretch his Master's money.

"Sure," said Stretch, and he headed straight for the bar, using the line to think. If this story was true why wouldn't Finn have come home? What a thing to come home with—a quarter of a million TropCredits! Stretch tried to imagine his father walking out of the Spinning Wheel, the money burning in his pockets. Maybe someone had followed him, challenged him, murdered him for the Credits! No, no, no. Too CrimeFlik again. Besides, there would have been a body. It was much more likely that Jenks had just confused Finn with someone else or simply invented the whole story. He bought the drinks and returned to the table.

"Cheers, mate," said Jenks. "Who says you Clodrones aren't the generous sort?"

"One more thing," said Stretch. "Can you tell me where the Spinning Wheel is?"

25

Outside the Mescat House, Gala said, "We need to get back."

"But we're so close now, Gala, can't you see that? And they said it's only a few blocks."

"A few blocks and four long years!"

"Are you afraid?" he challenged her then.

And she realized suddenly that she was. If they got to the truth and that truth was that her father was dead, then the matter was closed. There would be no more hope.

There was a pause, and then he said simply, "Please, Gala—for me."

"But Daz . . ."

"He'll cope."

Once more they headed across the Polis. The Estates were dark at night, even when the electricity was on. Here streetlights blazed. The walk was not far and Gala was glad of the night air. Stretch was glad of the other Clodrones on the streets, obviously out running errands for their Masters. They nodded at him as he passed, a conspiracy of the unseen. No one else was in the least interested in what was going on beneath his brown Clodrone cap and his brown Clodrone ambisuit.

The Spinning Wheel was right at the heart of the Entertainment District: here were GamblaDomes, Virtual Date Palaces, ElectricFlik Houses and hundreds of PoppaPill Joints. All these places were lit in cascades of multicolored neon, but the Spinning Wheel topped them all with a hundred gyrating rooftop rings of gold. The rings seemed to melt in and out of one another, disappearing for a moment only to reappear like liquid fire against the night sky. It was mesmerizing, Stretch thought, his head in the air.

The steps to the front entrance were ballroom, a wide sweep of white marble with a red carpet so plush their feet half disappeared as they ascended. At the entrance they were cursorily inspected by two middle-aged men in sharply cut, slightly military-looking uniforms of red and gold. The men wore breeches, polished black boots, gold braid, and shining black-peaked caps. Where an ambisuit had a breast pocket, these suits had the Spinning Wheel crest (four interlocking gold rings) and the embroidered word "Flunkey" followed by a number. They were interacting with Flunkeys 12 and 31.

"Proceed," Flunkey 12 announced.

They proceeded. The GamblaDome itself was designed as a series of concentric rings, leading, Stretch presumed, to the central roulette chamber. The outer ring was dominated by the ping and zing of electronic slot machines. If they weren't being played they spoke to you as you passed: "Hey, winner, I just feel it's your lucky night." Or there might be a sultry woman's voice: "Hi, handsome, are you looking for me tonight?" Every few minutes there would be the sound of cascading coins, or TropCredit tokens as Gala saw they were when some fell to the floor in front of her. She thought of these credits, hundreds of thousands of them in her father's hands.

Flunkey 26 sidled up behind Stretch. "Want to play?" he asked softly, and he picked up a couple of tokens from the floor and handed them back to a breathless, glassy-eyed man sitting at the VirtualSectorSex Machine. "So much to play for."

"No," said Stretch rather too fast. "I'm on business. I need to find someone, someone for . . . my Master."

"This is not a MeetZone," said Flunkey 26, "this is a PlayZone. You come here to play, to have fun." He paused. "Even Clodrones need fun."

"I want to speak to someone, someone who's been working here at least four years. Maybe you've been here that long?"

"One forgets how long one's been here," said Flunkey 26. He turned to Gala. "Can I get you a drink?"

"Finn Lorrell," said Gala precipitously. "Does that name mean anything to you? He won money. Quite a lot of money. Four years ago."

"Ah," Flunkey 26 sighed. "He won't have it now."

"Why not?"

"Do you want tokens?" said Flunkey 26. "I can exchange TropCredits for tokens."

"No," said Stretch. "We want information."

"Wrong place," said Flunkey 26. "Wrong time." And he moved away, zeroing in on another client who wasn't yet playing, paying.

They continued on to the next ring; it was quieter here, but still very bright, as bright as it had been in the Securi-Cell. Stretch thought of Clodrone 1640 then, he hoped he

238

could sleep in that brightness. In this ring the men (it was mainly men) were playing cards. They sat in alcoves, a Flunkey at each table, vials of mescat sparkling beside them. As all the Flunkeys here seemed occupied, they passed unhindered through to the inner chamber. It was a huge room, domed like an OldTime cathedral. Suspended from the very center of the dome, like some gigantic chandelier, was the four-tiered Roulette Wheel. Now he saw it, Stretch remembered people in the Estates talking of this wheel but, as you had to have TropCredits to play, few people had actually been here, so they spoke of it as a dream, a vision. And it was a kind of vision, Stretch thought, as he stood a moment, dazzled. Each of the gyrating roulette tiers was a different set of colors, black and green for the smallest top tier, black and red for the next layer down, then black and pale blue and, finally, black and gold. Each of the numbers on each of the first three layers had a tiny hole beside it. When the highest croupier, the one controlling the top layer, released the ball (or balls, there seemed to be maybe five or six balls falling at any one time), the wheels revolved and undulated with an extraordinary hypnotic rhythm. They watched the circles slew this way and that. But the most extraordinary thing was not the mesmerizing wheels but the mesmerized people. There were hundreds of them suspended in rings at the four different levels, strapped into chairs from which there seemed to be no escape. They were literally floating about the wheels. Stretch had no idea how the chair rings worked, but the look on the gamblers' faces was of maddened exhilaration. All the chairs were taken and there was a long line at each of the levels for the first available seat.

"Place your bets," screamed the Croupiers, who were also Flunkeys, only these ones were women. "Place your bets now!"

There was the frenzied sound of TropCredits being downloaded from ambisuit pockets all around the room.

"Balls go," shouted the top-level Croupier, a big, blonde Flunkey. Out of nowhere there was a crescendo of music and the frantic flash of strobe lights as gold ball after gold ball twirled and fell.

"We have a winner," screamed the Croupier.

"Which level line do you wish to join, sir?" said a tone-less voice at Stretch's shoulder.

"I . . . ," said Stretch, turning his attention from the frantic brightness of the flying rings to the Flunkey beside him and unable to focus for a minute. "We're not looking to line up, we just need some information."

"If you're not playing," said the Flunkey in his flat way, "I must ask you to leave the RouletteRoom." His face was shadowed beneath the black peak of his uniform cap. "For safety reasons no spectators are permitted."

"Please . . . ," began Gala. The Flunkey—22 according to his breast insignia—was taller than her brother, but his body seemed to have been crushed into a too small suit, or maybe, Gala thought inconsequentially, that it wasn't that the suit didn't fit him but rather that he didn't fit the suit. "We're trying to locate someone . . ."

"I'm sorry," said the Flunkey, "please follow me." He turned, trying to lead Stretch back to the outer rings of the GamblaDome.

"Finn," Stretch said. "Finn Lorrell."

Flunkey 22 stopped in his tracks, his feet planted on the

floor as if they had taken root. The chief Croupier called "Balls go," and there was the clash of music and the flash of strobes.

"Do you know him?"

Flunkey 22 turned around then, turned slowly like a corkscrew and seemed to lengthen in the process, grow taller. For the first time he looked out from beneath the rim of the cap. His eyes were a startling blue.

In his gaze, Stretch and Gala stood transfixed. Seconds passed, which seemed liked hours.

"Papa?" said Gala at last, only the word didn't come out quite right, as most of it seemed to be sticking to the back of her throat.

The man beneath the cap looked on and on, drinking them in. "Is it you?" he whispered at last. "Oh, my darlings, is it really you?"

Above them, the roulette wheels spun, the gamblers hovered, and the tiny gold balls kept on falling, falling.

"Flunkey 22," said a commanding voice behind them both, "are you helping this customer to a line?"

"This customer doesn't want to line up," said Stretch without taking his eyes from Finn. "He wants to talk to his f—"

"Friend," interrupted Finn immediately and inexplicably. "We're friends."

So Stretch never got to say the word *father* and maybe he wouldn't have been able to say it anyway, given how his whole body was shaking.

"This is WorkTime, 22, not RelaxHour, get back on the job." The man, who was wearing a red dinner suit, was obviously some kind of manager. If Stretch had been in control of his limbs he might have reached down, taken the knife from his boot, and stabbed the man through the heart.

"I'm due a break," said Finn Lorrell, his tone drained again, respectful. "I've been working for seven hours without a break." And then he added, "sir."

The manager pointed a LoggoWand at the Flunkey's number, ran a scan, humphed. "I'll give you ten minutes," he said. "If you're not back on duty by then, you'll forfeit half a day's pay."

"Thank you," said Finn Lorrell, and the deferential way he bowed his head made Gala's heart hurt.

"Place your bets, place your bets," screamed the Croupiers.

Gala realized then she'd never imagined this moment, never really believed that her father could be alive and not have made his way back to them.

"Shall we go outside?" Finn asked at last.

He led the way out of the jangling rooms. A gambler stopped him in the card room to ask a question. "Don't speak to him!" Stretch begged of Finn, and then he said to the man, "He's off duty!" But Finn patiently, quietly, flatly, gave the man the directions he required. Stretch could hardly breathe. The shock was still electric in him. His head was like one of the gyrating wheels and his brain the little balls, falling through.

After a lifetime's walk they arrived outside. Finn walked down the flight of steps, out of the bright lights, stopping only when there was a little shadow.

"Let me look at you both," he said then, and he drank them in all over again. "You're so grown," he said, "so grown-up."

"Is that all you can say!" Stretch exploded finally, the suddenness and the ferocity of his anger taking him by surprise.

"Stretch . . . ," began Gala. She couldn't bear it if, after such a long separation, there was to be bitterness.

"What is it you need me to say?" asked Finn quietly.

"Something!" spluttered Stretch. "Some explanation! All these years and we didn't know if you were alive or dead! Have you any idea what that feels like? Why didn't you at least just say, send a message. Something!"

"I just . . . couldn't."

"Couldn't? Why couldn't you? The not knowing—it's nearly killed our mother!" he claimed on Perle's behalf, because it was Perle who had wept, but he was also talking about himself. "Did you never think of that? And . . ."

"Let him speak," cried Gala, "for pity's sake let him speak."

But for long moments, Finn seemed either unable or unwilling to speak, then finally he said, "I think of your mother from the moment I wake till the moment I sleep again. And I think of you, Phylo. And you, Gala. And Daz. In fact the only reason I keep on getting up, going on, is because of you. Because I know that you are all still free," he paused, "even if I am not."

"I don't understand."

Finn shook his head, or maybe it was a shudder that passed through him. Then he reached out his hand and touched the Clodrone suit: "Phylo—what is this, why are you wearing this suit?"

"Don't change the subject. It's not important!" But it was important, it was part of the journey that had brought

Stretch here. If he wasn't careful, Gala thought, Stretch was going to cry. He was going to become ten years old again. A boy who wanted to tell his father everything.

Finn waited as if the Clodrone tale was more important than his.

"It's a long story," conceded Stretch. "But I'm hiding. Because of the lies on the TropScreen. Is everyone too fuddled to look at a TropScreen in the GamblaDome? I, Phylo Lorrell, am Most Wanted. I apparently committed the Atrocity at the hospital."

"You did that?"

"Of course not!" How could his father think that even for a moment? Finn Lorrell always knew what was right, what was wrong. "Where are you at, Papa? We have ten minutes. Talk to me! Tell us what happened, where you've been, what's going on. Tell us everything."

"Of course. You deserve to know. But it's not a good story."

"It'll be all right," said Gala, and she held out her hand to him. But he didn't take it, just shrank away into the dark, leaned against the shadowed wall of the GamblaDome. "That day I came to donate," he began, "we were hours waiting. I was one of the last to get called. One of the lucky ones." Here he paused and a bitter sound came out of his mouth. "How wonderful those few TropCredits looked in my hands. A small plastic docket with a few golden credits coded on. Finn Lorrell's recompense."

"Only you used them on drink," said Stretch savagely.

"Stretch . . ."

"Yes," said Finn. "I did."

244

"And then you came here to the Spinning Wheel," continued Stretch, "to blow some more."

If Stretch hadn't been here, would the anger have fallen to her, Gala wondered? No, she just wanted to scoop her father up, hold him, he looked so bereft.

"Yes, I came here," Finn said. "How did you know?"

"People talk," said Stretch. "They also say you won a quarter of a million."

"Not quite. But near enough. I took a four-tier bet. The numbers, not the colors, the highest bet you can make on numbers alone. One, thirty-seven, seventy-four, ninety-eight. Afterward they told me the odds on those four numbers coming up were over nine million to one."

"But you did win?"

"Yes. I won."

"And then?"

"Then I lost. Lost everything."

"I don't understand."

"I had a few drinks. Of course. I was euphoric. Such things don't happen to people like me. I was just a Scavenger, a rubbish merchant, but I'd take home to Perle the biggest prize of all, a one-way ticket out of the Estates."

Gala wanted him to stop there. She wanted the story to have another ending.

"Only I had another drink," said Finn.

"And another, no doubt," said Stretch.

"They asked me to play again. The management, they said everyone did, it was traditional. All big winners got a free roll, to double their money. One chance only. GamblaDome policy."

"You never fell for that!"

"I chose again. It didn't matter if your numbers didn't come up, they didn't mind. It was a free roll."

"And your numbers didn't come up again," said Gala.

"But they did, that's the point. My numbers came up again. And then I had another drink. And then I thought I couldn't lose. That I'd take your mother home a million."

"Only next time you lost," Stretch breathed. "You must have seen it coming. The oldest trick in the book!"

"Only I didn't just lose the initial stake—but another ten thousand Trops on top. I borrowed more than I had. Because I wanted it exactly—the full million."

"They had you!" Stretch cried. "It's what the Enhanced do, it's the Plastics-Take-All way of life. They had you!"

"No," said Finn Lorrell, "I had me. My greed. That's all it was."

Such a small flaw, thought Gala.

"They got you drunk!" There was something desperate in Stretch's voice.

"I got me drunk."

"But it's a fix, a scam." Stretch was shouting again. "Like everything in this Polis. It's all lies. Flimflam. Dad . . ." He wanted his father back again, he wanted Finn to be the man waving the flag on top of the GarbageDump. *There are things that are right and things that are wrong, son.*

The four interlocking gold rings on Flunkey 22's suit began to glow.

"What's that?" asked Stretch.

"My warning bell. My ten minutes are almost up." Finn Lorrell stood up.

"You're not going back in there," said Stretch defiantly.

"I am," said Finn Lorrell. "I will be going back in there every day for the next eight years. That's how long it will take me to pay off the debt."

"Come home," said Gala, "come home. I beg you come home."

"I can't," said Finn.

"She will forgive you," said Gala. Is that what he was afraid of? "Mama will forgive you."

"But I will not forgive myself. Besides, I have given a false name here. If they knew my real identity, they could go to the Estates and take what little the family has. Against the debt. That's the way it works."

"We have nothing to take!"

"You have your liberty."

"What?"

Finn looked about him, lowered his voice to a barely audible whisper. "I've had to sign things. Swear I have no family. It's the GamblaDome's policy to have debts paid off as quickly as possible. If they knew you existed they could take you, your labor. You'd have to come here to work, Phylo, you and Gala and—as soon as he's thirteen—Daz, too."

"They can't do that, Dad. It's not right."

"It's not right, son, but it's what happens here."

"Then you've got to fight it—we've got to fight it!"

"With what?" asked Finn.

"They've crushed you!"

"I made a mistake," said Finn. "I did something wrong and now I'm paying for it." He pulled himself up, stood taller. "They have taken many things from me but my dignity is not one of them." For a brief instant there was a flash of the former man. "Now, at least," Finn said, "I am doing what is right."

"You have to come home," Gala said doggedly. "Mama is ill. Very ill."

"I know," said Finn.

"You know!" repeated Gala.

"She's going to die," said Stretch brutally. "Do you know that?"

"Yes," said Finn.

"And yet you still won't come?"

"I tell you, they are without mercy. They will take everything."

"Mama doesn't have anything," said Gala, "except you."

"Of course she does. She has you. You and your brothers. Do you think I don't know how you look after her? Bless you, Gala. Bless you forever. And you, too, Phylo."

"How can you know?"

So Finn Lorrel finally told them. "One day, every week, I don't eat. With the money I save I can afford, once a month, to get information about you. Gubbins, you know Gubbins who gives your brother paints? He sends word, though he doesn't know it's me to whom the word is coming. Just a few details, a snapshot, a postcard of how you are, how your mother is, what Daz is painting this week." He paused. "That's how I survive, by holding all the pictures in my mind."

"And you couldn't have sent us one picture," pressed Stretch relentlessly. "One message. To say you were okay. Just one."

"I'm not okay," said Finn. "And I knew you'd come for me. I *know* you, Phylo. I couldn't chance it."

"Well, we're here now."

"Yes. And it's almost too much. Almost unbearable."

Gala flung herself at him then, but he fended her off again, pushed her away.

"Don't think I don't want to hold you," he said hoarsely. "Hug you. Kiss you. You, too, Phylo. But I know if I held you for just one minute I couldn't go on, do what I have to do. I'd just lie down here on the pavement and die."

The interlocking rings glowed a final time.

"Dad . . . ," began Stretch.

"No," said Finn. "I beg you, let me do it my own way." He paused. "I shall pretend that you never came. It was just a dream. The most marvelously beautiful, impossible dream. Now go. You are still in danger."

And when they wouldn't go, Finn went. Walked back up the plush ballroom steps into the GamblaDome. Gala cried out for him to turn around one final time, but he did not.

Daz sat by the front door of the apartment, or rather he sat by the space where the front door had been.

How many "visitors" had they had since the TropScreen had announced that Phylo Lorrell was responsible for the Atrocity? He didn't know, no longer remembered. The early ones had come in pairs, men mainly, big men who claimed to be "friends" of Phylo's, who just wanted to "see if he was all right."

Gala had still been at home then.

"How dare they!" she had exclaimed. "Bounty Hunters. They're sick."

"How did they get our address?" Daz had asked.

She'd called him naive. People in the Estates had few

enough ways of making money, she'd said, to disregard the value of information. If the price was right, there was always someone who knew someone who knew the answer.

"Don't open the door," Gala had said after the first visitation. "Don't open it, Daz."

The bell didn't work, so the men had hammered with their fists.

In her room Perle had shaken with the noise.

Daz had opened the door. "He's not here. Sorry."

The men were disbelieving, they had moved from the apartment entrance but not from the building. They'd hung about in the stairwell, they'd watched who came and who went.

And then Gala had gone.

"You'll be all right," she had said. "Stretch needs me. I have to go."

Daz had looked at her.

"Just don't open the door to them. It'll be all right, Daz. I promise you."

It was less than an hour after Gala had left that the hammering began again.

"Let them in," called Perle from her bed. "What have we to hide? If they see he isn't here, maybe they'll go away."

There were three men this time, dark skinned and bearded, Migrasylas, Gala thought, economic refugees from some other Trop.

"We can offer a place of safety," the front man began.

"For a price," said a second, smaller man.

"Take him somewhere where no one will find him."

"Leave us alone," said Daz. "My mother is ill, leave us alone."

"They'll find him," said the third man. "If we don't find him, the Plastics will. Do you want that?"

Daz didn't want that, of course not. But he couldn't quite believe what was happening. Phylo was innocent! How could the Trop hold him if he was innocent?

"Go away," he said, and he shut the door.

The next visitors didn't bother to knock. There were seven of them and they simply kicked the door in. They were all wearing black and, at their throats, they each had a tattoo of a crystal vial. Members of the MesCat Gang.

"Where is he?" Their leader was a thin, blond youth with glassy eyes. As he spoke, his Adam's apple bobbed so that the vial at his throat seemed to be throbbing. Beneath the throb his name was tattooed: Acid.

Perle struggled into the hall and stood alongside Daz.

"Have you no shame?" she asked.

"Shame?" Acid spat. "Wozzat?" He laughed. Then he turned to his fellow gang members. "Let's go, boys!"

The black-clad youths howled and whooped as they pushed past mother and son and began to ransack each room in turn. There was little enough to disturb, but they disturbed it all. They wrenched the kitchen cupboard doors off their hinges and threw china against the walls; they strew clothes from the makeshift wardrobes on the floor; they kicked over chairs and upended beds. The bottle of dark medicine the doctor had prescribed for Perle fell from beneath Gala's mattress and smashed on the floor.

Perle watched as the liquid—her poison, her release— soaked into the floorboards.

"Oops," said one of the gang. "Sorry."

251

Daz ran then, squared himself in front of the door to his own room. The three MesCats that pushed past him barely registered his presence, they seemed to walk straight over him, through him.

"What's this?" asked a thickset, grinning boy, with the word *Bull* at his throat.

It was Daz's painting on a sheet, his fabulous sun of red and gold. "Please leave it, please, I beg you. It's all I have."

From somewhere near his ankle Bull extracted a small knife with a curved and shining blade. He poked the knife in the heart of picture and then tore the sheet in half: It made a satisfying ripping noise. "Well, you don't have it now."

"Phylo is not here," Daz screamed then. "He's not here!"

"Then where is he?" said Bull. "You must know."

"I don't," said Daz. "He left." And then, because Gala had left him in charge, he added quickly, "Do you think he'd tell us where he was going? 'What you don't know you can't tell,' that's what he said."

"Liar," said Bull amiably.

"Any luck?" Acid came into the room, throat bobbing.

"Done some lovely ripping," said Bull.

"I'm talking the main target," said Acid. "Lorrell—any sign of Lorrell?"

"Ner. He's bolted. But I'd say Baby Face here knows where he is. And"—he leaned toward Daz—"with a little encouragement . . ." The knife shot up toward Daz's neck.

Labored breathing announced the arrival of Perle. "Leave him alone," she said.

"Sure," said Bull, and he spun his bulk around as if he was a dancer. The knife ended up at Perle's throat.

Daz saw the blade wink, he saw his mother close her eyes.

"Phylo's in the Polis," he shouted. "He's gone to Gem-Corp, Dr. Igo Strang's Lab."

"Daz!" cried Perle.

"Oh," said Bull disappointed. "So easy. And I was rather looking forward to a bit more ripping." His knife hand fell away.

Perle opened her eyes. "You're disgusting," she said to the youths.

"Oh yeah?"

"Phylo's one of us."

"Us?" queried Bull, looking about him. "The only *us* is the MesCats."

"Come on," said Acid. "We got what we came for. Let's go."

As they left, Perle choked at their backs: "One of us. A Natural. You should be supporting him, not leeching off him."

Acid turned back. "You know nothing, but you have a big mouth, mother, I suggest you keep it closed."

"I . . . ," began Perle, but was unable to continue for the hand around her jaw. The hand was Daz's.

"Glad to know there's one smart member of the family," said Acid, and with a few final random kicks at the corridor wall, the Gang left.

Daz let his mother go and dropped to his knees by the torn sheet.

"Is that all you care about?" Perle breathed. "Your painting? You told them where Stretch is! How could you!"

Daz looked up from the floor. "He would have used that knife." He paused. "Besides, they won't be able to get to Stretch at the Lab. They have Poldrones there. Unlike us."

253

Perle steadied herself against a wall. "I apologize," she said.

Which Daz couldn't bear, so he said quickly: "Anyway, Gala will talk Stretch out of the cells. She will. She'll bring him back safely."

"You think? You think Phylo is all right, he'll be all right?" He heard the desperation in his mother's voice.

"Gala promised, didn't she?"

But neither of them quite believed it.

Daz righted his mother's bed and Perle crept, in silence, beneath a cover. Daz took half his picture and sat by the smashed door. He'd been made man of the family and he'd failed.

26

Gala and Stretch were still on the steps of the Gambla-Dome.

"I'll wait for him," said Stretch. "They can't make him work every hour, day and night. I'll wait till he's off duty."

"He won't come home with us," said Gala. Her brother didn't understand, wouldn't understand. "You heard him. He's made his decision."

"But it's all wrong!"

Right, wrong, Gala was beginning to feel she didn't know which was which anymore. Just as she couldn't tell whether her father was a strong or a weak man. She'd wanted him to be a hero, Stretch had always talked of him as a hero, as if his return would make everything right in their world. Yet here he was, flawed but also obstinate, still holding out, in his small way, for what he believed in. Perhaps one could only do what one could do. Which is why she needed to get back. "Daz," she said, "we need to get back for Daz."

"You go," said Stretch. "I'll stay."

"No. It's not safe for you in the Polis. You know that."

"With what you said about the Bounty Hunters," said

Stretch, "it's not safe for me at home. At least here I'm invisible. Nobody looks at a Clodrone, Gala."

There was some truth in that, but she needed Stretch to be with her now. She couldn't bear any more losses.

The TropScreen behind them, which had been blaring on inconsequentially, burst into MajorAnnouncement life.

"Atrocity perpetrator apprehended," screamed the Announcer.

Stretch and Gala turned—astonished. They weren't the only ones, immediately a crowd began to gather.

"The Leaderene, may her name celeb forever, is proud to announce that due to SupremeVigilance, the suspected Atrocity perpetrator, Phylo Lorrell, has been taken into Isolation by the InternalSecurity Forces."

"Bravo," shouted an ambisuited figure beside Stretch.

"Isolation's too good for him," roared another. "Raze him!"

"Raze the Estates!"

"What!" exclaimed Stretch.

"Shh," said Gala. "Ssh." Quickly, she drew him aside, whispered, "It's good, don't you see?"

"It's a lie!"

"But if everyone thinks you're already locked up, they won't be looking for you anymore, will they? You can come home."

"You think? You're as mad as they are. I'm not locked up. They must know that. It must be a ruse, a ploy. To get me off my guard. To get me home. That must be what they want!"

He was as intransigent as her father. "Right," she said at last, "well, it's a long walk back and I at least have to start."

"You don't have to walk," said Stretch.

"No?" said Gala. "Thanks to you, I'm clean out of bribes, remember?"

Stretch tapped his breast pocket. "Call it a gift from Clodrone 1640."

He hailed a car.

"Stretch . . ."

"I will come back, Gala. I promise you that."

Stretch gave the driver the address and presented 1640's CreditLog for payment details.

Gala wanted to hold him, to say a proper good-bye—perhaps because her father had denied her and the ache was still in her arms. But, as Stretch had previously made clear, Clodrones neither hug or are hugged. So she just had to drive away.

Stretch stood on the street until the car was out of sight. He was surprised by how very alone he suddenly felt. It would no doubt be a long time until the end of his father's shift. He would go back to the Mescat House.

After all that had happened, he deserved a drink, didn't he?

Maxo Evangele Strang lay on the MassageCouch of Living Space 1 in his favorite black ambisuit. The couch was trying to entice him "to take some relaxation," but he was too bruised, so he shut the couch off. He had put on the black ambisuit in an effort to feel normal, but he did not feel normal, as evidenced by the walls around him, which were finding it so difficult to program his mood that they were shifting uneasily between various shades of soothing green and jollying pink. The only thing that seemed obliviously unchanged was the TropScreen and the voice of the Announcer who was updating the Trop on different aspects of the Atrocity. There was to be a mass GemX funeral apparently, arranged by none other than his own GenMa, Glora Orb, which meant, Maxo thought, not without bitterness, that she wouldn't answer her 'cator (and he'd checked using the landline) for hours if not days. His GenPap's 'cator was registering "incommunicado," which meant Igo Strang was probably traveling in some part of the Trop currently suffering a network suspension—a fact borne out by Maxo's call to the Lab. Igo Strang's AnsaMach informed him that the chief scientist of GemCorp InterTrop was "not in the Lab at this time," and advised him, very politely, "to try again later."

On another day, in another life, Maxo might have called Bovis. But Bovis was dead. He might even have called Lydida. But Lydida was dead. Maxo lay and lay and looked at his hands. There was a pattern of lines on them not unlike the pattern of OldTime honeycomb, only slightly less regular. It was quite pretty, Maxo thought hollowly.

NewsFlash, shouted the Announcer. *Intensive investigation by the Trop's Senior Security Team has revealed that Atrocity perpetrator, Phylo Lorrell, was not working in isolation. InternalSecurity, headed for this Emergency by Fikk Powell . . .*

Chavit, wondered Maxo, what happened to Chavit?

. . . believe there may be up to a dozen other insurgents working in close collaboration with Lorrell. . . .

The footage cut to a small, brutal-looking man in a dark green and military gold ambisuit outside HighCommand. *Earlier Mr. Powell had this to say. . . .* The man opened his tight little mouth: *"Apprehending these Treasoners is a Priority-One. The Leaderene, may her name celeb forever, has sanctioned all measures to this effect. . . ."*

Maxo sat up, the walls jangled green and yellow. Where had he heard that anodyne little phrase *"all measures to this effect"* before? At Bovis's apartment, after the last Atrocity, that was it, exactly the same announcement had been made and the next thing they knew was that RazeMachines were rolling into the Estates. Fourteen Dreggie blocks had been flattened. The residents had been given five minutes to vacate their homes. Bovis and Maxo had drunk mescat while they watched.

"Let's have a vial for every block that goes down," Bovis had said.

And Maxo had laughed. He had laughed and drunk a Vintage Six.

Now he was on his feet. The Security Forces would go to Gala's block, of course they would, that would be the first to be razed, the Perpetrator's own block. It would be a warning. It would be revenge. And Gala?

Gala would die.

Did he still care about her? No, of course not. Gala had made her feelings—or lack of them—extremely clear. But then there was her foot, her little tiny foot. . . . But it wasn't even that, no. It was the unfairness, the fact that he knew Gala's brother could not be the Perpetrator. It was about the truth.

Maxo Strang had never had to examine the truth before. He'd always just accepted that things were the way they were, never questioned the natural order of things. Natural. The Enhanced order of things! How could he have been so

259

blind? He put a hand up to his swollen eye. They'd punched him in the eye and now he saw more clearly.

He pushed back his tiredness and made for the SkyLift. The PriorityCar was waiting where he'd left it on the street outside his building. He stepped in and ordered the driver to take him immediately to the Estates, Block 213. He hoped he wouldn't be too late.

Rumors were rolling into the Estates faster than any Raze-Machines. There was so much activity on the low-level 'cator frequency that the networks jammed and were temporarily suspended. Half messages and half-truths abounded.

Daz, using Edwin Challice's 'cator, was "reliably" informed (before the networks went down) that there were at least fifteen RazeMachines on their way.

"At least one of them," his informant told him, "is apparently a remote-controlled, armor-plated RazeAll with swamp treads and a twin-shank ripper."

Daz walked in the apartment; paced. Up and down. Up and down.

On the back of the rumors there was frenetic activity in the block. Those above and below the Lorrells were packing things, moving things, clearing out. Through the open door of the apartment, Daz could hear grunts of anger and fatigue coming from the stairwell. Some of their neighbors stopped long enough to shout: "If the RazeMachines don't get you, Phylo Lorrell, we'll be back for you!"

A while later Gubbins, the old man from Floor 12 who traded paints with Daz in exchange for Daz running his errands, came by.

"I would knock," he said, looking at the kicked-in door. Daz nodded, there was nothing to say.

"I'm sorry," Gubbins continued, "about, you know, Phylo."

"And I'm sorry," said Daz, "about everyone having to leave . . . you having to leave."

"Well, they might never come," the old man said. "But, if they do, well, I never liked the twelfth floor much, as you know. Maybe I'll get better luck next time."

"Yes," said Daz.

"Look, I know it's hardly the time." Gubbins had something in his hands, two small tubes. He held them out. "Prussian blue and titanium white," he said. "Probably more than you'll want to carry, but . . ."

"Thank you," said Daz. "Thank you so much."

The old man nodded. "You'll be all right, I think you'll be all right. There are people, you know, looking out for you."

"You think?" Daz gestured at the devastated apartment.

"Yes. Well, maybe. One never knows. Hope, that's the thing."

"Suppose so," said Daz.

"Bye then." Gubbins and his small suitcase continued their slow way down the last four flights of stairs.

Daz sat twiddling the tubes; he unscrewed the white and smelled it.

He should take his mother. He should be taking charge, getting out. But where would they go? And, if they went, how would Gala and Stretch ever find them?

Daz opened the Prussian blue, smelled that.

* * *

Gala ran up a flight of stairs that everyone else was bumping down with whatever they owned closed up in cases or tied up with string.

"What's going on?"

"RazeTanks. They're sending RazeTanks!"

Gala ran faster. She came to the ex-door of her apartment, saw a young boy smelling paint. She only had to look at her brother's face and see the first of the mayhem in the hall to guess what had happened.

"Oh, Daz. I'm so sorry."

He looked small and dazed.

"Is Mom okay?"

"Asleep. She's asleep."

Gala stepped over her brother, stepped over the broken door.

"Have you packed?"

"What's to pack?"

"Mom's medicine. Come on, Daz, what are you waiting for?" She hugged him, shook him. "Come on."

"It's gone, they came and it's gone," said Daz, and he began to cry.

"What?"

"The medicine," he blubbed. "They smashed it. I couldn't stop them. I couldn't stop anything."

She left him there. There wasn't time for comfort. There wasn't time even for shock, for anger. But her mother's medicine . . . She had to pack. She had to get them out. It would take a lifetime to get Perle down the stairs and they didn't have a lifetime. Five minutes, that how long you had to get out once the RazeTanks arrived.

Gala found herself a light canvas bag. She packed one change of clothes for herself, for Daz. She packed a flashlight, and what little food she could carry. Then she went into Perle's room.

"Is that you, Stretch?" said Perle from the bed, eyes closed.

"It's me. Gala. Stretch is safe. He's still in the Polis. He'll come soon."

"And Finn?" said Perle.

Gala had spent the entire journey back to the Estates arguing with herself about how or what to tell her mother. Perle deserved to know the truth, but she was so weak now that sometimes Gala thought it was only the hope that Finn would return that was keeping her alive at all. If Gala told her mother that she'd seen her father, but that he would not come, not now, not ever, what then? Perle might just give up, she might slip away, and Gala wasn't ready for that, which is why Gala Lorrell—grateful that there was no time for pause—found herself saying: "Nothing yet, not yet, Mama."

Perle opened her eyes, looked at her daughter.

"There are RazeMachines on the way," said Gala. "We have to go."

"Where?" said Perle. "We don't have anywhere to go."

"Then we'll find somewhere," said Gala, thinking, please, don't make this more difficult than it already is.

"You go," said Perle. "I'll stay."

"What!"

"If Finn comes, and I'm gone, how will he find me?"

That tore at her, but she still managed to say: "But there won't be any place to find you in, that's the point, they're going to raze the building, don't you understand?"

"You go and take Daz," said Perle. "I'll stay."

And then Gala understood: Her mother was giving her and Daz a chance. Carrying their sick mother, going at her pace, having to care for her, find an appropriate place for all three of them, that would be hard if not impossible. She and Daz would be better off on their own.

"No," said Gala. "Whatever you say—no. You're coming with us." And then she shouted, "Daz, Daz, help me!"

The RazeMachines arrived first—but only just. Maxo saw them pull up in front of Block 213, three machines in an arc. On Bovis's TropScreen the machines had looked formidable enough, close-up they were terrifying. They were huge, grim fortresses on wheels, or rather on caterpillar treads. Each vehicle had an armored bulldozer arm at the front and a ripper at the rear. Only one—the central one—had a turret, which meant, Maxo supposed, that the outer two machines were remote controlled. The turreted machine also had a gun, a gray blunt-nosed gun, which was swinging like a stiff animal trunk right and left as the machine took up its position. It must be a RazeTank then—often considered the most fearsome of the various RazeMachines, although some people said it was the remote-controlled RazeAlls that were the most lethal, because they didn't notice if they rode over people.

In the PriorityCar, Maxo had had a plan. He would stand in front of the RazeMachines and prevent them bulldozing

Gala's home. He'd speak up for the truth, others would join him, maybe form a human ring around the building. It had seemed simple enough; now, looking at the machines, it seemed the dream of a madman. Maxo got out of the insulated car. Immediately the noise assaulted him, not just the ordinary din of the Estates but an additional, terrified scurry. There were people running, shouting, screaming, cars revving and swerving, and a kind of generalized panic which, though Maxo had thought himself quite calm, seemed to clutch at his throat. And then there were the RazeMachines themselves, the constant, low, threatening throb of their engines.

The RazeTank gun stopped turning and, from cone-shaped loudspeakers mounted on either side of the turret, the RazeTank's commander's voice boomed above the melee: *"In accordance with PolisSecurityLaw 2018, the Leaderene, may her name celeb forever, has ordered the total annihilation of Block 213 for the crime of Harboring. Block 213 has been identified by InternalSecurity as the headquarters of numerous insurgents and anti-Trop Treasoners. . . ."*

"Lies!" shouted Maxo, but nobody could possibly have heard him.

". . . Demolition will therefore begin in precisely five minutes. . . ."

Like the gun turret of a few minutes ago, Maxo's head swung up toward the fourth floor of Block 213. There was someone at the window of Gala's apartment. They hadn't left! They hadn't got out. Perle would never make it down the stairs in five minutes. Perle would die and so Gala—attending to her—would die, too! Maxo Evangele Strang stepped in front of the RazeTank.

"People of the Estates," he began. But he could hardly hear himself speak, let alone make others hear him. He was barely as tall as the top of the caterpillar treads and his head was well below the level of the gun, and therefore, presumably, the VidEyes of the tank. The RazeTank commander couldn't hear him and couldn't see him. That gave Maxo an idea. The arm of the bulldozer was low enough to the ground for him to grab on to it, so he did; in one swift movement he swung himself up onto the RazeTank. The armor plating was riveted on with huge bolts and the metal clanged as he climbed, along the bulldozer arm and up the gray fortress of the tank itself. The VidEyes swiveled as if they sensed him, but he kept himself low, beneath the level of the ScanBeam, scrambling his way over the nose of the machine and then, clinging to the barrel of the gun, making for the turret itself. At first, he thought the top of the turret was too high above the main body of the tank for him to be able to make the final ascent, but he had to make it, he had to. He found a bolt, positioned his left foot, and forced himself upward.

On the fourth floor of Block 213, Daz had gone from mute to hysterical. "Come on," he was screaming. "Come on! What are you doing!"

Gala was looking out of the window, watching transfixed as a figure scrambled up the shank of the RazeTank.

He'd come back. Maxo Evangele Strang had returned. She had thought, after the encounter with her father, that there weren't any heroes anymore, that there could be no heroes. But here was one, standing on a RazeTank. If it was insanity, then it was an insanity to swell your heart.

"We'll never do it," screamed Daz.

She watched Maxo climb along the gun barrel, haul himself up onto the turret, where he stood in his black ambisuit. Shining. He was shining! But why had he come? What—or who—had he come for?

"We'll never be out in five minutes!"

"Yes," said Gala with certainty. "We will. Now we will!" She had never been so sure of anything in her life. "Only we have to stop the machines. Here's what we're going to do. . . ." And she gave Daz some instructions and then she began to pelt downstairs toward the three tanks and the ludicrous desire to be loved.

The top of the turret was surprisingly flat and Maxo found himself able to stand quite easily.

"People of the Tropolis," he began again, "I, Maxo Evangele Strang . . ." But it was no use, people could see him all right, there were people pointing, amazed, but no one could hear him over the general noise and the drone of the Raze-Tank engine. To have come so far and still to be silenced—it was impossible, it was maddening.

"Four minutes," shouted the commander, still apparently unaware of the presence of the interloper. The announcement was so loud it nearly knocked Maxo off balance. The loudspeaker cones! They were not part of the armor plating, just metal mounts to help amplify the sound. Natural megaphones! Maxo knelt and wrenched at the left-hand cone; with a strength he didn't know he had, he pulled it from its fitting.

"People of the Trop," he shouted, mouth to the jagged edge of the metal, "you know as well as I do that Block 213 contains no insurgents. I was with Phylo Lorrell on the day of the Atrocity. I was standing right next to him at the moment of the explosion. And I, Maxo Evangele Strang, GemX, do swear by . . ."—what should he swear by? People in the Polis swore on the life of the Leaderene because, so Maxo had been taught, you had to swear on the most important thing in the world—". . . do swear," Maxo continued, "on the life of my . . ." He wanted to say "mesh," his mesh, Gala Lorrell. But she wasn't his mesh and, in any case, mesh seemed to be entirely the wrong word. What was the right one? "On the life, on the beautiful foot of Gala Lorrell . . . my love," he ended. *Love.* Love—wasn't that on the Eradicated List?

"Crazy," shouted someone from the small but gathering crowd. "CrazeMachines as well as RazeMachines. What will they think of next?"

"No," said a second voice, that of an old man. "Listen to what he's saying . . ."

"He's saying he's a GemX," interrupted a thin woman, "which makes him one of Them. A Plastic. What else do we need to know?"

"My name's Gubbins," said the old man, "and I live in this Block and I say we hear him out. When has anyone from the Polis ever spoken up for people in the Estates before?"

"He's not speaking up for anyone," said the woman grumpily. "Except perhaps himself."

"He's standing on a RazeTank," said Gubbins. "He's risking his life."

"And ours, too, probably," said the woman.

"Let's hear him out," said a second man.

"No," said the woman. "Let's get out, while we still can."

"What I'm trying to say," continued Maxo, "is that I was there. I know Phylo Lorrell did not commit the Atrocity. And I believe the Leaderene knows that, too!"

Now there was a stunned gasp. This was TropTreason of the most heinous kind. The crowd looked to the tank commander for a reaction but, after an agonizing few moments, it became clear that there wasn't going to be a reaction. Maxo thanked Gala's little foot that though the RazeTank's VidEyes could look frontward and backward, they were not, apparently, able to look upward.

"And I say we should defend this building," he continued, "defend this family against the Polis lies. Make a stand, stand up for what's right!"

Three minutes, yelled the commander.

"It's a trick, a Polis plot," shouted the woman. "I tell you—he's a GemX, a Plastic, and they're all the same. He wants us to join in so we can be done for Complicity, for Incitement. Then they can destroy our homes and us—bang us up for life!"

"Funny face for a Plastic," said Gubbins quietly. "Too many lines."

A third man picked up a rock and lobbed it at Maxo: "Plastic scum," he yelled.

"Wait," said Gubbins, but they didn't.

More rocks zinged through the air. Most of them missed Maxo, clanged on the side of the RazeTank. But even if one had hit him, Maxo would probably not have noticed, because his whole attention was suddenly focused on the small figure of a running girl. She'd emerged from a crowd at the entrance to Block 213 and now she was running, running.

"Gala," he yelled. She was safe! Oh—CelebHigh! And then again not safe, she was running toward the RazeTank. "Gala, no!"

But still she ran, light-footed and slightly airy, barely stopping when she came to the tank, but swinging herself up, along the bulldozer arm, just as he had. She was faster than him and more graceful, she was the most beautiful thing he'd ever seen on a tank. The VidEyes swiveled again—had they seen her? You'd want to look at her. The crowd were looking, they'd stopped throwing rocks. She was at the turret now, at the base of it. But she was too small, she could not get up.

"Take my hand," Maxo cried, crouching down and reaching for her. "Take it." And she did. As her fingers twisted into his, he felt the electricity surge through him. Kill me now, he thought, right now, who cares? This is happy. And here was another word to astonish him: *happy.*

"Two minutes," yelled the commander.

Gala pulled herself upright, stood tall on the turret overlooking the gun. She let go of his hand but remained unbearably close.

"I know this man," she cried, but her voice was lost in the din and engine rumble. Maxo passed her the metal cone, watched her put it to her lips. "I know Maxo," she began again. "And he's right, my brother Phylo Lorrell did not commit the Atrocity. I was with him that day, too. And with my hand on my heart, I say it's lies."

"Lies!" It was Gubbins shouting, supporting her.

"And even if he had committed such an act," Gala continued, "would it be right to come here with RazeMachines to the homes of innocent people, giving them just five minutes to evacuate their lives? My mother is in that building, she's ill, she can barely walk, do you think she can get out of a building without a lift in five minutes?"

"A lift that's been out of action for over eighteen months," remarked Gubbins.

"And she's only on Floor 4. What about those on Floor 24?"

"And 18," yelled a young boy suddenly. "We think my dad's still up there. We can't find him. We think he's still there!"

Maxo grabbed the megacone, put his lips where hers had been. "Make a ring," he yelled, "We'll make a ring and surround the building. If everyone joins in we'll be powerful. They won't raze the building if we all stand together!"

"One minute!" yelled the commander.

27

In the bowels of the PoliticoPalace, Leaderene Euphony Clore watched SecurityScreen 402 with some satisfaction. Maxo Strang and some Dreggie girl had just jumped off the RazeTank and headed for the entrance to Block 213.

"They make it so easy," she remarked to Fikk Powell. Maxo Strang would have needed liquidating at some point and here he was, offering himself up for execution. She was only glad that so many GemXs had died in the hospital blast. It would have been intolerable to watch an entire generation disintegrate the way this boy seemed to be doing. The lines on his face were quite shocking, he looked about forty years old. But it was his mind that was really going; he appeared to have lost all grip on reality. It was difficult to believe now that he'd come from such good stock and had seemed to have a glittering future in front of him. One had to be so careful, she had to be so careful, thought Euphony Clore, so thank the Leaderene (she laughed a little at this) that she herself had such a large brain.

"Do you want me to radio now?" asked Powell.

"I'm a woman of honor," said the Leaderene. "I said five minutes and they shall have their five. It is not, after all, long to wait."

"Of course," said Powell.

"Only put it on the TropScreen, delayed action. Start the film from the boy's Treason talk. That, and the final assault, should be warning enough for anyone else thinking of fomenting trouble in the future."

"Do you want the boy brought in?"

"Oh, I don't think so," said Euphony Clore, tolerantly. "I mean, if the tank commander has his wits about him, I don't think Mr. Maxo Strang is going to survive, do you?"

There were too many people still exiting from the building for the Block entrance to be a good place to begin the chain. "Further along," said Maxo, "quickly." He took Gala's hand again, it was easier to run that way and he was doing it for her, wasn't he? (And for the Truth, of course.)

"Come on," Gala shouted at the crowd, "join us! Aren't our homes worth saving?"

"Not really," muttered Gubbins, but he was quickly beside her, extending his old, bony hand. She grasped it, squeezed it hard, as if he'd know what she meant, as if he'd understand her wordless gratitude. Next came the small boy who thought his father was still inside the block and next to him a woman who must be his mother and then the beginning of a chain of total strangers.

"Demolition," shouted the tank commander. *"Demolition!"* The remote-controlled RazeAlls lurched forward.

"A ring," Gala screamed, "make the ring now." She looked to the Block entrance. So many people emerging, but not her mother or Daz. "Close the ring!" But the chain wasn't nearly long enough. It didn't even stretch halfway across the building front. But they were standing directly in front of the main RazeTank, which hadn't moved a tread. If the commander was a Poldrone, the tank would advance, she knew that, but if it was one of the security men, then maybe it wouldn't, maybe they could hold it off a few vital minutes.

"We beg you," she cried at the monumental machine, "spare this Block. There are no insurgents here. Only ordinary families. Have pity."

The RazeAlls jerked to a halt. And in the shocked stillness of that moment, Gala saw her mother emerge from the building being supported by Daz and a man she didn't know. They must have carried her, Daz and a stranger. And from the cry that came from the mouth of the little boy beside her, it seemed that the stranger was the boy's father. Gala's heart pounded with joy: her mother was safe, Daz was safe, the child's father was safe, and here was Maxo, who'd come back for her, who cared about her whole community. Savior. Lover?

In the Bunker, the Leaderene was not quite so impressed.

"What's the fool waiting for?" Euphony Clore grabbed the Communicator from her head of Internal-Security and barked into the ears of the RazeTank commander.

"Priority override 534. Shoot to kill."

The noise of the gun blast was deafening. Gala didn't move at all, but Gubbins did, he simply fell away. It took Gala a few shocked moments and the clearing of some smoke to see what had happened.

"Idiot," shrieked the Leaderene, "buffoon! He got the old man."

* * *

Gubbins lay in the dust looking pale and slightly surprised.

Gala was on her knees now. "Are you all right?"

"No," said Gubbins softly. "I'm not."

She saw the blood then, but it didn't seem part of him, it seemed separate, someone else's blood. How could there be so much blood and Gubbins be still alive?

"I'm so sorry," she whispered, and she wanted to say more but his face stopped her, that and the terrible realization of what she'd done.

"My choice," Gubbins said, and, for a moment, she thought he smiled, but he couldn't have done so, because his eyes rolled and his body twitched and then he was gone.

"No," she cried, "I know who you are, I know what you've done for me, for my father. I know!" But she was crying over a lifeless corpse.

"Come on," Maxo said, and pulled at her. Only the two of them were still in front of the tank. The others had all broken away, the others were fleeing for their lives. "Come on."

"No," said Gala. "It isn't right!" If Gubbins was dead it had all been for nothing. They'd lost. She stood up in front of the tank, opened her arms wide, made herself a big target.

"Shoot," she said.

The RazeTank engine roared, the huge machine rumbled forward a few treads, gun cranking, this way, that way finding its aim. Maxo grabbed for her hand then, pulled it and her toward him. "Stop it," he said. "It's not your fault. It's

theirs, don't you see? Don't give yourself to them, Gala."
And all the time he spoke he was pushing her, trying to
force her out of the line of the swinging nose of the tank,
so when the second shot came it would miss her. And it did
miss her, missed them both, but only just, the heat of the
blast singeing her hair.

"Gala!" He lifted her now, stumbled with her toward
the Block entrance. The RazeAlls were moving in toward
the building, and she could hear the whine of their bulldozer arms; they must have Grinders as well as Rippers.

"Mama!" Gala cried, finding her voice at the same time
as her feet.

Daz had got their mother out of the entrance, but now
he was supporting her alone. The man had run to join his
child, get them away. Gala would have liked to have
thanked him.

"It was Gubbins," said Daz, "wasn't it? He shot Gubbins."

"Yes," said Gala. "I'm so sorry, Daz."

"Gubbins, who never hurt a soul in all of his life."

"Daz . . ."

"Come on," said Maxo. "We have to get out of here."

His words were reinforced by the first huge crash as the
two remote-controlled RazeAlls slammed into the building, making all twenty-four floors shake. The RazeTank
meanwhile was turning, lumbering about, trying to locate
them again.

"I'll take your mother's legs," said Maxo to Daz. "Come
on, this way."

"What way, exactly?"

"I know somewhere," said Maxo. "Trust me."

Daz looked at his sister.

"Trust him," she said.

The PriorityCar was still where Maxo had left it, the Clodrone driver sitting patiently in the shaking shadow of Block 213 waiting for instructions. Maxo heaved open the back door.

"Get in," he commanded Gala and then helped Daz ease Perle into the backseat between her children. He shut the door with care, remembering how last time he was in a car with the Lorrells it was Gala who was stretched out on the backseat. How many things had changed since then.

He made his way swiftly around the car to get into the front seat, but before he could open the door a huge hand landed on his shoulder. He tried to spin about but couldn't, the hand was like a bar of iron holding him down.

"Poldrones," screamed Gala from inside the car, and he saw her lean for the door handle.

"Museo," yelled Maxo at the PriorityCar driver. "Take them to the Museo. Now!"

The Clodrone slammed the car into action and before Gala could disembark, he was speeding away. Through the glass of the rear window, Maxo saw Gala's face set into a mask of horror. But she was safe. She would be safe.

It wasn't Poldrones, Maxo realized then, it was just one Poldrone, albeit a particularly hefty, ugly one.

"This way," said the Poldrone.

Maxo hardly had a choice, he was spun around and marched across the teeming road to another car and unceremoniously dumped in the back.

"Oh, CelebHigh," said a voice, "CelebHigh and Praise the Leaderene forever!" In the front seat of the car, his eyes shining, sat Maxo's GenPap, Dr. Igo Strang. "You're safe," he cried. "You're safe at last. Oh, Maxo." Maxo thought Igo's eyes might be shining because they were wet. Could his GenPap be *crying*?

Igo leaned through the gap in the car seat and touched his GenOff's hand. He knew it was inexcusable, but he couldn't quite help himself. "You're going to be all right," he said, "I swear it on the Leaderene."

"I am all right," Maxo managed then. "Or I was all right, until just now."

"Proceed," said Igo joyfully to the Poldrone, who obediently slid the car into gear. Then Igo took the car 'cator and spoke a number. "Glora, GloraMesh, I've got him, I've got Maxo. He's alive!" He clicked off. "AnsaMach," he said apologetically. "The HoloFuneral, you know."

Maxo knew.

"But she'll be thrilled, thrilled."

Maxo wondered.

"Oh, but you're bruised," cried Igo then. He was trying not to look at the cracks on his GenOff's face and so was concentrating on his eyes, where there seemed to be a ring of purple and black. "What happened?"

"Long story," said Maxo. "Mainly to do with this city, this sick city. And its sick Leaderene."

"What?" cried Igo, unable to stop himself scanning the car for bugs even though it was his car and, therefore, any surveillance equipment was entirely his own.

"They put me in an IsolationCell," continued Maxo. It

was good to tell his GenPap this, his GenPap should know. "They beat me up."

"What? I don't understand."

"They thought I was Phylo Lorrell."

"Lorrell, the Atrocity Perpetrator?"

"Or not," said Maxo, "depending on your point of view."

"They didn't hurt you?" asked Igo. "Did they?"

"Yes," said Maxo. "A bit." And then he added quickly, "Stretch, Phylo—did he come to the Lab, did you see him?"

"Yes. He came asking after his father, but, of course, I couldn't help. How could I know his father?"

"You didn't hand him over, did you?" asked Maxo urgently. "Not to the Security forces, tell me you didn't?"

"I didn't," said Igo truthfully. "He's . . . quite safe." Well, a person would be safe in a GemCorp SecuriCell, very safe.

"So you let him go?"

"Why do you care?" said Igo. "Why do you care anything about him?"

"He's Gala's brother," said Maxo.

"Gala of the little foot," said Igo. The boy was very damaged, Igo'd have to get to work very fast on the mental side of things.

"Yes," said Maxo, pleased. "How did you know?"

"A Clodrone told me."

"A Clodrone?"

"Don't worry about that. Don't worry about anything, Maxo. I already have a team working on the aging problem. We'll have a stabilizer very soon. Very very soon. I'm just glad to have you back in . . . whatever state."

"Can we go to the Museo?" said Maxo.

"No, we have to go to the Lab. I need to run some tests. Define exactly what the problem is, although . . ."

"There isn't a problem," said Maxo, "and I'm not going to the Lab."

He doesn't know how badly he's affected, thought Igo, he cannot hear what he's saying.

"Not a problem," said Igo carefully, "at least not a problem we can't—I can't—solve. Everything's solvable."

"Is it?" asked Maxo.

"Yes, yes, of course. This is the most advanced Polis in the world, first in progress and perfection . . ."

"My perfection," said Maxo, "is on her way to the Museo."

"It'll pass," said Igo. "You will take the pills and it will pass."

"No," said Maxo. "It will not pass. Because I don't want the pills. And I'm not going to take any pills, because I like what's happening to me. You see"—the paused struggling to express himself—"I . . . have never felt so . . . *alive* in all of my life."

Igo took a deep breath. "Maxo, Maxo, my GenOff, my best, my most perfect boy, listen to me. The degradation has affected your brain—nothing we can't rearrange, of course, but alive you are not. You are aging, Maxo. You must be able to see that with your own eyes. If the process is not reversed you are in danger. Grave danger." Igo Strang left a gap.

"Do you mean I'm going to die?" asked Maxo.

"Yes," said Dr. Strang.

"How long?"

"I can't know that, not without the tests. But I do know

that it's degenerative, progressive, so you could have years, but you could also just have months. That's why we need to get to the Lab."

"If you take me to the Lab," said Maxo, "I will open the door and walk to the Polis to get to the Museo. My need—my only need—is to be where Gala is."

"Even if it kills you?" asked Igo.

"Yes," said Maxo Evangele Strang.

Perle Lorrell lay in a bed belonging to the custodian of the Museo. The ants in her head had changed into ball bearings, tiny spheres of steel, which were ricocheting about inside her brain, flinging themselves against the bone of her skull. It was difficult to think through the pain, but Perle was thinking. How had she got here?

She remembered the journey in the PriorityCar and how her head had slewed when they turned corners, skidded when the driver braked. She remembered coming into the Museo supported between her daughter and her son. Couldn't she walk anymore? She remembered the custodian, an old man with a gentle face. The man had welcomed them, asked what they'd come for. Did they want to see the DefunctReligions or Manuscripts, he could recommend Manuscripts, it was his favorite room, is that why they'd come?

"No," Gala had just blurted out: "No, we've come from Block 213, Block 213 is our Block. Or was our Block. And my mother's ill and Maxo—Maxo Strang—told us to come."

"Ah," said the custodian, as though this was the most natural explanation in the world, "this way please."

He'd led them along a corridor and then upstairs in the

elevator ("A working elevator," as Daz had remarked, she did remember that) to the apartment labeled Custodian of the Museo. The apartment had one bedroom and one bed. The custodian had offered Perle that bed.

Perle was glad to be lying down, glad that her limbs at least were still. Finn had always said she would end her days in the Polis, that was his promise to her.

"I will take you from the Estates," he said, "I will give you a better life." She had not thought to be in a bed in the Polis because her home had been destroyed and her menfolk taken. The ball bearings whirled and crashed.

Finn.

Phylo.

How had it all happened? How had she managed to lose so much? Despite herself, a terrible cry came out of her throat.

"Mama," said a voice at her shoulder. It was Gala's. "Can I get you anything?"

"Phylo," whispered Perle Lorrell. "Get me Phylo."

"Mama . . . ," said Gala.

"And Finn," said Perle Lorrell. "Please get me Finn."

In the Mescat House, Stretch did not know for how long he'd been drinking or how much he'd drunk. The bar never appeared to shut. Certainly he'd been here since his father had walked away from him—but had that been four hours or four years? He felt very tired, he did know that, and a little fuzzy. Had he slept here? Maybe he had, maybe he hadn't, maybe he'd just drunk. Drunk. He looked about, there was something different going on but, at first, he couldn't quite identify what it was. Then it hit him, the noise. Or the lack of it. Everyone in the bar had gone silent.

Why?

He tried to focus, follow the stares of the others, because they were staring at something, something mounted high on the wall. The thing was big enough for him to see (if somewhat blurred at the edges). It was a TropScreen. Unsteadily, Stretch tried to move a little closer to the screen, as if that would make the picture clearer. There was something big and blockish in the center of the screen that was wobbling, swaying even, although the swaying might have been in Stretch's head. He concentrated: There were also two, possibly three, smaller blocky things apparently attacking the big blocky thing. They were all swinging and swaying and lurching.

Stretch hung on to the back of a chair.

"Wass goin' on?" he said.

"Can't you see?" a voice said from the haze. "It's Block 213. They're RazeMachining it."

"Oh," said Stretch. They did that sometimes, the Plastics, RazeMachined things, it was part of the . . .

"What block you say?"

"213," said the man. "The Perpetrator's Block, Phylo Lorrell."

"No!" shrieked Stretch, experiencing a flash in his brain almost bright enough to cut through the mescat haze. He grabbed a 'cator that was lying on a nearby table.

"Oi!" shouted the owner of the 'cator.

Stretch began dialing furiously. No answer. No tone. He'd dialed the wrong number.

"Oi, I said," said the 'cator owner emphatically. "What you think you're doing, Clodrone?"

"Just a minute, pleasch," said Stretch, and he dialed again. Daz picked up.

"Oh, thank . . ." Stretch couldn't think of anyone to thank.

"Stretch?" queried Daz. "Is that you?"

"They're RazshMasschining our Block, Daschz!"

"You don't say," said Daz.

"But you're out! And Mama and Gala, are they okay?"

"We're fine. We're in the Polis. At the Museo. But where are you? Mama's going mad. You've got to come. You've got to come now."

"I'm . . . ," began Stretch, but he didn't have time to finish because a large fist landed on his nose.

"He ran out of time," announced the Oi Man, to no one in particular.

28

"If you care about me, you'll take me where I ask—to the Museo." That's what Maxo had said.

Care.

Of course Dr. Igo Strang cared about his GenOff, why else would he have been so fearful after the hospital explosion, so determined through the "kidnap," so zealous in driving the length and breadth of the Trop to find his Maxo? Dr. Strang knew, of course, that it was important to care more for the good of the Trop itself than for any single individual (this is how Progress was achieved, putting the Trop first, the germline first, this led to Perfection) but yes, he cared for Maxo. Which is why, after a bitter argument, Igo Strang had finally taken Maxo to the Museo. Though there had been a condition.

"Please," said Igo, "just do one thing for me in return, Maxo. Let me have a SkinScrape, just a few cells, please, Maxo."

"There's no point," said Maxo. "I told you, whatever you can develop, whatever pill, whatever stabilizer, I will not take it. Not now. Not ever."

"Please," said Igo, "if not for you, then for me."

Maxo had relinquished something then, held out his

285

hand toward the RazorKnife Dr. Igo Strang always carried with him. It had been the smallest of nicks, no blood, of course, just a few cells and, because Igo had not had a glass slide with him, he'd had to make do with slipping the knife and the cells inside a plastic SpeciWallet.

After that, they'd driven in silence. At the entrance to the Museo, Igo had watched his GenOff alight from the car and almost run to the door of the building. A RazorKnife seemed to turn in Igo's heart then. Maxo was embarking on a new life. Or a new death.

Just inside the entrance, Maxo had turned and mouthed the words "Thank you." A moment later he was gone.

Igo drove alone with the Poldrone back to the Lab. He knew exactly what he was going to do when he arrived. He was going to let Phylo Lorrell go free.

"You do not know me anymore." That was another thing Maxo had said. Phylo Lorrell was a boy who'd lost his father but who wouldn't give up searching for him. And Dr. Igo Strang was a man who seemed to have lost his GenOff, but he wouldn't give up the search either. He'd find Maxo again, find out who he was now. Letting Lorrell go, not handing him over to the authorities, that would be part of it. Igo's attempt to demonstrate that he did care and he could know.

He iris-scanned himself into the GemCorp InterTrop. His iris-scan gave him access to all parts of the building, including the SecuriCells, so he made his way immediately to Floor 24. The Security Poldrones who would be watching the screen that monitored the door would not challenge him. Igo would let Lorrell go and deal with the administration afterward.

As soon as he was through the door, Dr. Igo Strang knew there was something terribly wrong. Afterward he couldn't have said whether it was the smell of the blood or the sight of the body askew on the floor, which assaulted him first. He did know that he stood and stared for what seemed like an eternity before it came to him that the corpse did not belong to Phylo Lorrell. It was not thin or angular enough and it didn't have the right face. The face of the corpse was rather simple, Igo thought, it had the happy look of an OldTime angel. Igo dropped to his knees, covering his nose to try and protect himself from the drenching stench of the blood (which seemed to have leaked copiously from the man's wrists). Igo had wanted to be wrong, but he was not wrong. Despite the incongruous purple (and now bloodied) ambisuit, Igo was looking at the body of Clodrone 1640.

Dr. Igo Strang's proto-enhanced rationality deserted him. He felt sick, he felt shocked, he was distressed, angry. Phylo Lorrell had murdered Clodrone 1640! How could that possibly have happened? Then the scientist recovered himself, he looked more closely. He saw the bloody slit about 1640's wrist; he identified the murder weapon, a shard of glass with dried blood along its lethal edge. Only it wasn't a murder weapon, of course, it was a suicide one, for Clodrone 1640 appeared to have taken his own life.

Dr. Igo Strang stood up. Suicide made even less sense than a murder. Clodrones were bred to be content with their lot, that was a factor about which he himself had been most particular. He'd worked very hard on modifying even low-level discontent. He'd adjusted the patterns, sought to eradicate vexations of all sorts. That was part of the glory of the Clodrones. How happy they were. And yet here was 1640 making a statement about the insupportability of his life. Igo Strang tried to recall all the mad things 1640 had said—about Lorrell's father, about the cells multiplying inside him. Something had gone wrong, wrong with the Clodrones, wrong with the GemXs but . . . it wasn't that. No. It was that, looking at 1640's twisted body and his beautiful calm face, Igo Strang felt an emotion he couldn't ever remember feeling before. At first, he thought it was pity and then he realized it was sorrow. He minded that 1640 was dead. 1640 had been part of his life, and that of his family, for over a decade. And now he was dead.

Dead.

Dr. Igo Strang stumbled into the HoldingRoom outside the SecuriCells and screamed up at the screens and the unseen Poldrones who would be watching them: "You imbeciles! Do you realize what you've done!" Apparently they didn't. "You've let your charge escape . . ."—the realization that Lorrell had clearly absconded was only just dawning on Igo—"and there's a man dead in here!" Igo said "a man" when he meant a Clodrone, but he stumbled on, "I mean, don't you check on your charges, bring them food and water?"

There was a pause and then the buzz of the 'Com: "Orders of Dr. Strang," came a Poldrone voice, "no food, no water."

His own orders. No food, no water.

To which a second voice added: "But we let 1640 bring water. 1640 said you'd authorized it, Dr. Strang, sir."

1640 had brought water to Lorrell. A Clodrone, a Clodrone who seemed to care (that word again) for the boy. *If you care about me then . . .*

"Get this place cleaned up. Get the body out of here," Igo screamed at the screen. "Now!"

Igo Strang left the door swinging behind him. There was no one to escape now. Except himself. Where would he escape to? The Lab. The Lab would calm him, in the Lab there was order, things could be controlled, if he could get to the Lab maybe things would begin to make sense again.

He took the lift to LabFloor1 and walked through the benches of his staff without looking right or left. He strode straight into his office and shut the door. His own bench beckoned, his own stool, his Micon10 Scope, just looking at them eased his breathing. He sat down and carefully extracted the RazorKnife package. He edged the skin scraping from the blade onto a pristine glass slide and clamped it beneath his Scope.

There was no machine faster in the world at identifying and isolating a single DNA strand and yet, to Dr. Strang, the process seemed to take forever.

"Come along," he shouted at the Scope, "come along!"

And then it was there beneath his gaze, the damage event as clear to him as daylight. Maxo had regressed, his DNA had reformed into a pre-enhanced (Dr. Igo Strang could not bring the word *natural* to his lips) state. The adjacent bases bonded across the helical ladder, and what was more, he could see the increase (the huge increase) of the chromatin compacting, which signaled age, old age. Of course, he could try an excision repair. He'd need

289

enzymes, a team of enzymes, but since the damage was only in one or two strands of the DNA, it might just be possible but . . .

But Maxo wouldn't want the treatment. He would refuse it. So he would die. Could Dr. Strang kidnap his own GenOff, force him onto the operating table? Impossible. Mad. He wasn't thinking rationally, scientifically. All because of 1640. Somehow 1640 had got under his skin. Skin. Cell damage, realigned DNA strands, strands that had degraded, twisted back into their original shape. Perhaps it was lucky after all that so many GemXs had died in the explosion, if they were all like this, all like Maxo. Because Perfection mattered, Progress mattered, that's what he'd been working toward all of his life, wasn't it?

But Maxo.

1640.

What was it that Lorrell had said about the Clodrone project? *You're developing a huge obedient workforce . . . which, if you can get them to live long enough, will obviate the need for workers from the Estates. We won't be needed. We'll be surplus to requirement.*

Ridiculous. Of course it was ridiculous. But then the explosion: if Phylo Lorrell was really innocent, then who had detonated all those lives? Something very icy crawled down Igo Strang's spine. Was there something—something very big—that he'd been missing? He felt the answer must be in the cell he was looking at. The degrading, aging human cell of Maxo Strang.

Glora.

Glora was fully Enhanced. He would speak with Glora and rationality would reassert itself. He grabbed his 'cator and cried out her number. Glora Orb's beautiful perfect face assembled itself on screen.

"Glora Orb is engaged in the HoloFuneral of the Century. Your image has been logged. Voiceprints may be left after the star."

Then Dr. Igo Strang did something he hadn't done for thirty years: he keyed in the word *MeshBabe*. This had been his and Glora's secret code when they had first met, their little subversive message to each other when things were urgent between them. Glora Orb had never failed to respond to MeshBabe. Igo waited. He waited some more. After a lifetime of waiting, three words appeared on the screen. "Not now, Igo."

That's when Dr. Igo Strang began to wonder if it wasn't all his fault. That, perhaps, if he hadn't been staring quite so hard down his Micon10 Scope at the tiny things, he might have seen some of the bigger things. Science, technology, that's what he'd concentrated on, the art of the possible. But had he ever stopped, even once, to ask himself if what he was doing was good? Was right? Progress, Perfection, they were mantras, his mantras, but what did they mean? The words swam in front of his eyes. The Leaderene's face swam in front of his eyes. Could the things he was now thinking about the Leaderene really be true? And Glora.

Oh, Glora.

He adored her. She was everything he'd ever wanted, everything he'd aspired to, she was the peak and pinnacle of Perfection. And yet—a veil fell from his besotted eyes— she was a monster! She was totally without feeling; she hadn't cared at all about Maxo and she didn't care about him. *Not now, Igo.* At the bench in his laboratory, which had been the heartbeat of his whole life, Dr. Strang heard someone (who couldn't have been a scientist) burst into uncontrollable sobs.

Some considerable time later, having wiped his nose on an asbestos mat, Igo walked out of his Lab and his life and into the streets of the Polis. There was one final thing he needed to know. The journey took fifteen minutes. He'd never walked in the Polis before, he thought vaguely, as he ascended the steps to the CloHouse. The Clodrone receptionist jumped to attention.

"Which floor for 1640's pod?" asked Igo.

"Fifth," came the reply.

Igo ascended in a very small elevator, which opened onto a dark corridor. Igo wanted to have some light, but he didn't see any switches. Each of the doors that led off the corridor had eight numbers listed on it. Igo peered until he identified 1640's pod. He knocked. There was no reply, so he entered. The eight (empty) LieDowns were stacked like shelves four high on either side of the room. If eight people had been in here simultaneously, Igo did not see how they could all have stood up together. An emotion that might have been shame crowded in on him, he had overlooked so much.

1640's LieDown was the bottom tier on the left-hand side. He had just enough space to sleep there and one drawer for belongings, which slid into the wall behind him. Igo Strang opened that drawer. In it there was a freshly pressed Clodrone cap and spare brown ambisuit. Igo moved the suit to see if there was anything else in the drawer, anything at all. But there wasn't.

Very slowly, Dr. Igo Strang began to undress. He folded

his own ambisuit as neatly as he could (he'd never had to fold anything in his life before) and put it into the drawer. Then he took out 1640's spare suit and put it on. He put on the cap. Under the cap he pretended there was nothing in his brain. Clodrones didn't have to think. They were excused from thinking.

For a brief, happy, moment, Dr. Igo Strang sat down on 1640's LieDown to wait for the arrival of the PodMaster who, he hoped, would tell him what to do.

29

Glora Orb sat in the front row of the gigantic Stadio-Perfecto. The seating capacity of the stadium was seventy-five thousand and, Glora Orb congratulated herself, there was not a vacant space anywhere. The friends and family of the 6,014 GemXs known to have died in the Atrocity numbered approximately 37,000, which meant that at least half the gathering (they'd had to pay, of course—nothing was free these days) had come because they knew, under the ArtisticDirection of Glora Orb, this would be the Funeral of the Century.

The mood in the front rows (where the families of the dead were seated) was relatively muted, as were the colors, most of the GenParents choosing to dress in their darkest ambisuits. But behind them the colors got gayer and the mood more expansive. In the seats furthest from the arena, people were clapping in time with the military music being piped around the stadium. Flasks of mescat flashed in the sun and Clodrone Sellers were doing a brisk trade in Poppas, Uppers probably, pills designed to lift the spirits in difficult times.

A loud roll of SteelMach Drums and a perfectly synchronized (coordination was a speciality of Glora's) blast of trumpets heralded the arrival both of the stadium roof and Her Celebship, Leaderene Euphony Clore. Every man and woman in the stadium (Glora Orb had banned children from the ceremony, it would all be wasted on them) immediately rose to his or her feet and stood in silent attention. The huge stadium roof slid on invisible WheelDrags across the sky, blocking out what remained of the day. As the halogen lights began to spot the auditorium, the Leaderene made her entrance. She walked slowly with a small train of dignitaries (Glora Orb thought the blunt-looking man behind her might be Fikk Powell) to the HighDais where she turned, paused, and raised her hands as if in welcome. There was an apparently spontaneous burst of applause, which the Leaderene (wearing a bright scarlet ambisuit with a wide black belt and wider smile) acknowledged with a small nod.

Glora Orb wished then that Igo could be beside her, witnessing this event, which was so clearly going to be a triumph. She'd told anyone who had been interested (mainly Mortimer Malkin, Lydida's GenPap) that the Atrocity had resulted in a PriorityOne WorkSchedule for all those engaged in the difficult job of preserving the germline. Otherwise, she informed Mortimer, Igo wouldn't have missed his GenOff's funeral for the world.

This wasn't entirely true. There was another explanation for Igo's absence: Glora hadn't quite managed to issue her mesh with a ticket so, even if he had arrived at the stadium, he would have been denied entry. The reason for this was simple: Glora Orb suspected, from the various different messages she'd received over the past few days, that Maxo wasn't dead at all. And, naturally, if he wasn't dead (and wouldn't that be wonderful!) then the Strang-Orbs would not be entitled to the take-home HoloJar (with its permanent, fully voice-imprinted miniature HoloImage inside) that Seud Quac had designed for each of the grieving families. The HoloJars were numbered, 1 to 6,014, and there could be no replicas. They were one-off works of art which would, in time, command immense sums of money. Especially in the extraordinary circumstance that one of those 6,014 HoloJars had been made for a dead GemX who turned out not to be dead after all. Imagine it! It would be like finding one of those OldTime stamps printed back-to-front or without the head of the monarch, an incredible, monumentally valuable rarity. Which is why Glora Orb had been deliberately rebuffing calls from her Igo (and MeshBabe was quite an incentive) because if they'd spoken, and he'd accidentally informed her that Maxo had survived after all—well then, the game would have been over.

The Leaderene was speaking, her voice amplified in all parts of the stadium. She was talking of the contribution of the GemX Progenitors, she was announcing the successful razing of Blocks 213, 301, 412, and 422.

"This Atrocity," said Euphony Clore, "will not defeat us. On the contrary, it will make us stronger. We haven't made the Progress we have or indeed the Sacrifices we have, to be turned back from our goal now. Together we will root out the Evil that threatens our Advancement. The Enhanced Project, and all it implies for the Health and Wellbeing of our Society, will continue unabated." The Leaderene raised her right hand in a small tight fist. "This I swear to you!" she yelled.

"And we to you," seventy-five thousand voices screamed back at her, fists also raised.

The Leaderene let the moment hang huge in the air for a minute, then she dropped her arm and her gaze. "Now," she said demurely, "let the Procession of the Honored Dead begin."

She sat down on the little golden throne that had been erected for her on the HighDais. Perhaps, she thought, she should really build a bigger stadium? Seventy-five thousand people, it wasn't really enough, was it? They didn't make enough noise.

The overall lighting in the stadium dimmed, the halogen spots intensified, as the first of the Honored Dead appeared to walk through the door, whence the Leaderene herself had come not ten minutes earlier. There was a gasp from the crowd, and a little shriek from Broda Frank. Leading the Dead was a full-size HoloImage of Bovis. As he walked around the Arena, his golden head swung this way and that, as if he was looking for something or someone. After doing an almost complete circuit of the ground, he came to a halt in front of Broda. The ethereally beautiful Bovis, (more beautiful perhaps in death than he had ever been in life) bowed to his GenMa and to his GenPap and then stood radiantly quietly while the rest of the Dead began to file in.

"Marvelous," shouted people from the upper tiers, swinging that mescat.

"Sensational!"

"Perfect!"

The Leaderene liked the word *perfect*. She smiled, but not at Llublo Quells who seemed to be leering across the stadium at her. What was wrong with the man? When this nasty little GemX episode ended she would need to get to grips with Llublo Quells.

More and more of the Dead filed in, a tediously long line of them, in fact, thought the Leaderene. Still, they were pretty enough to look at. Seud Quac seemed to have chosen a defining color for each individual rather than going for a naturalistic look. She watched the image that stopped in front of Mortimer Malkin. It was pink. That must be Lydida, the Leaderene supposed. As his GenOff stared up at him, Malkin's body seemed to give way slightly, as though he was being crushed by some unseen force. It was unpleasant to look at, thought Euphony Clore, unseemly. Any minute now, the man would blub. She was almost sure now that he was a ThrowBack; she'd get Fikk Powell to put a PriorityTail on him. He'd give himself away sooner or later. They all did in the end.

The last of the Dead to arrive went to stand in front of Glora Orb herself. Maxo Strang! Or rather a glowing blue impression of him. The Leaderene experienced a frisson of delight. So—the RazeTank commander had not been so idiotic after all. Euphony had had to leave the Bunker before the end of the Raze and hadn't known that Maxo had definitely been shot. That was one job off her list then, the Leaderene thought. All credit to Glora Orb for seamlessly weaving Maxo into this Funeral, as though he was one of the innocent dead, that would stop any awkward questions arising. Good woman. And how clever of her to assemble Maxo's HoloImage so fast. She must have had an Image-Plate already made up, just in case. What forethought that showed, what progressive thinking. Glora Orb's body was not bowed, she held herself upright, she displayed perfect dignity. Perhaps, Euphony thought, Ms. Orb should be brought closer to the InnerCircle?

A long, low trumpet note brought the stadium to silence again. There was half a second's pause and then 6,014 separate voices (each one voiceprinted with total accuracy by Seud Quac) began talking in unison.

"We, the Honored Dead," the HoloImages said, "salute you, our GenFamilies and our Polis. From beyond the grave we commend our lives and thoughts to you, to strengthen you in your resolve to advance toward Grand Vision. Let nothing stand in your way in the fight for Progress and Perfection."

"Yes!" cried the crowd in the pause left for just such a shout. "Oh yes!"

There was more such talk (a little too much for the Leaderene's liking, though the import of the words, she believed, had been entirely her own suggestion) and more fervor from the crowd, especially those at the mescat level, who seemed to be well away now.

And so it went on until there was a last trumpet call. Euphony Clore rose to her feet and the stadium hushed a final time. "I invite you, Honored GenParents, to take your LastLeave." She held the moment. "You may embrace your Dead."

More than twelve thousand hands stretched immediately toward the glittering images. Those who were near enough to touch found their fingers passing into and through absolutely nothing.

Stretch still had a lump on his head from where the Oi Man had hit him, but at least he was almost sober now. He'd had to walk to the Museo. He'd tried flagging down a Clodrone car but no one would stop for him. Perhaps because he had been reeling about the pavement. Well, it had been a long, long walk and he wasn't reeling now. People had heard of the Museo but nobody, it seemed, had ever actually been there, so directions had been vague. It was always one street this way, or two that, a mirage, always just out of reach. But now, finally, he had arrived. Right in front of him were the huge open doors of a PublicBuilding and, above them, written in gold, the word *Museo*. So why was he hesitating? He was afraid again, just as he had been before he went to confront Igo Strang. So many things had been lost. His home was gone, he'd seen it—razed to the ground. His hopes and his dreams—those invested in his father anyway—they were gone, too. What was left of anything that had been his was—supposedly—here at the Museo. But what if he walked through those doors and there was nothing?

Maxo Strang was crossing the foyer of the Museo with an empty glass in his hand. He had been sent by Gala to beg PureWater from the custodian.

"Edwin," said the custodian, "call me Edwin."

But Maxo couldn't, quite. When he looked at the old man he felt awe and gratitude and something he thought was shame. He'd shouted at Edwin, stolen from him, sneered at and disregarded him.

"Don't think about it," said Edwin Challice. "It is all as nothing."

And what had Edwin done? This near total stranger had

stood by Maxo, spoken up for him, defended him, tried to shield him from Burton Chavit, taken the StunDart in his own breast. Why? Why had he cared? How could he have cared!

And Edwin couldn't have said (even if he'd been asked, which he wasn't): "because we are, after all, both human beings." And if Edwin mumbled about things lost and found (and how glad he was to have found whatever it was that he had found) then this all might just have got mislaid among his nods, his smiles.

Only it didn't, because the smiles made Maxo feel that Edwin saw in him something he had never seen in himself, made him experience possibilities. It was difficult to explain. There were so many words Maxo didn't seem to have, but miracle came close. It was like a miracle, like seeing Edwin for the first time standing upright in his blue custodian's tunic without a blood-edged hole.

"Thank you," said Maxo. "Thank you."

Edwin nodded, walked on, left Maxo to other things.

Gala.

In coming to the Museo, Maxo had felt he was in some way coming home, that things must now turn out well. He'd thought, that after he and Gala had stood so close together on the tank, they would somehow be joined forever. Hopeful, foolish thoughts. Gala's mother was dangerously frail and Gala, it appeared, had no eyes or ears for anything else. Maxo was prepared to wait, of course he was. He had some control over the frightening urges now, his yearning seemed to have become deeper, quieter—though just as needy. But it was hard watching Gala with

Perle. Gala whispered to her mother, sang to her, held her hand. Maxo looked from a distance at that hand-holding, those intertwined fingers. It made him feel intrusive, as if he was, in fact, in the wrong place; it also opened something inside him that hurt. So he skirted around the edges of things, was grateful when Gala asked him to get water, because he knew what getting water meant. It was something he could do, could understand.

Then there was Stretch. Gala wanted Stretch. Perle wanted Stretch. Gala told her mother that Stretch would come, said it like an OldTime prayer, as though she really believed it. Stretch had phoned apparently, had been told that the family were at the Museo, so he would come, he had to come. There was something frantic in the way Gala said these things, as though there wasn't much time left. But Gala knew things, Maxo thought, that weren't always spoken. For once he could see the connections, the invisible threads that bound this family together even when they were far apart. There was a thread like that between him and Igo, but with Glora? Maxo stood in the foyer and thought of Glora Orb—stretched a hand out as though she was there in front of him, but, of course, she wasn't.

"No!" The shout was loud and it was behind him. Maxo wheeled about. Coming through the open doors of the Museo was the brown ambisuited figure of a Clodrone. "Not you," it shouted.

Only it wasn't a Clodrone. It was Stretch, an exhausted, haggard-looking Stretch.

Maxo couldn't help himself. "Thank Gala," he exclaimed, "you're here."

"What?" said Stretch, and he seemed to fall; luckily he landed in the custodian's chair.

"Gala!" shouted Maxo. "Gala! You said he'd come and he's here!"

"Gala?" said Stretch.

"They're all here. Gala, Daz, your mother."

Breath seemed to leave Stretch then, as though his whole body was exhaling.

In response to Maxo's yell, there was a wild clattering on the stairs, the sound of running feet. Gala arrived full tilt.

"Stretch!" Without a glance at Maxo, she flung herself across the room at her elder brother. Found his sitting knees, clung to them. Words tumbled out of her. "Oh, Stretch, I've never been so glad to see anyone in all my life. Mama's been calling, calling for you."

Those hands again. Those embracing hands. Maxo wished he could be Stretch's knees, have, just for one moment, those arms about him. Gala's arms, her hands. Just once.

"Get him water," Gala cried at Maxo then. "Are you all right, Stretch?" Because Stretch hadn't said anything to her at all.

And Maxo thought he should get water. He'd been asked to get water for Perle and now he'd been asked to get water for Stretch. He'd get water for whomsoever Gala wanted him to get water. He had turned to leave when they all heard the urgent voice of Daz coming from the custodian's apartment.

"Gala, Gala—come quickly, it's Mom!"

Then, like a storm, Gala rose and, pulling Stretch to and with her, she began to run again. And Maxo wanted to run, too, to go with them, to face whatever it was that they were going to face. But they didn't want him, they didn't need him. Maxo Strang went to get water.

Perle opened her eyes and saw an angel.

"Phylo," she whispered. The whisper was because her breathing was difficult now, the air going in and out of her body in hard, sharp rasps.

"Mama," said Phylo.

"Kiss me, Phylo," she breathed. If he kissed her, some of the pain would go away, she knew that.

She felt, but did not see him bend down, come close to her. His lips touched her forehead.

"I was so worried," she said.

"Don't talk," he said, "don't say a thing. It's all right now. Everything will be all right." She looked so frail, so shrunken, how could it have happened in such a short space of time? He remembered her exclaiming, when he'd first spent time away from her, "Oh, how you've grown," when he returned. And now he'd been away this brief, brief time, and she had shrunk.

"Finn," she said. "Did you find my Finn?"

"What?" Didn't she know? Hadn't they told her? Stretch whipped around to look at Gala standing at the end of the bed. His sister swallowed hard, shook her head. Stretch felt the ground shift beneath his feet, he felt he was falling. His mother didn't know.

"Tell me," said Perle.

Gala shook her head again, this time at Stretch, warding him off. Daz swung his gaze from his sister to his brother and back again, mystified. Gala clearly hadn't told him either.

Why not? It was the truth wasn't it? *There are things that are right, son, and things that are wrong.* But his mother looked so frail. . . . What if the knowledge burst her heart?

No, please, no, mouthed Gala.

"I didn't find him," said Stretch tightly. "I couldn't find him, I'm sorry."

"Liar," Perle said softly. If Finn was not to be found, if he had died, she would have known, her bones would have known. Just as they knew from the quality of her daughter's silence and the tone of her eldest son's words that her children were lying to her.

Stretch looked once more at Gala.

Perle, blind in the bed, felt that look. "Phylo," she said, "be braver than your sister."

And he found he wanted to tell her, was desperate to tell her, not just because it was the truth but because she deserved to know. Knowing things could hurt—as the knowledge had hurt him. But knowing also made things complete. So he told his mother everything, everything his father—her husband—had said. He omitted nothing: not the hope or the heroism, the love, the care, nor the obstinacy, the fear, and the defeat. Gala sobbed at the telling but Perle listened without making a sound of any kind. When Stretch finally came to a halt she said: "He's a good man. Don't ever forget that, Phylo." It was too many words, the effort of saying them all seemed to exhaust her. Yet still she went on, though so quietly now that he had to bend down to hear her, "But things can be different. Do things differently, Phylo."

"I got drunk," Stretch burst out then. "Things went wrong and I couldn't cope either. I got drunk, too."

"Promise me," Perle rasped.

So Stretch did. He held her dying hand in his living one and he swore to do things differently, to forge a different future.

Perle didn't speak again. Not then or ever.

The pyre was Gala's idea. In the internal courtyard of the Museo logs had been laid by an AllWeather notice: Old-Time Primitive Tribes Cremation.

"I won't give her body to the Polis," said Gala. "I refuse."

"It's all burning," said Daz brutally.

He doesn't know how to deal with this, thought Gala. Why should he? But she pushed him away, and Stretch, too. Not that she blamed Stretch for telling their mother the truth. Her brother had done what she had been too selfish to do, he had released Perle, let her go. But she needed to be by herself now, wanted to prepare things, make things right in her own way.

"Can I help?" asked Edwin Challice.

"No," said Gala. It was kind of the custodian to offer, but Perle wouldn't have wanted strangers about her. Besides, Gala knew she had to wash the body. She did the soaping alone, held each of her mother's fingers in turn, honored them. Honored every part of her mother's body, refusing to be embarrassed, for these were the loins that had borne her, these were arms that had cherished her all her life. When the body was ready, when Gala felt herself ready, she wrapped her mother in a single white sheet, leaving an opening so her brothers could have one last look at their mother's face.

She did accept help then. The boys carried their mother between them, downstairs, past OldTime Mythologies and out into the courtyard. They laid her gently on the wood. She felt someone looking. Maxo. He was there in the background. She was grateful for his silence. There would be a time for talking later.

She didn't know which of them would be able to light the match.

Stretch.

He finally walked forward and struck a flame. And then another and another until the kindling caught. It was terrible seeing the fire lick about her mother, hearing the logs and the bones begin to fracture.

"I love you," Gala said in farewell, but she didn't cry. Daz was crying. Stretch was sobbing his heart out.

Maxo watched them all: Gala, Daz, Stretch, and, standing bent in the shadows, Edwin Challice. He felt like a piece of stone beside them. He wanted to break, too, he wanted to break deep inside, but it wasn't his loss and in any case he didn't yet know how. But he wanted to know. That's what he felt, looking at them all, that, no matter how bitter it was, that these people had something that he had never had and it mattered.

"I will learn," he told himself. Because he knew he wanted to be able to feel what they felt, understand what they understood. Perhaps, he also thought, that if he shared their pain, it would lessen their load, Gala's load. So much, he realized long afterward, that he hadn't known that day as he watched the black smoke curl over Perle Lorrell's body.

It was dusk when Edwin called them in.

"Someone has come for you." He led them to Salon 22 of Manuscripts.

307

There was a man standing there in a black ambisuit, leaning on a black cane, as though he had one leg shorter than the other.

"Mr. Malkin!"

"Maxo," greeted Mortimer Malkin, and then he turned to the Lorrells. "I'm so sorry about your mother."

Gala nodded at him, but Daz and Stretch said nothing, withheld.

"I know this may not feel like the moment," said Mortimer Malkin, "but I have reason to believe you are in danger here. You need to leave. Right now."

Daz laughed bitterly. "And go where exactly?"

"What danger?" asked Stretch.

"And who are you?" asked Gala worn out. "And why should you care?"

"There isn't time to explain everything now," said Malkin. "I need you to trust me."

Now it was Stretch's turn to laugh but Maxo cut him off.

"Do it," he said to Gala. "Trust him. Please." Then he turned to Stretch. "They put me in an IsolationCell because they thought I was you. You don't want to go in an Isolation-Cell, Stretch."

"What!"

"There's a lot you don't know, Stretch," said Gala.

Stretch took a breath. "Fine. But I do know that I don't particularly want to get involved with some member of the Enhanced I don't even know."

"I know him," said Maxo.

"So what? You're one of them, too. The Enhanced. You would know him. You belong together. We don't. We'll find our own way." *Forge a different future.*

"It's not about us and them anymore," said Malkin. "We need to work together."

"Work for who? For what?"

"The Polis," said Malkin. "The good of the Polis."

"Where have I heard that before!" said Stretch.

"Look," said Maxo. "InternalSecurity know this place, that's where they picked me up first time. If Mr. Malkin says we should go, we should go."

"You go then," said Stretch to Maxo. "No one's stopping you from going." And he stretched his hands protectively toward Gala as if he could take her away from all this, keep her under his wing.

"No," said Gala, and she slipped from him. "If Maxo goes, I go, too." And she crossed the room to stand at Maxo's side. She'd paid Maxo no attention at all, she realized suddenly. Once again she'd shut him out, turned away from him. And just as he'd come back when she needed help with the RazeTanks, so he'd come back to her when she needed support at the Museo. He'd been there by her side in the big things and he'd been there for her again, in the small ones. If she'd asked for water, he'd brought water. If she wanted silence, he'd somehow known that, he hadn't said a word. He had never intruded, he'd just done whatever was necessary when it was necessary. And she hadn't said anything to him at all.

"Thank you," was what she said now, and she finally looked deep into his eyes. What she saw there that day she could never quite describe, some combination of hope and pain and terror and love. Yes, a huge, trembling love.

"If it wasn't for Maxo," said Gala, turning back to the others, "Mama would have died in Block 213. She never would have got out. And nor would you, Daz. That's good enough for me."

Maxo felt her presence like fire. He couldn't speak.

"Daz?" pressed Gala.

Daz havered still, looked from his sister to his brother and back again.

"Phylo," said Mortimer Malkin. "We need people like you, Phylo. People with brains and passion. Questioning people, doubtful people."

"*We*?" questioned Stretch. "Who's we? ThrowbackIntellectuals?"

"ThrowForward," Mortimer said quietly. "Perhaps. There is no back now."

"And in any case what else can we do, where else can we go?" said Gala. "Be with us, Stretch. I need you to be with us. With me. Please, Stretch. Please, Daz."

In a few minutes they were gone. There was nothing to pack. Daz followed Mortimer Malkin out into the night with nothing more than a tube of titanium white and a tube of Prussian blue. In time he chose to believe these paints were not just the last of Gubbins's gifts but the first of his father's. *Hope's the thing.* That's what Gubbins had said. Stretch took his anger and his hurt and also his promise to his mother; it whispered in his ear: *forge a different future.* It would be a long time before he learned what that meant. Gala went shrouded in her exhaustion; there was part of her that night that didn't care whether she lived or died. And another part, of course—what Perle would have called the coping part of her—that cared very much indeed. They journeyed in silence for some while before Gala realized that, behind her in the dark, Maxo had broken his

310

stride and he was walking pace for pace as she walked. She could hear his breath as if it were her own, the soft ins of it, the steady outs. She stretched out her hand then, to draw this comfort closer, to bring him alongside.

Maxo perhaps knew more than the others about what a life with the ThrowbackIntellectuals might mean. It would be difficult, it would be dangerous, it would cut him off from everything he'd known. But, as Mortimer had said, there was no back now. Besides he owed it to Lydida, to Bovis. And also to himself. Which is why, when Gala slipped her hand in his (although her fingers held his for only the briefest of moments) he felt the sudden exhilaration of a man who knew, at last, where he was going.